# PRAISE FOR LEE

## PRAISE FOR *GATED PREY*

"I whipped my head back and forth reading *Gated Prey*. So twisty, so funny, and so LA—a few of my favorite things. After zooming through these pages, I'll ride shotgun with Lee any day!"
—Rachel Howzell Hall, bestselling author of *And Now She's Gone*

## PRAISE FOR *BONE CANYON*

### A *Mystery and Suspense Magazine* 2021 Best Book of the Year Selection

"Lee Goldberg proves again that he is a master storyteller with this piece. His ability to develop strong plots and use a fast-paced narrative keeps the reader on their toes as things progress. Poignant characters also help keep things enthralling until the final reveal for the attentive reader."
—*Mystery and Suspense Magazine*

"Goldberg follows *Lost Hills* with a riveting, intense story. Readers of Karin Slaughter or Michael Connelly will want to try this."
—*Library Journal* (starred review)

"Goldberg knows how to keep the pages turning."
—*Publishers Weekly*

"Lee Goldberg puts the *pro* in *police procedural*. *Bone Canyon* is fresh, sharp, and absorbing. Give me more Eve Ronin, ASAP."
—Meg Gardiner, international bestselling author

"Wow—what a novel! It is wonderful in so many ways. I could not put it down. *Bone Canyon* is wrenching and harrowing, full of wicked twists. Lee Goldberg captures the magic and danger of the Santa Monica Mountains and the predators who prowl them. Detective Eve Ronin takes on forgotten victims, fights for them, and nearly loses everything in the process. She's a riveting character, and I can't wait for her next case."

—Luanne Rice, *New York Times* bestselling author

"*Bone Canyon* is a propulsive procedural that provides high thrills in difficult terrain, grappling thoughtfully with sexual violence and police corruption, as well as the minefield of politics and media in Hollywood and suburban Los Angeles. Eve Ronin is a fantastic series lead—stubborn and driven, working twice as hard as her colleagues both to prove her worth and to deliver justice for the dead."

—Steph Cha, author of *Your House Will Pay*

## PRAISE FOR *LOST HILLS*

"A cop novel so good it makes much of the old guard read like they're going through the motions until they can retire . . . The real appeal here is Goldberg's lean prose, which imbues just-the-facts procedure with remarkable tension and cranks up to a stunning description of a fire that was like 'Christmas in hell.'"

—*Booklist*

"[The] suspense and drama are guaranteed to keep a reader spellbound . . ."

—*Authorlink*

"An energetic, resourceful procedural starring a heroine who deserves a series of her own."

—*Kirkus Reviews*

"This nimble, sure-footed series launch from bestseller Goldberg . . . builds to a thrilling, visually striking climax. Readers will cheer Ronin every step of the way."

—*Publishers Weekly*

"The first book in what promises to be a superb series—it's also that rare novel in which the formulaic elements of mainstream police procedurals share narrative space with a unique female protagonist. All that, and it's also a love letter to the chaos and diversity of California. There are a lot of series out there, but Eve Ronin and Goldberg's fast-paced prose should put this one on the radar of every crime fiction fan."

—National Public Radio

"This sterling thriller is carved straight out of the world of Harlan Coben and Lisa Gardner . . . *Lost Hills* is a book to be found and savored."

—*BookTrib*

"*Lost Hills* is Lee Goldberg at his best. Inspired by the real-world grit and glitz of LA County crime, this book takes no prisoners. And neither does Eve Ronin. Take a ride with her and you'll find yourself with a heroine for the ages. And you'll be left hoping for more."

—Michael Connelly, #1 *New York Times* bestselling author

"*Lost Hills* is what you get when you polish the police procedural to a shine: a gripping premise, a great twist, fresh spins and knowing winks to the genre conventions, and all the smart, snappy ease of an expert at work."

—Tana French, *New York Times* bestselling author

"Thrills and chills! *Lost Hills* is the perfect combination of action and suspense, not to mention Eve Ronin is one of the best new female characters in ages. You will race through the pages!"

—Lisa Gardner, #1 *New York Times* bestselling author

"Twenty-four-karat Goldberg—a top-notch procedural that shines like a true gem."

—Craig Johnson, *New York Times* bestselling author of the Longmire series

"A winner. Packed with procedure, forensics, vivid descriptions, and the right amount of humor. Fervent fans of Connelly and Crais, this is your next read."

—Kendra Elliot, *Wall Street Journal* and Amazon Charts bestselling author

"Brilliant! Eve Ronin rocks! With a baffling and brutal case, tight plotting, and a fascinating look at police procedure, *Lost Hills* is a stunning start to a new detective series. A must-read for crime fiction fans."

—Melinda Leigh, *Wall Street Journal* and #1 Amazon Charts bestselling author

"A tense, pacy read from one of America's greatest crime and thriller writers."

—Garry Disher, international bestselling author and Ned Kelly Award winner

# PRAISE FOR *FAKE TRUTH*

"A winner from first page to last. Lee Goldberg has single-handedly invented a new genre of thriller. At once nail-bitingly suspenseful and gut-bustingly hilarious . . . but never less than a pedal-to-the-metal, full-on page-turner. *Fake Truth* is clever, edge-of-your-seat entertainment that I read in one glorious sitting. And that's no lie!"

—Christopher Reich, *New York Times* bestselling author

"Timely, satirical, and funny. Lee Goldberg's *Fake Truth* is deftly ironic and painfully observant."

—Robert Dugoni, *New York Times* bestselling author

"Hilariously surprising. The author's juggling of truth and fiction is almost as dexterous as his hero's."

—*Kirkus Reviews*

## PRAISE FOR *KILLER THRILLER*

"*Killer Thriller* grabs you from page one with brilliant wit, sharply honed suspense, and a huge helping of pure originality."

—Jeffery Deaver, *New York Times* bestselling author

"A delight from start to finish, a round-the-world, thrill-a-minute, laser-guided missile of a book."

—Joseph Finder, *New York Times* bestselling author

"*Killer Thriller* is an action-packed treasure filled with intrigue, engaging characters, and exciting, well-rendered locales. With Goldberg's hyper-clever plotting, dialogue, and wit on every page, readers are in for a blast with this one!"

—Mark Greaney, *New York Times* bestselling author

## PRAISE FOR *TRUE FICTION*

"Thriller fiction at its absolute finest—and it could happen for real. But not to me, I hope."

—Lee Child, #1 *New York Times* bestselling author

"This may be the most fun you'll ever have reading a thriller. It's a breathtaking rush of suspense, intrigue, and laughter that only Lee Goldberg could pull off. I loved it."

—Janet Evanovich, #1 *New York Times* bestselling author

"This is my life . . . in a thriller! *True Fiction* is great fun."

—Brad Meltzer, #1 *New York Times* bestselling author

"Fans of parodic thrillers will enjoy the exhilarating ride . . . [in] this Elmore Leonard mashed with *Get Smart* romp."

—*Publishers Weekly*

"A conspiracy thriller of the first order, a magical blend of fact and it-could-happen scary fiction. Nail-biting, page-turning, and laced with Goldberg's wry humor, *True Fiction* is a true delight, reminiscent of *Six Days of the Condor* and the best of Hitchcock's innocent-man-in-peril films."

—Paul Levine, bestselling author of *Bum Rap*

"Ian Ludlow is one of the coolest heroes to emerge in post-9/11 thrillers. A wonderful, classic yet modern, breakneck suspense novel. Lee Goldberg delivers a great story with a literary metafiction wink that makes its thrills resonate."

—James Grady, *New York Times* bestselling author of *Six Days of the Condor*

"Great fun that moves as fast as a jet. Goldberg walks a tightrope between suspense and humor and never slips."

—Linwood Barclay, *New York Times* bestselling author of *Elevator Pitch*

"I haven't read anything this much fun since Donald E. Westlake's comic-caper novels. Immensely entertaining, clever, and timely."

—David Morrell, *New York Times* bestselling author of *First Blood*

# GATED
# PREY

# OTHER TITLES BY LEE GOLDBERG

*King City*
*The Walk*
*Watch Me Die*
*McGrave*
*Three Ways to Die*
*Fast Track*

## The Ian Ludlow Thrillers

*True Fiction*
*Killer Thriller*
*Fake Truth*

## The Eve Ronin Series

*Lost Hills*
*Bone Canyon*

## The Fox & O'Hare Series (coauthored with Janet Evanovich)

*Pros & Cons* (novella)
*The Shell Game* (novella)
*The Heist*
*The Chase*
*The Job*
*The Scam*
*The Pursuit*

# The Diagnosis Murder Series

*The Silent Partner*
*The Death Merchant*
*The Shooting Script*
*The Waking Nightmare*
*The Past Tense*
*The Dead Letter*
*The Double Life*
*The Last Word*

# The Monk Series

*Mr. Monk Goes to the Firehouse*
*Mr. Monk Goes to Hawaii*
*Mr. Monk and the Blue Flu*
*Mr. Monk and the Two Assistants*
*Mr. Monk in Outer Space*
*Mr. Monk Goes to Germany*
*Mr. Monk Is Miserable*
*Mr. Monk and the Dirty Cop*
*Mr. Monk in Trouble*
*Mr. Monk Is Cleaned Out*
*Mr. Monk on the Road*
*Mr. Monk on the Couch*
*Mr. Monk on Patrol*
*Mr. Monk Is a Mess*
*Mr. Monk Gets Even*

# The Charlie Willis Series

*My Gun Has Bullets*
*Dead Space*

## The Dead Man Series
## (coauthored with William Rabkin)

*Face of Evil*
*Ring of Knives* (with James Daniels)
*Hell in Heaven*
*The Dead Woman* (with David McAfee)
*The Blood Mesa* (with James Reasoner)
*Kill Them All* (with Harry Shannon)
*The Beast Within* (with James Daniels)
*Fire & Ice* (with Jude Hardin)
*Carnival of Death* (with Bill Crider)
*Freaks Must Die* (with Joel Goldman)
*Slaves to Evil* (with Lisa Klink)
*The Midnight Special* (with Phoef Sutton)
*The Death March* (with Christa Faust)
*The Black Death* (with Aric Davis)
*The Killing Floor* (with David Tully)
*Colder Than Hell* (with Anthony Neil Smith)
*Evil to Burn* (with Lisa Klink)
*Streets of Blood* (with Barry Napier)
*Crucible of Fire* (with Mel Odom)
*The Dark Need* (with Stant Litore)
*The Rising Dead* (with Stella Green)
*Reborn* (with Kate Danley, Phoef Sutton, and Lisa Klink)

## The Jury Series

*Judgment*
*Adjourned*
*Payback*
*Guilty*

# Nonfiction

*The Best TV Shows You Never Saw*
*Unsold Television Pilots 1955–1989*
*Television Fast Forward*
*Science Fiction Filmmaking in the 1980s*
(cowritten with William Rabkin, Randy Lofficier,
and Jean-Marc Lofficier)
*The Dreamweavers: Interviews with Fantasy Filmmakers of
the 1980s* (cowritten with William Rabkin, Randy Lofficier, and
Jean-Marc Lofficier)
*Successful Television Writing* (cowritten with William Rabkin)

# GATED PREY

## LEE GOLDBERG

THOMAS & MERCER

Text copyright © 2021 by Adventures in Television, Inc.
All rights reserved.

Published by Thomas & Mercer, Seattle

www.apub.com

Amazon, the Amazon logo, and Thomas & Mercer are trademarks of Amazon.com, Inc., or its affiliates.

ISBN-13: 9781542029346 (hardcover)
ISBN-10: 1542029341 (hardcover)

ISBN-13: 9781542029360 (paperback)
ISBN-10: 1542029368 (paperback)

Cover design by Shasti O'Leary Soudant

Printed in the United States of America

First edition

*To Valerie and Maddie, as always and forever.*

# CHAPTER ONE

Eve Ronin was topless under her black Chanel suit jacket, so everybody she encountered at Bristol Farms supermarket had their eyes on her chest. That was fine with her. She wanted to draw attention to herself but not to her face, which she feared people might recognize, despite hiding it behind a big pair of sunglasses. She also didn't want anyone studying her blazer's long cut, which hid her holstered Glock and the Los Angeles County Sheriff's Department badge that were clipped to the waistband of her skinny jeans.

Her partner, Duncan Pavone, a fat man in his late fifties, leaned on a walker beside her in the checkout line. He wore an untucked oversize Louis Vuitton blue camouflage silk shirt that matched his cargo pants and sneaker boots. He would've been invisible in a jungle of Vuitton logos, which Bristol Farms often was, but not on this foggy February morning.

He pulled out a thick wad of cash from his pants pocket, peeled off a crisp hundred-dollar bill with a flourish, and handed it to the middle-aged female cashier to pay for their deli sandwiches, an apple pie, and a bottle of wine.

"Keep the change, honey. I don't do small bills." Duncan winked at the woman and shuffled out, leaning heavily on his walker, leaving Eve to handle the groceries. Eve snatched up the bag and as she passed Duncan, he smacked her on the butt.

She didn't mind the swat. It was all part of the act. Now anybody watching who was trying to decide if she was his twentysomething lover or his daughter would have their answer.

Eve took a leather-wrapped key fob out of her pocket as she emerged from the store and aimed it at the white Rolls-Royce Cullinan SUV parked in the handicapped spot.

The suicide doors of the Rolls automatically yawned open, revealing the decadent leather, wood, and milled-aluminum interior, and the plush lambswool floor mats. She tossed the groceries on the back seat. Duncan hobbled up and she held his walker steady for him as he climbed into the front passenger seat.

She folded his walker, stuck it in the back seat, closed the doors, and walked around to the driver's side.

"You don't do small bills?" Eve asked as she climbed in.

"My money clip can barely hold all the cash I've already got."

"It's all singles under that other C-note."

"The money roll and my Glock are weighing down my pants. They're only held up by a drawstring and I don't want them to fall."

"Is that how you're going to explain the expense to the captain?"

"What's he going to do, fire me?" Duncan said. "I'm retiring in eighty days."

Eve started the ignition and they both watched as a slot opened at the tip of the impossibly long hood and the silver Spirit of Ecstasy ornament, a winged woman ready to fly, rose up from hiding and snapped into place. It was a grand performance to mark the beginning of each journey.

"I wish my Buick Regal did that," Duncan said.

With one hand on the wheel, Eve looked over her right shoulder and slowly backed out of the parking spot. It was like looking down the aisle of a 747, but she didn't trust backup cameras and wasn't going to start now when she was responsible for a half-a-million-dollar Rolls-Royce. Twisting in her seat made her blazer gape open. Duncan peeked at her cleavage. Slight yellowing traces of bruising still colored her skin where she'd broken her sternum a few weeks earlier.

"Stop looking at my boobs," she said.

"You know I can't resist a mystery. How are they staying in there?"

"Tape."

She faced forward again and steered the Rolls out of the shopping center, which was across the street from the woodsy campus of the Motion Picture and Television Country House and Hospital, where her estranged father, Vince, a retired TV director, lived in a bungalow. The Rolls weighed three tons but it felt like the Spirit of Ecstasy had somehow lifted them into the air and they were flying above the road.

"You mean like Scotch tape?" he asked.

"Of course not."

"Duct tape?"

"Boob tape."

Duncan shook his head. "I've been married for thirty years, I've got two adult daughters, and I've never heard of boob tape."

Eve hadn't, either, until last week, when her mother, Jen, a struggling actress, came down from Ventura and helped her choose the wardrobe for this assignment. "It prevents wardrobe malfunctions."

That was something Eve never had to worry about before in either her professional or personal life. All of her clothes were practical, simple, and not the least bit flashy. It was a reflection of her life, or at least how she tried to live it. But that hadn't been easy since she became the youngest female homicide detective in the history of the LASD, a promotion five and a half months ago that generated lots of publicity and that the rank and file, and Eve herself, knew she didn't deserve. Her most recent case, only her second as a homicide detective, ended with the arrest of several deputies and the suicide of another, putting her in the media spotlight again, deepening the resentment toward her in the department. Duncan was one of three people with badges who she completely trusted.

Eve made a left onto Calabasas Road and headed through the center of Old Town Calabasas. The Leonis Adobe ranch house and the clapboard storefronts were authentic, harkening back to the mid-1800s, but it still felt like she was driving through a movie studio back lot. That feeling was especially strong today, since they were riding in a Rolls-Royce confiscated from a drug dealer, and pretending to be a couple, hoping to attract the gang responsible for a series of increasingly violent home invasion robberies.

"I should buy a couple of rolls of boob tape," Duncan said, kicking off his shoes and running his toes through the furry floor mat.

"For your wife or for your daughters?"

"Are you kidding? I don't want them walking around with everything hanging out."

She glanced at him. "Then what do you want the tape for?"

Duncan patted his belly. "To hold this back and create the illusion that I have six-pack abs."

"You should call David Copperfield instead."

"Maybe I should," he said. "Then we can take this show on the road."

"Isn't that what we are doing now?"

Over the last four days, they'd visited all the local grocery stores and shopping centers, making a spectacle of themselves—as an obscenely rich, hobbled old man and his much younger gold-digger wife—on the off chance that was how the robbers picked their targets.

"I don't see the point," Eve continued. "All of the homes hit so far were in one of the gated communities along Parkway Calabasas. A robber can't just follow the victims home through the gate." She'd made the argument before, and was overruled, but she was growing more irritated with the assignment as time wore on.

Eve stopped at the light at the intersection of Park Granada and Calabasas Road, facing the Commons shopping center on their left and the Courtyard shopping center on their right. The Commons was an upscale re-creation of an Italian village with a landmark clock tower topped by the world's largest Rolex. The Courtyard was a mundane, architecturally forgettable collection of shops, fast-food restaurants, and banks, anchored by a Trader Joe's. Eve and Duncan had performed their act at both shopping centers.

"The point, Grasshopper, is we don't know how the targets are getting picked, or how the thieves are getting in or out of the gated communities," Duncan said. "And when you don't know shit, you try everything."

Like luring the thieves to them rather than tracking the thieves down, which was why they were spending their days in a 4,500-square-foot furnished McMansion they'd rented in Vista Grande. It was one of the four gated communities built atop a ridge that overlooked Parkway Calabasas and the Calabasas Country Club's golf course on the east side, the high-end dealerships along Calabasas Road and the Ventura Freeway on the north side, and Las Virgenes Road on the west, which snaked its way through Malibu Canyon to the Pacific Ocean.

"You should make a note," Duncan said.

"Of what?" She made a right onto Park Granada, passing the side entrance to the Commons as she headed up the road.

"My little nuggets of wisdom. You're going to miss them when I'm gone."

"No, I won't. You're going to haunt me like Obi-Wan Kenobi."

"Who the hell is that?"

She gave him a look, unsure if he was joking. "Why do you keep calling me a grasshopper?"

Now he gave her a look, unsure if she was joking. She wasn't.

Duncan shook his head. "I feel so old."

"You aren't old," she said. "You're ancient."

Park Granada ended at a T intersection with Parkway Calabasas and the ornate wrought-iron front gates of Vista Grande, which had two massive rocky fountains, one flanking the exit side and one on the entrance side, that spilled into large ponds. It could have been the entrance to one of the Las Vegas Strip's hotel-casinos. All that was missing, Eve thought, was a volcano, dancing water, and a Frank Sinatra tune blaring from speakers hidden in the lush tropical landscaping.

The light turned green and she drove through the busy intersection into Vista Grande, where the entranceway forked into two lanes, one for community guests that passed by the window of the Spanish-Mediterranean-style guardhouse and one for residents who had decals on their windows. The resident's lane was also used by vehicles from utilities like Edison, Spectrum Cable, and PacBell, from official state and local government, from law enforcement agencies and the fire department, as well as for regular deliveries from the post office, FedEx, Amazon, UPS, and, Eve believed, anybody with a car with a base sticker price over $75,000. She took the resident's lane.

"I don't see why they bother with the gates," Eve said as she waved at the uniformed guard, a young man who waved back at them and hit the button that opened the rolling gate, proving her assumption. She hadn't bothered to put a Vista Grande resident decal on the Rolls and hadn't been stopped at the gate yet. "It's a joke."

"Maybe so, but they get a lot less crime in the gated communities than they do in the ones that are wide open," Duncan said. "The cameras catch the license plates and faces of everyone who drives in and out. That's a big deterrent."

"Not to the home invaders we're after."

Eve drove up the steep hill. Both sides of the street were lined with mini-mansions in the same Spanish-Mediterranean style as the front gate guardhouse with red-tiled roofs, perfectly manicured landscaping, lots of German-made cars in the driveways, and hardly a security camera in sight. Or, she knew, even out of sight.

"The gates give the residents a false sense of security," Eve said. "They have Ring doorbells, simple alarms they rarely turn on, and are too lazy to lock their doors and windows. They might as well have lighted signs on their front lawns that say 'Come and get it.'"

"Maybe that's what we need," Duncan said. "Though I am in no hurry for this assignment to end."

"It's a bore," Eve said.

She made the comment just as they pulled into the pressed-concrete faux-cobblestone driveway of their two-story house, which they'd told neighbors they were renting until they could build a new home in Malibu. It was on a corner lot and had a low stucco wall around the front perimeter for decorative purposes rather than for providing any privacy or security.

Eve got out and walked around to the other side of the Rolls to get the grocery bag and the walker out of the back seat. Duncan didn't actually need the walker, but she wanted to play it safe. She didn't know who might be watching. There were gardeners working next door. A pool man's truck was parked across the street. An Amazon truck cruised up the hill. She opened his door and held the walker for him.

Duncan slipped his feet back into his shoes, got out of the car, and smiled. "I could stay here until my retirement party."

"This *is* your retirement party."

Eve walked past him to unlock the front door, which was mostly glass and ineffective from a security standpoint. Not only could the glass be broken, allowing easy access to the dead bolt and doorknob, but anybody walking up to the door could see the marble foyer, the grand staircase, and the two-story great room with its massive windows that looked out over a lagoon-style pool, waterfall, and the homes on the opposite ridge.

They went inside, and Eve typed the alarm code into the keypad on the wall. It deactivated the alarm and also alerted the sheriff's deputy assigned to watch them at Lost Hills station that they'd arrived home. Eve and Duncan also waved at the camera in the entry hall, one of a dozen throughout the house that were being monitored by the deputy at his computer screen. As an extra precaution, Eve and Duncan each had a tiny key fob in their pocket that, if pressed, activated all the hidden microphones in the house and alerted the observing deputy that they were in danger. Armed backup would be there in five minutes or less.

Duncan left the walker in the hallway as they went to the enormous kitchen, which was larger than Eve's Calabasas condo and had a marble island with a dozen barstools around it. They sat down at the island and started unpacking the grocery bag from Bristol Farms, though the wine would go untouched, along with all the other alcohol they'd bought over the last four days. They were on duty 24/7 during this assignment.

"I don't know why you're whining," Duncan said as he unwrapped his sandwich. "Living in this big house has got to be better than your room at the Hilton Garden Inn."

She'd been staying at the hotel while her condo was being gutted and renovated after the fatal shooting that had occurred there, though, as time went on, she wasn't entirely sure that she could ever move back. Eve went to the giant subzero refrigerator, took out a Diet Coke for each of them, and used her hip to close the door.

"This doesn't feel like police work to me." She handed him his Diet Coke.

"It's an undercover assignment," he said, popping open the can. "The problem is you can't stand the luxury."

"I feel like I'm being intentionally exiled."

Eve picked up the iPad that was on the island and checked out the security camera video feeds, just to be doing something productive. The iPad screen was divided into a dozen screens, each with a different live feed.

There weren't any cameras mounted outside, to make the place seem like easy pickings, but there were plenty of them hidden inside, strategically aimed at the windows to show them, and the deputy on duty at Lost Hills, all sides of the house. One camera in the guest bedroom upstairs showed them a view of the back hillside, all the way down to the golf course and Parkway Calabasas, while another in the master bathroom gave them a view of the front yard. Other cameras in the house were placed to record video and audio that would be used as evidence if they were ever robbed.

"You're being eased back into active duty after being seriously injured on the job," Duncan said, talking with his mouth full. "But don't fool yourself. This is a big case. The department is spending a fortune on it. If it doesn't pay off in another day or two, we'll be back in our cubicles at Lost Hills and you'll miss this."

"You mean that *you* will. You're getting paid to ride around in a Rolls-Royce, eat free food, and sit in a plush home theater all day watching westerns."

Duncan washed down a mouthful of corned beef and sourdough with some Diet Coke. "Would you feel better if we were undercover as homeless people, eating rancid scraps from garbage cans and living in cardboard boxes on urine-soaked dirt beside a freeway off-ramp?"

"Yes," she said.

"You're just feeling guilty because soon you could be living like this."

She unwrapped her sandwich. "Never."

"You just optioned your life story as a TV series."

The first episode would probably begin with her off-duty arrest of a violent movie star, hero of the globally successful *Deathfist* movies, and the viral video of the takedown that was shot by onlookers. It would tell how she'd leveraged her popularity with the public, during a time when the LASD was embroiled in scandal and bad press, to get the sheriff to promote her from a lowly deputy to the robbery-homicide division just to keep her at the front of the news cycle. And it would cover her first murder case, the capture of a killer who'd slaughtered a family.

"That doesn't mean the series will happen," Eve said. "And even if it does, I'm not giving up this job."

The idea of her life becoming a TV series made her nauseous. She pushed her sandwich aside. She'd only accepted the deal because a series would be made with or without her involvement and so she'd have the money to hire a decent lawyer. Eve knew it was only a matter of time before she was sued by the widow of the deputy who'd killed himself as a result of her last investigation, the one that left her with a broken sternum.

"The job may give you up first," Duncan said.

"The department is certainly trying."

"Yeah, this is brutal," he said, shaking his head. "Seriously, you need to learn how to relax or you're gonna burn yourself out before you hit thirty."

He took another bite of his sandwich. They were quiet for a long moment, then she said, "Urine-soaked dirt?"

"What?"

"Why would we put our cardboard boxes on urine-soaked dirt?"

"Because you enjoy suffering."

Movement on one of the iPad feeds caught Eve's eye. She picked up the iPad and saw three men in sunglasses wearing orange-and-yellow SoCalGas company vests over their khaki shirts and blue SoCalGas baseball caps, the brims pulled low over their faces, approaching the front door. The man in the lead held a clipboard. She turned the iPad so Duncan could see the feeds, too.

"We have some visitors," she said. "I don't see a gas company truck on the street, do you?"

"Maybe it's parked around the corner." He didn't say it with much conviction.

Her heartbeat jacked up. "Do you think this is it?"

He nodded and slid off his barstool. "Let's not call the cavalry until we're sure. You answer the door when they knock. I'll be in the living room."

Duncan went to the hallway and got his walker. Eve watched the iPad as the men came to the door. She knew the deputy at Lost Hills was seeing the video feeds, too, and she hoped that he'd already told the dispatcher to alert the nearest patrol cars.

The doorbell rang.

*Here we go.*

# CHAPTER TWO

Eve hid the iPad in the silverware drawer and walked to the front door. The three men were standing outside. Anytime she saw three men she didn't know, she dubbed them Manny, Moe, and Jack, the Pep Boys, until she had their names. Manny was facing the door, but Moe and Jack were behind him, with their heads bowed down, the brims of their hats obscuring their faces. But she could still tell the Pep Boys were white.

Eve opened the door a crack. "Can I help you?"

"We're with the gas company," Manny said. "You have a leak."

She guessed that Manny was in his mid- to late twenties, just like her. Moe appeared to be about the same age. Manny was blocking her from getting a good view of Jack's face.

"You must have the wrong house," Eve said. "We didn't call you."

"It's showing up on our readouts at the office." Manny held up his clipboard, displaying a piece of paper with a graph on it. "We need to come in, make sure there's no gas buildup or the house could explode. There'll be nothing left but a smoking crater."

Duncan hobbled up on his walker behind Eve. "We don't smell any gas."

"Maybe you have a stuffy nose," Manny said.

"I don't."

"We have to check anyway," Manny said, irritation creeping into his voice. "It's for your own safety."

Eve reached into her pocket and squeezed the button on her key fob, alerting the deputy at Lost Hills that the invasion was going down. "Come in, but take off your shoes. We don't want you scuffing up the travertine."

She stepped aside, and opened the door wide, to let them in.

As Manny entered, he smacked Eve's face with the clipboard, taking her by surprise. When she looked back at him, her cheeks stinging and her eyes tearing up, he was holding a gun in her face. "Fuck your travertine, bitch."

The other two men spilled in behind Manny, both pulling out guns before Duncan had a chance to go for his, which was hidden under his big untucked camouflage shirt.

Moe pressed the barrel of his weapon against Duncan's forehead and said, "Empty your pockets and take off your watch."

"You can have whatever you want. Please don't hurt us." Duncan took out his wad of cash, which Jack grabbed from his hand and stuffed into his own pocket, and then Duncan slipped the fake Rolex off his wrist, which Jack took, too.

Manny kicked the front door shut behind him, then yanked off Eve's gold Tiffany necklace from her neck. "Give me your ring."

She pulled off the wedding ring, with its huge fake diamond, and dropped it into his open hand.

He stuffed the jewelry into his shirt pocket. "Where's the safe?"

"We don't have one," Duncan said.

Moe pistol-whipped him across the face. "Bullshit."

Duncan staggered back but held his balance. The gun's front sight had slashed his cheek like a knife. Blood streaked down his face and dripped onto his camouflage shirt. Eve stole a glance up at the security camera lens, as if it were the faceless, distant deputy's own eyes.

*Are you seeing this?*

"I won't ask nicely next time," Manny said.

"It's upstairs, in the master bedroom," Eve said, making eye contact with Duncan, who gave her a slight nod, letting her know he was okay. They only had to keep things under control for another minute or two before backup arrived. The station was only five miles away but there had to be a patrol car nearby that could immediately respond.

Manny smiled at her. "Do you know the combination?"

"Yes."

"Lead the way." Manny followed her up the stairs, his gun pressed into her back. He looked down at Moe and Jack. "Get to it. Shoot the old man if he gives you any trouble."

Moe grabbed Duncan by the arm, dragged him to an easy chair in the great room, and pushed him into it. Jack started looking around the house for valuables.

Eve reached the second-floor landing and headed for the master bedroom, which had a four-poster bed, a vaulted ceiling, a fireplace, and a balcony that overlooked the pool. The sliding glass door to the balcony was open for the fresh air and as an invitation to burglars.

"Where's the safe?" Manny asked.

"In the closet."

His-and-hers walk-in closets were on either side of a short hallway that led to the master bathroom. Eve started to go into one of the closets, but Manny grabbed her arm and yanked her away from the door.

"Not so fast." He pushed her toward the bathroom and turned to give the closet a quick glance, perhaps in case she had a weapon stashed there.

The closet was empty. There weren't any clothes hanging inside. Just as he was registering that puzzling fact, Eve whipped out her Glock and aimed it at him.

"Drop the gun," she said.

Manny's eyes went wide. "What the fuck? Where did you get that?"

"I'm a cop. You're under arrest."

He dropped his gun and the clipboard, turned his back to her, and bolted across the bedroom toward the balcony. His reaction surprised her, because it was such a dumb thing to do, but she didn't shoot him. Her life wasn't in immediate danger and there was nowhere for him to go.

That's when she remembered the pool.

"No!" She ran after him, but it was too late.

Manny vaulted over the wrought-iron railing and dropped from sight.

Eve heard a moist smack and a tiny splash before she reached the railing. She saw his broken body grotesquely bent over the edge of the pool, his face in the water.

At that same instant, there were two gunshots.

Moe crashed through the living room window in an explosion of glass shards and landed on his back on the patio, two bullet wounds in his chest, his wide, dead eyes staring up at the sky.

*Duncan . . .*

Eve dashed back inside to the bedroom door and peered cautiously around the edge of the open doorway to the staircase, looking for movement on the landing, stairs, and entryway below, in case Jack was waiting to take a shot.

She called out: "Duncan?"

"We're clear," he yelled. "The third guy scrammed through the back door in the kitchen."

Eve rushed down the stairs, reaching the entry hall to see Duncan standing in the great room, the window shattered behind him, and the two bodies on the patio. Duncan was breathing hard, his gun held at his side, blood streaming from his cheek wound. She started toward him but he irritably waved her away.

"I'm fine. Go!"

She dashed out the front door just in time to see Jack yank a woman out of her Cadillac Escalade at gunpoint and take her seat behind the wheel. Eve raised her gun but couldn't get a clear shot at Jack without endangering the woman, the gardeners next door, and a pool man walking to his truck across the street. The Escalade tore down the hill.

Even if the sheriff's patrol cars arrived now, they'd pass the speeding Escalade on their way up to the house without realizing they were letting a gunman get away.

*Shit!*

That's when Eve remembered she still had the Rolls-Royce key in her pocket.

*This isn't over yet.*

She holstered her gun, jumped into the Cullinan, and backed out of the driveway fast, whipped the car around, shifted into drive, and floored it.

The Escalade was a block ahead of her, blasting through Vista Grande's half-open front gate as it was rolling closed. She watched as Jack ran the red light and charged into the busy intersection. The Escalade T-boned a BMW 3 Series and kept going, turning the sedan into a makeshift bulldozer scoop that clipped a passing Mercedes C-Class. The two sedans spun off in opposite directions, freeing the Escalade to barrel on down Park Granada, its front end mangled, but leaving a snarl of wrecked cars in its wake.

Eve was speeding toward the rapidly closing exit gate. The open space between the center post on the left and the gate on the right was narrowing fast in front of her. But she didn't stop.

The Rolls-Royce passed through the tight opening, the post shearing off the driver's side mirror and the leading edge of the gate scraping the entire length of the SUV, shooting off a spray of sparks, each one a flaming hundred-dollar bill.

Eve dodged the clogged intersection by making a hard right and driving through the exit-side waterfall, plowing through the shallow pond and across Parkway Calabasas. She mowed over the landscaped median, crossed the opposite roadway, and turned left back onto Park Granada, heading north.

Through it all, the Rolls-Royce's ride was almost supernaturally smooth and silent. It was like she was driving in a sensory deprivation chamber, which gave her an unsettling sense of detachment, as if she were watching the chase rather than participating in it.

Jack made a sharp, screeching left into the Commons shopping center, the Escalade fishtailing as he fought for control, shearing off his dangling front bumper and sending it cartwheeling into the air.

The bumper ricocheted off the Rolls-Royce's massive chrome grill, and right over the Spirit of Ecstasy, as Eve followed the Escalade into the Commons.

Jack came to a tire-squealing stop in front of the supermarket, bailed out of the Escalade, and ran into the store.

Eve pulled up behind his Escalade, drew her weapon, and rushed into the supermarket after him. She was nearly mowed down by the rush of panicked customers fleeing the grocery store like a spooked herd of cattle, but she managed to catch a fleeting glimpse of Jack, on her far right, running toward the liquor section.

She stayed low, moving swiftly but methodically through the store, stopping to glance down each aisle before she crossed them and became an open target. People were still running for the exits and she was worried that Jack might double back on her or slip away in the crowd.

"I know you're here," a man called out from somewhere in the liquor aisles. She hadn't heard Jack speak before but she knew it was him because of the angry desperation in his voice.

Eve peered around the edge of the aisle. Jack was down at the other end, standing near the meat case at the back of the store. He was half turned to his left, holding an open vodka bottle by the neck in one hand and his gun in the other.

"Show yourself," he said. "Don't be a coward."

"Here I am," Eve said, stepping into the aisle in a firing stance. He turned and looked at her, confusion on his face, his gun aimed loosely in her direction. Three shots rang out in rapid succession, shattering the vodka bottle in his hand and dropping him to the floor.

But Eve hadn't pulled her trigger.

She dropped back and peered around the other side of the aisle. At the far end, she saw a young uniformed security guard, still holding the gun he'd just fired.

Eve removed her badge from her belt and held it up. "I'm a sheriff's deputy. Put down your gun."

The security guard, a man she pegged as being in his early twenties, bent down, gently laid the gun on the ground, and backed away from it with his hands raised.

"Oh God, oh God," the guard said, his voice cracking.

Behind Eve, two male deputies rushed in, guns drawn. She knew them by face, but not by name. They knew her, too.

"The assailant is down in the next aisle. The security guard shot him." She gestured to the guard, then looked at one of the deputies. "Call an ambulance and stay with the guard." She met the eye of the other deputy. "Clear the rest of the store and lock it down. No one in or out until the ME and CSU get here."

She returned to the other aisle, her gun aimed at Jack's body, and moved cautiously toward him. His body was still, lying in an expanding pool of blood and vodka, but his gun was still within his reach and she wasn't taking any chances.

She reached him, saw the bullet hole in his forehead and the brain matter all over the packaged meats, and holstered her gun.

"Is he dead?" the security guard asked.

Eve turned to him. He seemed to her like a scared child wearing an adult's oversize uniform.

"I'm afraid so," she said.

The young man dropped to his knees and started to cry.

# CHAPTER THREE

Eve knew before she stepped outside that the media would already be there. The paparazzi haunted the Commons parking lot 24/7, hoping to grab a shot of a celebrity buying groceries, eating at a restaurant, getting a cup of coffee, getting ice cream cones with their kids, or catching a movie. And there would be a hundred civilians, each one an aspiring social media influencer, filming the scene with their phones for a live global audience, making the TV reporters, once they showed up in their lumbering satellite broadcast trucks, feel like the last few dinosaurs left staggering around after the asteroid strike 65 million years ago.

But she went outside anyway, knowing it would beam her face to the world. She needed the fresh air. Her adrenaline rush was crashing, leaving her feeling light-headed and queasy. What she saw in the parking lot, though, stoked her anger, causing her to find new reserves of adrenaline that she didn't know she had.

There were a half dozen patrol cars, sealing off the entry and exit to the shopping center, and uniformed deputies were out unrolling yellow police tape to establish a wide crime scene boundary that would also encompass space for the arrival of more official vehicles. Other deputies were already taking statements from the people who fled the grocery store. And she saw Captain Moffett get out of his plain-wrap Explorer and start marching toward her, his uniform starched and creased as stiff as a suit of armor.

The Lost Hills sheriff's station was located on Agoura Road, on the northwestern boundary of Calabasas, five miles from the Commons shopping center. The captain and the deputies somehow got here, the commercial center of Calabasas, within three or four minutes. She knew that backup should have arrived at the sting house just as fast. Or faster.

*But it didn't.*

And that was infuriating.

Moffett glanced at the bashed-in Rolls-Royce SUV and grimaced with what looked like physical pain before facing Eve. He'd told her before that she didn't deserve a desk at his station, that she was an attention-seeking, backstabbing novice who'd used politics to get what she couldn't earn through skill and experience. She'd been imposed on him by Sheriff Lansing. She was sure the two homicide cases she'd solved hadn't changed Moffett's opinion of her. If anything, they'd hardened his dislike and distrust.

"What's the situation?" he asked.

"An attempted home invasion. Three men with guns. Two of them are dead at the house, the third carjacked a woman and fled here. I gave chase. He's dead in the store."

"You shot him?"

"The store security guard did."

Moffett cursed under his breath and glanced again at the Rolls-Royce.

"That's a half-million-dollar vehicle that's going to need a quarter-million dollars in repairs." She wasn't sure if he was talking to himself or to her. He looked out into the parking lot, at the paparazzi and the civilians with phones and at the first TV news van arriving. "This clusterfuck is going to make national news tonight. Hell, it's probably on CNN right now."

"This could have been contained at the house if we had backup," Eve said, keeping her voice even and tight, trying to tamp down her anger. "Where was it?"

"There was a glitch at the station."

"What kind of glitch?"

"Gastrointestinal," Moffett said. "The deputy assigned to watch the video feed was in the bathroom when the invasion began. He ate a bad taco for lunch. Damn food trucks."

Out of a 24/7 surveillance, the deputy just happened to walk away the instant the invasion occurred? Eve didn't buy the coincidence. It was obvious to her that the deputy wanted them to die, that he'd waited to send backup until he was sure they'd survived. It was payback for what she'd done to the Great Whites, a secret clique of deputies that originated within the Lost Hill station and had members throughout the department.

"It's not what you think," Moffett said.

"It's *exactly* what I think."

Moffett pointed a finger at her and started to take a step forward but then, mindful of all the digital eyes on them, lowered his hand and stayed where he was. "That kind of reckless speculation is the last thing we need right now. Focus on the case."

"I will." Every aspect of it, she thought, including the deputy who'd abandoned his post and set them up to die. "Now, if you will excuse me, sir, I've got a crime scene to process."

"Stick to that and stay away from the media. I'll handle them."

"Yes, sir."

She walked away from him and took her phone out of her back pocket to call Duncan. But just as she was about to press the keys, a question occurred to her.

*Why didn't Manny take our iPhones? They're valuable.*

Probably because he knew a cell phone was essentially a tracking device and wasn't worth the risk.

These were smart guys, she thought, who had a very bad day.

She keyed in Duncan's number and he answered immediately.

"Are you okay?" he asked.

Eve took stock of her situation. Three men were dead and she hadn't fired a single shot. She got slapped with a clipboard, but that only hurt her pride.

"Yeah, I'm fine. How about you?"

"I may have to ditch my retirement dream of becoming a fashion model, but otherwise I'm fine."

"Do you need stitches?"

"The paramedic says butterfly bandages should do it."

"He's not a plastic surgeon," she said. "You should see one if you want to avoid a scar."

"It's just a scratch, and if it's not, it'll add the rugged to my good looks. What the hell happened upstairs?"

Eve turned her back on all the cameras watching her in case any-body was trying to read her lips. "I pulled my gun on the guy and he tried to escape by jumping into the pool. He missed. What about you?"

"My guy got distracted by your guy's swan dive and I drew my weapon on him," Duncan said. "He thought he could shoot me anyway. He was wrong. Did you get the runner?"

She told him briefly about what had happened.

He said, "You should thank the security guard."

"For what?"

"Saving your life."

"He didn't," she said. "I had the drop on the gunman. If I thought my life was in danger, I would have put him down before he got a shot off. Just like you did at the house. The guard overreacted."

"Maybe so, but it comes down to this: Do you want the guard to live with the guilt of killing a man? Or do you want to give him a chance to make peace with it?"

Eve wasn't sure Jack had to die, but he put himself in the deadly situation by running into the store with a gun. She'd never know if Jack was about to shoot her or not and she wasn't going to torture herself over it. The security guard shouldn't have to, either. He was only trying to do his job, to do the right thing, even if that ended up being a fatal mistake.

"Thank you, Obi-Wan," she said.

"You're welcome, Grasshopper," he said.

She disconnected the call, pocketed the phone, and noticed Deputy Tom Ross guarding one of the yellow-tape perimeters. He was an ex-marine and she was sure that anybody who looked at Tom, even if he were in a clown suit and makeup, would know he'd been in some branch of the military.

Eve walked toward him, he walked toward her, and they met each other halfway. She glanced at his arms and remembered how safe she'd felt a few weeks ago when, only a few hours after she'd been badly injured, he drove her from the hospital back to Calabasas and then carried her out of his car. It was a more intimate and naked moment for her in some ways than if they'd had sex, though they'd never been lovers nor had the possibility ever crossed her mind. She hardly knew him and yet trusted him implicitly.

"You're hard on vehicles," he said, tipping his head toward the Rolls-Royce.

"I wish it wasn't necessary. I've got a question for you, Tom. Who was the deputy assigned this shift to watch our video feed?"

"Bud Collier."

"I don't know him. What's he think of me?"

"Judging by today, I'd say he's a big fan."

"Does he have the tat?"

Many of the deputies at Lost Hills had Great White tattoos on their calves, including Tom, though it meant something different to him than it did to most of the others in the clique. For him, it was the same as the tattoos he had from the units he'd served with in the Marines. They reflected his devotion to his fellow marines but foremost they represented his allegiance to the flag. His first allegiance now was to the badge, and what it stood for, and not to the Great Whites.

"I haven't noticed," Tom said. "I keep my eyes to myself in the locker room."

She nodded. "Can I get some gloves from you and borrow your notebook and pen?"

He took a pen and a small notebook from his breast pocket and handed them to her, then reached into his back pocket for a pair of disposable rubber gloves, which he gave to her. "Watch your back."

"It's a little late for that," she said.

He shook his head. "Not as long as you're still alive."

Eve went back into the supermarket and found the security guard sitting on a folding chair by the florist's stand. He looked pale, and was hunched over a bucket, the wrapped roses that were once in it piled neatly on the floor beside him. A uniformed deputy stood near him, holding the guard's gun in an evidence baggie. The deputy didn't seem much older than the guard, but their bearing and maturity were entirely different. She motioned the deputy over and noted the name on his chest tag: Donald Helm. Every time she saw a uniformed deputy now, she couldn't help wondering: *Friend or foe?*

"What can you tell me about the guard?"

"His name is Grayson Mumford, age twenty-four. He's worked for Big Valley Security for five years. I did a quick background check. He's licensed to carry the weapon, his California guard card is valid, and he's got no arrests."

*Friend,* she decided.

She was familiar with Big Valley Security. It was founded by an ex-LAPD deputy chief and their officers were all over Calabasas, providing security patrols for the city's private lake, the country club, most of the gated communities, and several of the shopping centers.

"Did you get his story?"

Deputy Helm nodded. "You want to hear it?"

She glanced at Grayson. He was shivering and she could smell the puke in his bucket from ten feet away.

"No, thank you, I'd rather get it from him first, but please send me a copy of your report," she said. "Can you call a paramedic for him, just in case he's going into shock?"

"Already have," he said.

"Good, but keep them back until I'm finished talking with him."

Eve walked over to Grayson and crouched in front of him. He'd just shot a man, and he was deeply shaken, but his gaze still dropped to her cleavage. She'd forgotten how she was dressed and wished she could cover up.

"I'm Detective Eve Ronin. How are you feeling, Grayson? Is there anything I can do for you?"

He shook his head. "I can't believe this happened. I mean, we trained for a robbery or active shooter situation, but it wasn't enough."

"What did the training miss?"

"The horror," he said.

She spotted an empty bucket, grabbed it, turned it over, and used it as a seat, sitting beside him so he wouldn't be distracted by her cleavage. "Can you tell me what happened?"

"You were here. You know."

She took out the notebook and pen that Tom gave her. "I need to see it from your perspective."

"I was walking the back of the store, keeping my eye on things, when I heard a car skid to a stop outside and someone yell, 'He's got a gun.' I looked down the aisle and saw the guy going for the spirits section. So I went the same way."

"Why did you do that?"

He seemed perplexed for a moment. "I don't know. I guess I thought it was my job. Run towards danger, not away from it."

That was true for cops, soldiers, and firefighters, but Eve didn't think that was part of his training. It was more likely the concept of "flee, deny, defend." His first priority should have been to get people out of the store. Failing that, it would be to prevent the gunman from reaching people by getting them behind locked doors or other obstacles. And, as a last resort, attack the gunman. Grayson started with the final option.

"Go on," Eve said.

"I hid in the condiments aisle and waited to see what he'd do next . . . but, out of the corner of my eye I saw a woman go his way. It was you."

"Did you see my gun?"

Grayson shook his head. "All I registered was that you were a woman. Then I heard him say, 'Show yourself.' I thought he was talking to me. But then I heard the woman, you, say, 'Here I am,' and I thought, 'Oh shit, she's crazy, she's going to get killed,' so I stepped out, saw him turning to shoot you, and I . . ." His voice trailed off and he dry-heaved into the garbage can. When he looked at her again, he had tears in his eyes. "I killed him."

She thought about what Duncan told her, pocketed the notebook, and put her hand on his back to comfort him. "You also saved my life."

"Really? You mean I'm not going to prison?"

"Definitely not. You were defending another person who was in mortal danger and I'm grateful."

"But you had a gun," he said. "You could have defended yourself."

"You didn't know that," she said, patting his back to reassure him. "You did the right thing, Grayson. You should be proud of yourself."

"I don't see how I can ever be proud of this."

# CHAPTER FOUR

Eve left Grayson Mumford with Deputy Helm and the paramedics, sought out the store manager in the crowd outside, and brought her back in to get a look at the security camera footage of the incident.

The manager, a very thin woman in her fifties, wore her hair in a bun so tight, Eve wondered how she was able to blink.

"I saw you shopping with your husband the other day," the manager said as she led Eve to the back room. "The typical Calabasas midlife crisis wife. I had no clue you were a police officer."

"That was the idea. My partner and I were undercover."

"The Reseda midlife crisis wife is the same age as you but shops at Brandy Melville, drives a Mustang, and is very proud of her pierced nipple. If you ever want to play that part, I can give you a picture of my ex-husband's wife."

"I'll keep that in mind."

Next to the manager's office was a windowless room that contained an ergonomic office chair, a desktop computer, and three large monitors, each showing about a dozen thumbnails of individual security camera views from inside and outside the store. The manager typed some commands on the keyboard.

"Here's the playback from a few minutes before the crazy man came in. You can hit the space bar to stop and use the mouse to scrub back on any of the screens," she said. "I can give you a link so you can stream or download this from your computer or I can copy it all to a thumb drive to take it with you."

"The link will be fine," Eve said and handed her a card with her email address and phone number.

The manager left the room and Eve let the footage play out, focusing her attention on Jack and Grayson from multiple angles. Jack went straight for the liquor section and Grayson's actions followed the story he'd told Eve. She'd give the video a closer look later.

Eve took out her phone and contacted the day's on-call judge to get telephonic warrants for the footage from the grocery store cameras and also from the Vista Grande gate. The manager had volunteered the footage, and Eve expected the Vista Grande homeowner's association to be cooperative as well, so the warrants weren't necessary to compel compliance. But that wasn't why she wanted them. Her goal was to limit the opportunities for a defense attorney to get any evidence thrown out on a technicality.

Upon hearing the situation, the judge granted the warrants without question, as Eve knew he would. The legal justification for the video was obvious.

She ended the call and when she emerged from the back room, she saw the CSU team had already arrived and was taking pictures of the crime scene. Paramedics were also treating Grayson Mumford, who was wrapped in a blanket and sipping a bottle of water.

Eve put on the rubber gloves Tom gave her and walked along the back of the store to the body of the assailant. Jack had bled out and his upper body was now in the center of a wide puddle of blood. A tall, very thin CSU tech in a Tyvek jumpsuit, rubber gloves, and booties was taking photos of the body and the scene around it. The tech was Lou Noomis, who had an Adam's apple so large that his neck reminded Eve of a snake swallowing a rat.

"Hey, Lou. You got here fast."

"We were nearby, wrapping up a shotgun suicide in Canoga Park and heading to lunch. I'm starving, and now I've got to spend a few hours surrounded by food I can't touch."

"Must be hell. Could I get a look at the guy's wallet and personal effects?"

"Sure." Noomis' knees cracked as he crouched down and carefully extracted a wallet, a cell phone, and a key fob with a Hyundai logo on it from the dead man's pockets without stepping in the blood.

Eve flipped open the wallet and looked at the driver's license. His name was Paul Colter and he lived at an address in Sherman Oaks. She took out her phone and snapped a photo of the license. The credit cards were in the same name. The phone was a typical burner that could be bought for a few bucks just about anywhere. Noomis studied the key fob.

She asked, "Do you recognize it?"

"I think it's for a 2017 Hyundai Sonata, but don't hold me to it."

"He doesn't have any house keys?"

Noomis shook his head. "Maybe they are in his car."

Eve handed the wallet back to him. "Sorry about your late lunch."

"It's okay, it's how I stay so slim."

"You get any slimmer, you'll be invisible when you turn sideways."

She walked to the front of the store and met Deputy Helm. "What do the paramedics say about Mumford?"

"Mild case of shock. He'll be fine once he hydrates and warms up."

She spotted a man with a graying crew cut and wearing an expensive tailored suit over his muscled frame crouching beside Grayson. The man exuded "cop" but his suit was too nice for him to be in law enforcement and she'd never seen him before.

"Who is that?" she asked.

"Ethan Dryer. He owns Big Valley Security."

"What is he doing in my crime scene?"

Helm shifted his weight and averted his eyes from her. "Mumford is one of his guards. I figured the kid could use the emotional support right now."

It was an admirable reason, but it was still wrong.

"Did I say anything about letting family or anybody else besides CSU, the medical examiner, or paramedics in here?"

"Dryer is one of us."

"No, he's not. He's a civilian." Eve marched over to Grayson and Dryer. "How are you feeling, Grayson?"

"Better, thanks," he said.

Dryer stood up. "Is he free to go now?"

Eve tipped her head, gesturing for Dryer to follow her. She led him over to the produce section, out of Grayson's view and earshot. "What are you doing here, Mr. Dryer?"

"The store is my client and one of my officers was involved in a shooting. I'm here to provide support and act as his advocate."

"You know better than to walk into an active crime scene without being invited by the investigating detective. You ever do that again and I'll file a complaint with the BSIS," Eve said, referring to the state's Bureau of Security and Investigative Services that oversaw and licensed security companies, bodyguards, alarm companies, repo men, private investigators, and locksmiths.

He smiled. "I was allowed in by the deputies."

Most of whom, Eve thought, were thinking ahead about their post-LASD job options and the possibility of a soft landing in a lucrative private-sector job with Big Valley Security.

"They were wrong," she said.

"Then your problem is with them, not me."

She stepped close to him. "It's with you, Mr. Dryer. I just saw three men die. I'm in no mood for bullshit. Consider this a friendly warning."

His smile vanished and his face hardened. "There's nothing friendly about it. A friend would show me some professional courtesy."

"You aren't a cop. You're a businessman."

"I was a deputy chief at the LAPD."

"That doesn't get you any special treatment. You're no different than any other civilian to me."

"I heard you were hated by just about everybody at LASD. Now I know why. You're a bossy little girl."

She ignored his comment and walked back over to Grayson. "You can go home now, Grayson. But I may circle back to you with some more questions." Eve handed him her card. "You may have some hard days ahead dealing with all of this. Call me anytime if you want to talk."

"Thank you," he said and slipped her card in his pocket.

Eve walked away as Dryer helped Grayson to his feet and went outside. The sun seemed brighter and the loud whap-whap-whap of news choppers circling overhead filled the air. The crowd behind the crime scene tape in the parking lot had doubled and now four more TV news trucks were parked on the street, satellite dishes raised, the reporters standing on the sidewalk facing their cameramen, using the shopping center as the exciting backdrop for their live broadcasts.

She spotted Tom near his patrol car, took his notebook out of her pocket, tore out the pages she'd written on, and walked over to him.

"Thanks for the notebook and pen," she said, handing them back to him and stuffing the torn pages in her pocket. "The gunman had car keys for a 2017 Hyundai Sonata. Can you put out the word to check Vista Grande, Calabasas Road, the golf course, this parking lot, and the surrounding area for any old Sonatas? He might have parked, walked to Vista Grande, and jumped a fence to get in."

Tom nodded. "Roger that."

"Thanks," Eve said, then saw Captain Moffett coming her way. She left Tom to meet the captain.

"You need to talk to the Officer-Involved Shooting Team," Moffett said. "So does Duncan. They'll meet you at the station."

It was a waste of time, she thought. The incidents were all on video, here and at the house, and she had more pressing things to do.

"Can't that wait, sir? There's work I need to do first at Vista Grande. We don't know how the three men got into the community or how they were planning to get out. We also need to—"

"I know what needs to be done, Detective," Moffett interrupted. "I didn't get my captain's bars off a YouTube video. Vista Grande is locked down. I've got deputies canvassing the neighborhood looking for possible accomplices, collecting home security footage, and questioning gardeners, pool men, everybody that's still inside the gates. You'll get all the reports and footage. But, frankly, I think the spree of home invasions just ended."

Of course he did, she thought, because that might reduce the heat from the media, and the public, over the deaths at the house, the car chase, and the shooting at the supermarket before any outrage over the violent outcome came to a boil.

But she didn't think the case had ended with the deaths of Manny, Moe, and Jack. There were still too many unanswered questions.

He tossed her a set of keys. "Take my Explorer and pick up Duncan. You can go back to work once Officer-Involved is finished with you. I'll get a ride back with a deputy."

Eve nodded and started toward his car when he spoke up again.

"Oh, and Ronin? Bring back the vehicle in one piece."

There were news helicopters circling high above Vista Grande and Eve even spotted a couple of drones buzzing like flies overhead as she drove up to the sting house. She wondered if the drones were from the media or curious homeowners.

Crime scene tape was stretched around the house and vehicles from CSU and the county medical examiner's office were parked in the motor court. She parked at the curb and strode to the house. As she approached, she could see through the open front door out to the backyard, where white tents had been erected over the dead bodies to hide them from the media overhead. CSU techs were everywhere, taking photos.

Duncan met her in the entry hall. The blood had been cleaned off his face and his cut pinched closed by several butterfly bandages. The wound didn't look like "just a scratch" to her, but she kept her opinion to herself.

"You get anything off the shooters?" she asked.

"Just their IDs, car keys, and burner phones. Both are white males in their twenties who live in the valley."

"Same with the gunman at the supermarket," she said.

He told her that the name of the guy she'd dubbed Manny was Joel Dalander, who resided in Reseda, and that Moe was Greg Nagy, who lived in Santa Monica. "I sent deputies to look for their cars."

"Likewise," she said, and told him the name of the third man, the guy she thought of as Jack, was Paul Colter. "These guys weren't what I was expecting."

"You thought they were going to be gang members, probably Hispanic, didn't you?"

"Most of the time they are."

"Walking into a case with preconceived notions is the biggest mistake you can make. You have to approach each investigation as if it's the first one you've ever done, which should be especially easy for you."

"Because I have so little experience."

"There's always a silver lining."

"Hard to see it in this situation."

"It's right there." Duncan gestured to the backyard. "They're dead, we're alive."

"Speaking of which," she said, "Officer-Involved is waiting for us at the station."

"I don't see the point. They can just make some popcorn and watch the movies. I'd like to see what happened upstairs myself."

She started walking back to the door. "It's not very exciting."

"I want to see the expression on your face when the guy bolted." Duncan stumbled and Eve caught him by the forearm.

"Are you sure you're all right?"

"Yeah, I've just been sitting a long time and my blood sugar is low."

They started walking, but she kept her hand on his arm to steady him and he didn't shrug it off.

"You ate two hours ago," she said.

"Exactly, I'm starving. Let's swing through McDonald's on our way back." He stopped when he saw the Explorer, a look of disappointment on his face. "Where's the Rolls?"

"Trashed."

"How many cars have you destroyed in the last four months?"

The tally depended on whether she counted her Subaru Outback, which deputies had spray-painted with the words TRAITOR BITCH and stuffed with bags of dog shit a few weeks ago, though she couldn't prove that they were the culprits.

"I haven't kept track," she said.

"That says it all."

They got into the Explorer and Eve drove them away. As she passed a patrol car parked at the gate, she asked Duncan a question that had been nagging at her for the last hour or so.

"When did backup finally arrive?"

"Too late to be considered backup."

"I'm sorry," Eve said, turning left and heading north on Parkway Calabasas toward Calabasas Road and the freeway.

"It's not your fault the deputy assigned to surveillance fucked us."

"Yes, it is. I'm the one who is loathed by most of the department. It's me they want to hurt. You're collateral damage."

"I'm your partner. I was an active participant in everything they hate you for."

"You didn't get promoted to homicide, leaping over detectives with years of experience, because you were the star of a viral YouTube video."

"Good point," he said. "Apology accepted."

# CHAPTER FIVE

They stopped at the McDonald's on Las Virgenes Road, also known as Malibu Canyon, a half mile from Lost Hills' sheriff's station. Eve walked into the restaurant with Duncan, smelled the aroma of french fries, and realized that she was ravenous, too. Duncan ordered them each a Double Quarter Pounder with Cheese combo meal, Eve paid for it since his "show-cash" was now evidence, and they settled into a booth.

"I figure the department owes us lunch," he said. "And the upgrade to Double Quarter Pounders."

Eve couldn't disagree with that.

They were both drawing curious glances from the other McDonald's patrons because they were considerably overdressed for the place, which was filled with people in beachwear who were either on their way to or from Malibu.

"I think we're violating the dress code," she said.

Duncan took a look around. "If you take off that jacket, you'll fit right in."

Between bites of his burger, Duncan called the judge to get telephonic search warrants on the homes, vehicles, and phones of the three dead assailants, but in doing so, he dribbled some ketchup on his Louis Vuitton camouflage shirt to go with the blood.

The judge granted their warrants, which Eve knew was a no-brainer given the situation. Eve's phone vibrated in her pocket. She looked at the caller ID: SHARK. It was Linwood Taggert, her Hollywood agent. She ignored it.

They finished their meals and headed to the station, which was on the west side of Agoura Road, parallel to the freeway, and was up against the boundary line between the small cities of Calabasas and Agoura, both of which contracted with the LASD for law enforcement services.

Eve drove through the gates to the restricted parking area in the back, where the employees parked their cars among the patrol units, assault vehicles, mobile command center, and other official vehicles. There was also a large helipad, often used as a staging area for search-and-rescue operations in the Santa Monica Mountains.

She parked beside her freshly repainted Subaru Outback and they went inside, directly to their respective locker rooms, to change into their own clothes before their interviews with the Officer-Involved detectives.

Eve was eager to peel off her boob tape and get back into her usual blouse, blazer, and slacks. But since she didn't have a spare bra, she had to live with the tape for the rest of the day.

She was just buttoning her blouse when she heard what was clearly a brawl in the men's locker room next door and Duncan saying, "Confess or I'll break your fucking arm."

Eve ran into the men's locker room. A red-haired man, wearing nothing but a pair of tighty-whities, was facedown on the floor, his nose bleeding, a fully dressed Duncan Pavone on his back, pinning his right arm behind him at a painful angle. Three deputies, in various stages of undress, stood around them, tensely watching the scene.

Duncan looked defiantly at the men. "If any of you boys tries to pull me off, I'll snap this bastard's arm like a twig, so back the fuck away."

They did, which gave Eve room to step forward without having to shoulder anyone out of her way. "Bud Collier, I presume?"

Duncan gave the man's arm a twist, eliciting a cry of pain. "The bastard almost made me a cliché: the old detective killed three months before his retirement. Can you believe that?"

Eve squatted in front of Collier and noticed the Great White tattoo on his calf: two surfboards, a gun, and a great white shark arranged so the pointed front sight of the gun barrel, the fins and tail of the shark, and the tips of the surfboards evoked the six points of a sheriff's star badge set against the backdrop of a cresting wave.

Collier gritted his teeth and glared at her with hatred.

She sighed and rose to her feet. "He's not going to say anything, Duncan. He'd rather have the broken arm as a badge of honor, to show his buddies that he didn't talk and fool them into thinking he has some guts. Don't give the coward the satisfaction."

"You're probably right." Duncan leaned close to Collier's ear and whispered, "You want me dead? Next time, pretend to be a man and come at me yourself. Don't get someone else to do it for you." Duncan let go of Collier's arm, got to his feet, and stared down the men around them. "You boys have something you want to say?"

The men shared some awkward looks between them, then dispersed to their various lockers to finish getting into or out of their uniforms.

"That's what I thought." Duncan adjusted his food-stained tie, straightened his hopelessly wrinkled off-the-rack jacket, and headed for the door.

Eve kept an eye on Collier as Duncan walked away in case he tried to take a cheap shot in retaliation and then followed her partner out.

Once they were out in the hall, she turned to Duncan. "Beating Collier up wasn't a wise move."

"What are they going to do, fire me? I'm retiring. Besides, that coward isn't going to file a complaint and neither are any of his buddies."

"How did it feel to break his nose?"

"Great," he said. "Did I get any of his blood on my tie?"

"It's hard to tell with all the other stains."

"Then it's a good thing I haven't washed it."

"You've never washed a tie in your life," she said. "You just throw them away when they start to decompose and buy a new one."

"Now you know why," he said.

Eve spent nearly two hours being interviewed about the events at the house and the supermarket but the detectives weren't hard on her. They had no reason to be. She had nothing to do with Joel Dalander's ill-fated leap off the balcony, nor did she shoot Greg Nagy or Paul Colter. But her actions did end in two deaths, even if they weren't by her hand, so she didn't blame them for wanting an explanation from her.

She left the interview room and went to the squad room, where she was surprised to see Duncan already at his cubicle, hunched over his computer.

"How did you get out so fast?" she asked.

"I didn't have as much of a story to tell as you. I didn't leave the house. Speaking of which, I just watched the video of you in the master bedroom when Dalander bolted. The what-the-hell look on your face is priceless." Duncan pointed to his computer screen, where he'd freeze-framed on Eve's face. "I think I'll make a T-shirt out of it."

"Let me see the video of your shooting."

Duncan tapped a few keys and the videos came up. She saw Duncan, sitting in an easy chair in the great room, and Greg Nagy, his body half turned away from the backyard window, pointing his gun at him. Then, outside in the background, Dalander's body seemingly dropped from the sky and hit the patio, startling Nagy, who whirled around to look. That's when Duncan drew his gun. Nagy turned back, already in shock, and was doubly surprised to see a gun aimed at him. It was obvious to Eve that Nagy was a twitch away from shooting. But Duncan fired first, two shots right in the chest that sent Nagy stumbling backward and crashing through the window. He was dead before he hit the ground and Duncan hadn't even risen from his chair.

"It's a justified shooting," Eve said.

"Of course it was. The security guard's shoot was justified, too."

"Justified, maybe. Necessary? I don't know."

"You just hate that somebody, especially a civilian, saved you." Duncan gestured to the dry-erase board across the room. She saw that he'd taped eight-by-ten blowups of the assailants' DMV photos onto the board under their names. "I ran our three robbers through the system and confirmed their present addresses. They've never been arrested, by the way."

That was another surprise. Eve was expecting them to be career criminals, but she didn't say that because she didn't want to get another lecture about the pitfalls of preconceived notions.

"Whose place do you want to visit first?" he asked.

"Joel Dalander seemed to be the leader of the crew," Eve said. "Let's begin there."

She started for the door.

"Hold up," Duncan said, staying in his seat. "None of these addresses are in our jurisdiction. We need to call for babysitters."

The LASD's jurisdiction was limited to specific areas of Los Angeles County without police departments of their own. For Lost Hills, it was an area bordered by Santa Monica Bay to the south, Ventura County to the northwest, and the City of Los Angeles to the northeast and east. Within those boundaries, the LASD was the law in Malibu, the Santa Monica Mountains, and the surrounding communities of Calabasas, Westlake Village, and Agoura Hills. But stepping on the LAPD's toes, and vice versa, was a daily, if not hourly, occurrence.

"We're just going to talk to some people," Eve said. "Maybe take a look around."

"And there could be somebody with a gun waiting for us and the last thing we need is another shoot-out today."

Duncan picked up the phone and began making calls to arrange for LAPD patrol cars to meet them at each location.

After World War II, the farmland in the San Fernando Valley was leveled and subdivided to build thousands of charmless stucco boxes for returning GIs and their families to live in. Eve thought the homes in this particular Reseda neighborhood, between Sherman Way and Saticoy, hadn't aged well, many of them altered by slapdash second-floor additions and attached garages sloppily converted into rooms.

An LAPD black-and-white was parked in front of Dalander's place, which was among the most well-kept homes on the street. The paint wasn't peeling, the landscape was watered and trimmed, and the garage was still a garage, the roll-up door open, showing off a clean and orderly interior, not even an oil spot on the painted concrete floor.

Eve and Duncan emerged from the plain-wrap Explorer she was driving and met the officers on the street. Duncan handled the introductions.

"The garage was open when we got here," the officer said. "And we haven't seen any activity."

"How long have you been here?" Duncan asked.

"Maybe two minutes," he said. "What happened to your cheek?"

"I cut myself shaving."

"Jesus. What do you shave with?"

"A switchblade," Duncan said. "I have very hearty stubble."

While they were talking, Eve walked up Dalander's driveway toward the open garage. His next-door neighbor, a middle-aged man in a golf shirt, Bermuda shorts, and flip-flops, pretended to be watering his dead juniper hedge so he could observe what was going on. A dog barked loudly inside his house.

The man said, "If you're looking for Sherry, she's gone."

"When did she leave?"

"Bolted out of here like her house was on fire a couple of hours ago. She ran over a squirrel." He pointed to the roadkill on the street, not far from where Duncan and the officers were standing. Eve had run over it, too.

"Do you happen to know her full name?"

"Sure. It's Sherry Simms. With two *m*'s."

Duncan gestured to the officers to stay put and moseyed over, holding up his phone, which displayed the DMV photo of Joel Dalander. "Do you know this man?"

The neighbor shut off his hose, now that the pretense wasn't necessary to learn what was going on. "That's Joel Dalander, her boyfriend. They've rented that house together for about a year."

"What do you know about Joel and Sherry?" Eve asked.

"They have sex so loud it scares our dog. I wanted to call you about it, but my wife says it's not a crime. Is it?"

"I don't think so," Duncan said.

"It's disturbing the peace, isn't it? How is loud sex any different than loud music?"

"Loud music can go on for hours," Duncan said.

The neighbor gave Duncan a sad look. "I guess you've forgotten what it's like to be in your twenties."

Eve spoke up before this conversation could go too far astray. "Can I get your name, sir?"

"Neville Nussbaum."

"Do you know what Joel and Sherry do for a living?"

"Sherry works from home, some kind of mail-order business. Joel's a night manager at the Burger King on Vanowen. He always gives us a free order of fries or a shake when we go in but that doesn't make up for the megaphones they're holding in bed."

Duncan showed Nussbaum pictures of Greg Nagy and Paul Colter on his phone. "You ever see these two guys around?"

Nussbaum looked at the photos and shook his head. "Nope. But it's not like I had Joel and Sherry under surveillance. I'm not a nosy neighbor."

Eve handed Nussbaum her card. "Here's my card. Please give me a call if you happen to see her come home."

"Sure thing." Nussbaum nodded and studied her card. "What did they do?"

"We just want to talk with her."

Nussbaum tipped his head toward the two officers. "You always bring backup for a conversation?"

"Sometimes conversations can get heated," Eve said. "Do Joel and Sherry have any dogs or other animals in the house?"

Eve didn't want to walk in and get attacked by a pit bull.

"Nope," he said.

"Thanks for your help." Eve smiled and followed Duncan into the garage, both of them putting on plastic gloves as they walked.

"Very tidy," Duncan said. "I don't trust people with clean garages."

"Why not?" Eve asked, noticing that several of the shelves held packing materials: rolls of Bubble Wrap, bags of Styrofoam "popcorn," rolls of packing tape, and stacks of unassembled flat-rate priority-mail boxes in various sizes.

"Most normal people have too much going on in their lives to worry about keeping the garage clean."

That conclusion made no sense to Eve, who was most interested in Sherry's quick flight. "She knew we were coming, which means there was at least one accomplice in Vista Grande who knew what went down."

"Or she saw the news," Duncan said.

"We need to make sure there are squad cars at the other locations to keep anybody else from bolting, if it's not already too late."

"I'll contact the dispatcher, have her call the watch commanders in Sherman Oaks and Santa Monica, and tell them to send units to watch the houses and stop anybody who tries to leave. You can go ahead and start the search in the meantime."

Duncan went back to the Explorer.

Eve tested the knob on the door that led into the house. It was unlocked. She started to open it, then thought about how the garage door was left wide open, practically inviting them to come inside, and then she remembered a scene in a movie where a cop was in a similar situation. He opened the door to the house, triggered a trip wire, and the house blew up.

She hesitated and thought perhaps she should try a different door. Or a window.

Or maybe she'd just watched too many dumb movies. Things like that didn't happen in real life.

*Screw it.*

She opened the door and stepped into the kitchen, which was clean but looked as if it hadn't been touched since a remodel in the 1970s. Formica floors, yellow laminate countertops, and dark wood cabinets. Even the appliances seemed dated, except for a Nespresso machine and a microwave on the counter.

"Hello?" Eve called out. "Anybody here? I'm a police officer with a search warrant."

The air inside the house was still and undisturbed. She was certain that nobody was home.

She walked through the kitchen to the living room, which was dominated by a huge flat-screen TV, electronic gaming equipment, and an elaborate stereo system. The leather-upholstered furniture looked new.

Eve continued down a short hallway to one of the two bedrooms. The first one was being used as an office, and the shelves held more packing and mailing materials as well as handbags, wallets, belts, and various accessories from Gucci, Chanel, Vuitton, and other major designers, boxes of Air Jordan shoes, and assorted jewelry. There was a stack of mailing labels on the desk, a printer, a wireless touch pad, and a foam wrist rest for a missing computer.

She picked up one of the mailing labels. The return address was a Reseda PO box on Vanowen and the company name was It's A Steal.

*Cute.*

She pocketed the label. Duncan came in and said, "What do you bet all of this stuff is stolen goods?"

"I'm certain of it." Eve showed him the mailing label. "Cocky, aren't they?"

"Not anymore."

"There's a printer but no computer. She must have taken it with her." Eve spotted a shredder beside the desk and pulled out the bucket. It was full of confettied paper and bits of other material she couldn't identify. "I wonder what this is."

Duncan looked over her shoulder. "Let's get CSU to look at it. They probably can't put any of it back together, but at least they can tell us what it was."

He started sorting through the drawers and papers while Eve used her phone to take pictures in the office and throughout the house. She'd learned the hard way the importance of documenting a scene, that what might first appear to be an insignificant, mundane detail could break a case.

In the master bedroom closet, Eve discovered two tank tops from Brandy Melville, a box of unopened burner phones, and a carton of bullets.

Duncan put in a call to CSU to come over to process the shredder basket, the bullets, and all the stuff in the office that were likely stolen goods.

Eve asked the LAPD officers to stick around until the CSU got there, and then she and Duncan got into the Explorer to head to Paul Colter's house.

After Duncan radioed the dispatcher to let them know where they were going, he turned to Eve and said, "Sherry Simms drives a new Mustang. I saw the lease statement."

If Sherry didn't go to prison, Eve thought, she could become a Reseda midlife crisis wife. All she needed was a pierced nipple, if she didn't have one or two already.

"We can put out an APB on her car, track her phone, and attach an alert to her credit cards so we get notified when she uses them."

"No, we can't," he said. "We have no grounds for the warrant."

Eve held up the mailing label and waved it at him. "It's A Steal?"

"That won't convince a judge. Sleeping with a home invader doesn't make her an accomplice. We can't prove yet that she's committed any crime. And if she's smart, and I suspect she is, she's not going to use her phone or her credit cards."

"At least she didn't wire the kitchen door to a bomb."

"I saw that movie, too."

"Is that why you had me go into the house alone while you went to call the dispatcher?"

"Of course it was. I'm eighty days from retirement," he said. "If I'd opened the door, there *definitely* would have been a bomb."

# CHAPTER SIX

Eve pulled up beside the LAPD patrol car parked down the street from Paul Colter's Sherman Oaks house and rolled down her window. There were two uniformed officers inside. One Asian, one African American.

"Any activity?" Eve asked, eyeing the house. It was in the flats of Sherman Oaks, south of Ventura Boulevard, an area that was once part of Van Nuys until the residents seceded in the 1990s and joined their more affluent neighbor. The name change alone doubled the property values of the ranch-style homes almost overnight.

The Asian officer shook his head. "Just an Amazon delivery. A woman I'd say is in her sixties answered the door and accepted the package."

His partner spoke up. "That's probably Estelle Colter. I ran the address. The house belongs to Alan and Estelle Colter."

"Thanks," Eve said. "We're going to serve our search warrant. You mind watching our backs?"

"To protect and serve, that's our motto," he said.

Eve pulled the Explorer into the Colters' driveway and the patrol car pulled up to the curb in front of the house. The front yard was all gravel and cactuses. Eve figured the Colters probably had the lowest water bill on the block. She and Duncan got out and walked to the front door. The two LAPD officers stayed a couple of steps behind them.

Duncan tipped his head to Eve, his signal for her to take the lead, as he almost always did when a woman was involved. It was sexist and irritating but she'd learned to live with it. She leaned on the doorbell. A moment later, the door was opened by a woman Eve assumed was Estelle Colter. She was heavyset and wearing lots of turquoise jewelry.

"Can I help you?" Estelle looked past them to the two police officers and looked nervous. Anybody would be nervous, Eve knew, if cops showed up at their door.

Eve flashed her badge. "I'm Detective Eve Ronin, Los Angeles County Sheriff's Department, and this is my partner, Duncan Pavone. Does Paul Colter live here?"

Duncan held up Colter's photo. Estelle glanced at the photo, the concern on her face sharpening.

"Yes, he's my son," she said. "What's wrong?"

"Can we talk about it inside?" Eve asked.

Estelle stepped aside for them and Duncan gestured to the officers to stay put. Eve and Duncan walked past her into the house. It had the feel of a home that was professionally decorated. Everything was too perfectly put together, the knickknacks impeccably sized for their spots and all part of a unified, contemporary southwestern theme more fitting for Santa Fe than Sherman Oaks.

"Has he been in a car accident?"

"Why do you say that?" Duncan asked.

"Because he drives for Uber and Lyft and is working right now."

"What kind of car does he drive?"

"My husband's old 2019 C-Class."

Also known to Lost Hills deputies as the Calabasas Corolla. The Mercedes was the perfect car for cruising the streets without being noticed. It might even get him through the resident's lane at Vista Grande with just a nod to the guard.

Duncan asked, "Do you have his number?"

"Of course," Estelle said, and gave Duncan the number. He stepped into an adjacent hallway to make the call, mostly for show, and on the off chance somebody else might answer.

Eve gestured to the couch in the living room. "Can we sit down?"

They went into the living room, Estelle taking a seat on the couch and Eve sitting on the edge of a chair that was kitty-corner from her.

"Do you need to talk to Paul?" Estelle asked. "Is he in some kind of trouble?"

Eve held up her phone and showed her photos of Joel Dalander and Greg Nagy. "Do you know these two men?"

"No, I don't. Who are they?"

"We think they are two of your son's friends."

"Oh, is that what this is about? Those men? Whoever they are?"

Duncan came in, sticking his phone in his pocket. "Went straight to voice mail."

*No surprise,* Eve thought.

"He doesn't answer his phone when he has a fare," Estelle said. "You can try back later. Now, will you please tell me what this is about?"

Duncan said, "Do you mind if I use your bathroom?"

"It's down the hall," she said. "Second door on your left."

"Thank you." Duncan went away on what Eve knew was a pretense to snoop around and also leave her with the painful task of breaking a mother's heart.

Eve took a deep breath and plowed ahead. "There's no easy way to say this, Mrs. Colter. Your son was involved in an armed home invasion robbery in Calabasas today."

Estelle blinked hard and cocked her head, confused.

"I don't understand. Did it happen to someone Paul dropped off at home? Or do you think he unknowingly gave the burglar a ride?"

"Paul was one of the perpetrators."

"No, no, no, you're making a big mistake, it couldn't possibly be Paul." Estelle toyed with her turquoise sunburst necklace, running her fingertips over the sharp rays around the intensely blue stone. "He's not a gang member or a criminal. Call him again in a few minutes, you'll see."

Eve lowered her voice, softening her tone. "I'm sorry to have to tell you this. After the home invasion, he carjacked a vehicle, drove to a grocery store, and was shot by a security guard. Your son is dead."

Estelle shook her head repeatedly and held up her hands in a halting gesture, a smile on her face. Eve had noticed early in her job that people smiled at the strangest times, that smiles weren't always smiles. Sometimes they were pain.

"That's absolutely crazy," Estelle said. "You're not making any sense. *It's not Paul.* I'm calling my husband. He's an attorney, he'll sort this out."

"That's a good idea," Eve said.

Estelle got up, went into the kitchen, and emerged a moment later holding a cell phone. Her lower lip was beginning to tremble and Eve could see tears welling in her eyes.

"Alan? There's a police detective here. There's been a horrible misunderstanding. She says that Paul robbed a house in Calabasas, held up a grocery store, and was shot by—" She stopped, apparently interrupted by her husband, a bewildered expression on her face. "No, I haven't seen the news. You *know* about this?"

Eve held out her hand. "May I speak to your husband?"

Estelle spoke into her phone. "The detective wants to talk with you."

She handed the phone to Eve, who introduced herself.

"Oh God," Alan said. "You're the one."

"The one?" Eve said.

"On the news. The detective in the Rolls-Royce who chased the gunman into the supermarket. You think he's our son?" He posed the question with heavy incredulity.

"We know he is."

"It's . . ." He took a long moment to find the word. "Incomprehensible. On the news, they say he was shot dead."

"Yes, he was. I'm very sorry." Eve heard silence on the line. "You should come home. Your wife needs you."

He seemed to choke on something, and when he spoke again, his voice was barely more than a whisper. "Yes, of course, right away. Let me talk to Estelle."

Eve handed the phone back to Estelle, who was crying now. Duncan emerged from the hallway and Eve went over to him to give Estelle, and themselves, some space.

"It's a three-bedroom house," Duncan said, his voice low so they wouldn't be overheard. "One of the bedrooms, I assume it's Paul's, is locked with a dead bolt."

"He really wanted his privacy."

"Maybe he didn't want his mom coming across his gun while she was cleaning his room."

"Or it's stuffed to the rafters with stolen goods."

"We'll soon find out."

"His father's a lawyer," Eve said.

"A patent attorney. I looked on the web while you two were talking. He won't fight us on the warrant."

Eve looked back in the living room and saw Estelle set the phone down on the coffee table with a shaking hand.

"Alan is on the way," Estelle said.

Eve walked over to her. "Do you have a key to Paul's bedroom door?"

Estelle shook her head. Duncan shared a look with Eve, then went outside.

"Alan was furious about the lock." Estelle sniffled and wiped the tears from her cheek with the back of her shaky hand. "He said it was his house, he could go in any room he wanted. But I told him to let Paul have his space. If having a lock made him feel better about being a grown man living at home, so what? What do you care what he's doing in there?"

"Why was Paul living at home?"

"Rents are outrageous in Los Angeles and he's had a hard time finding a decent job. He was just staying here until he got on his feet."

Duncan came back into the house holding a small battering ram. Estelle's eyes widened.

"What is that for?"

Eve said, "We have a warrant to search Paul's room. We're going to have to break the door down. You'll be reimbursed for the damages."

"What do you think you're going to find in there?" Estelle asked. "An explanation?"

"Or something that will lead us to one."

Eve and Estelle followed Duncan down the hall to the locked door. He heaved the ram where the door met the jamb, splintering the wood around the dead bolt. Estelle flinched as if she'd been slapped. The door yawned open, torn free from the jamb.

Duncan set the ram down and put on his plastic gloves.

Eve turned to Estelle and put on her gloves. "You need to stay here in the hall. You can't go in or touch anything."

It was still a teenager's bedroom, frozen in time, but being occupied by an adult. A full-size bed was crammed into the tight space. The walls were adorned with posters of sports and music figures from Colter's youth. The shelves were crammed with books assigned for high school reading, action figures and spaceship models, and a bunch of soccer trophies.

"My daughter played soccer," Duncan said. "She was terrible. Her team ranked last in the league. But they all got trophies."

He picked up one of the trophies and showed it to Eve. There was no championship designation, just the name of his team in the valley youth soccer league and the year that he played.

"That's nice," she said. "It makes everyone feel good and reminds them that it's about sportsmanship, not winning."

Duncan put the trophy back. "It's touchy-feely bullshit. In my day, you got trophies for winning, not for showing up."

"In your day, coaches didn't give much attention to individual self-esteem."

"Yeah, and look where it got Paul," Duncan said.

The bed faced a large flat-screen TV that was mounted high on the wall above Paul's old student desk, where he had a new MacBook, the latest gaming console, a few Rolex watches, a men's gold necklace, and a pair of Gucci sunglasses. There was an iPhone charger plugged into the wall, but no phone.

Estelle gestured at everything on the desk side of the room. "Where did all that stuff come from?"

Eve glanced at her. "You never saw him bring it into the house or wear any of it?"

"Of course not. He couldn't afford any of that."

Duncan got on his knees, peered under the bed, and pulled out a slim box that contained porn DVDs, porn magazines, K-Y Jelly, and a hollow electronic device that looked like a flashlight missing the light and batteries. Eve didn't want to imagine what it was used for but couldn't stop herself from doing so anyway. Neither could Paul's mother.

Estelle covered her mouth and turned away from the door, repulsed by what she saw, and walked away.

Eve shook her head at Duncan. "Did you have to pull out the box while she was standing there?"

Duncan shrugged. "These things happen. At least now we know he didn't have a girlfriend."

He pulled out another box that contained a carton of bullets and a bunch of burner phones, identical to the ones they'd found at Dalander's house.

Eve picked up one of the Rolex watches and dangled it in front of Duncan. "Looks like Paul kept some bling for himself."

"We can leave this for CSU to process and collect as evidence."

"Maybe they can unlock his computer, too."

"It's probably full of porn," Duncan said. "I'll make the call."

Eve took photos of everything so she could create a virtual tour of the room if she needed to, then went out to find Estelle Colter, who was sitting on the couch again, her back straight and stiff. She'd made herself a drink.

"We need to go," Eve said, "but two officers will stay here and wait for the forensic team to arrive to take photos and remove evidence from your son's room. You can't go in until they say it's clear."

"But it's our home."

"That room is a crime scene now. I may be contacting you again with more questions. In the meantime, please feel free to call me if you have any questions or concerns." Eve handed her a card and turned to the front door.

"What Paul did . . . what happened to him . . . it's on the news?" Estelle asked. "Everybody already knows?"

Eve looked back at her. "His name hasn't been released yet."

"But it will be?"

Eve nodded, and dreaded having to inform the next of kin about the deaths of Dalander and Nagy, who might be as in the dark about their criminality as Estelle was about her son's.

Estelle took a long, big gulp of whatever she was drinking and looked at Eve again. "How are we supposed to live with this?"

Eve had no answer for that, so she went outside, where Duncan was giving instructions to the two uniformed officers. She went to the Explorer, got inside, started the engine, and radioed the dispatcher that they were on their way to Santa Monica. Her phone buzzed. She glanced at the screen. Her agent again. She let the call go to voice mail.

Duncan joined her a moment later. Neither of them spoke until they were on the San Diego Freeway, heading south over the Sepulveda Pass into the smog-choked LA basin. The sun was setting, giving the smog a sickly glow that made the landscape look to Eve like an alien world populated by creatures that breathed radiant vomit.

She said, "Maybe Colter was the guy who cased the neighborhood and picked the homes to rob."

"What makes you think that?"

"If he really is an Uber or Lyft driver, he could have circled Calabasas all day to pick up rides that originated or ended inside gated communities. That would give him an opportunity to get behind the gates and cruise the streets. We could get his plates and the gate logs to see when, and how often, he came into the communities where houses were hit."

"Sure we could. But even if that is true, I'd like to know how they were getting in and out for their invasions."

"They could have come up the ridge on foot from the golf course on Parkway Calabasas or from behind the car dealerships on Calabasas Road. All they have to do is climb the fences. A child could do it and there's zero security. They could leave the same way."

"In broad daylight? Carrying armfuls of Versace clothes and Chanel bags stuffed with jewelry, gold, cash, and credit cards down steep hillsides? I don't think so. Besides, they'd be out in the open, easily spotted by people in the homes on the ridge, the car dealership, the street, or even in cars on the freeway."

"I don't think people pay that much attention to who is on the hillsides," Eve said. "They could have had a getaway driver waiting somewhere, like in the Commons parking lot, for their call to pick them up when they hit the street."

"I suppose it's possible," Duncan said.

"But you don't buy it."

"Nope and neither do you."

He was right.

# CHAPTER SEVEN

Greg Nagy lived in a block of new apartment buildings on Seventh Street in Santa Monica. It seemed like everything had been torn down and replaced with apartments since Eve had last been in the area. Even the fire station next door to Nagy's building had a sign out front announcing it would soon be razed for more apartments.

A plain-wrap Dodge Charger, a standard make for unmarked police cars, was parked in the red zone. Eve pulled up behind it. The man who stepped out of the Charger wore an off-the-rack suit that could have come from the same rack that Duncan's suits came from at Men's Wearhouse. He was in his forties, with a nose that had been flattened by fists more than once, a receding hairline, and a tan that matched the unnatural brown color of his hair.

Duncan got out and went straight up to the guy, his arm extended for a handshake. "This is a surprise. Since when do they call out the big guns to be babysitters?"

The men shook hands. "I've been waiting for my invitation to your retirement party. I thought I'd find out personally what happened to it."

"It's coming, Gus. Engraved with a red ribbon."

"Good, because I thought you'd forgotten about me," Gus said. "Where's it gonna be? The Sizzler?"

"Nothing so swanky." Duncan gestured to Eve. "This is my partner, Eve Ronin. Eve, meet Gus Bellows, the most decorated cop in the Santa Monica Police Department. By that, I mean colored hair, fake teeth, and contacts."

Gus grinned and shook hands with Eve. "Pleased to meet you, Eve. Be glad that he's retiring. Donuts' last two partners started out thin like you and a few years later died of morbid obesity."

Eve grinned back, unaccustomed to being greeted warmly by veteran detectives on the LAPD or anywhere else. Most of them felt that they'd met her already on TV and decided they didn't like her. "I've been popping Lipitor tablets like M&M's since our first day."

"Smart woman," Gus said, then tipped his head toward the building, getting down to business. "Greg Nagy lives alone in a studio apartment on the third floor. Number 301. The management company gave me the keys so we don't have to break down the door."

"That was considerate of them," she said.

Gus typed in a key code that opened the door to the lobby, which was just big enough to hold the wall of mailboxes, and led them to the elevator, which was beside the door to the parking garage. Eve opened the door and glanced at the cars. No Calabasas Corollas were in sight. The trio got into the elevator and put on gloves as they rode up to the third floor.

"What's the rent on a studio here?" Duncan asked.

"Seventeen hundred a month."

Duncan whistled. "That's about as much as my mortgage."

"This building is reserved for low-income individuals earning seventy grand a year or less."

Eve was stunned. "That's poverty wage in Santa Monica?"

"And all of Los Angeles County," Gus said.

Duncan looked at Eve. "That's insane. Give me one good reason why anybody lives in Southern California?"

"In-N-Out Burger."

"That's right," he said. "I forgot."

They got out and found themselves facing Greg's studio apartment. Not the most desirable location in the building, she thought. He must hear people coming and going from the elevator at all hours of the day and night.

Gus used his key and opened the door to a narrow hallway, the bathroom on the left. At the end of the hall was the combined kitchen, bedroom, and living space with a window overlooking Seventh Street. To fit inside the hallway without colliding, the three of them had to walk in single file. Eve took the lead, followed by Duncan and Gus.

The kitchen was L-shaped, laid out along the intersection of two walls, with new appliances, contemporary cabinets, and a dozen cartons of sugary breakfast cereals lined up like a row of books on the faux granite countertops.

"The man's a gourmet," Duncan said.

Framed movie posters for *The Terminator*, *Avengers: Endgame*, and *Skyfall* decorated the wall above his bed, which also doubled as his couch, one side facing his desk and a wall-mounted flat-screen TV. She noticed a charger plugged into the wall for a missing iPhone. There was a MacBook on the desk beside a stack of screenplays bound with brass brads between heavy-paper covers with studio logos on the front, the movie titles written on the spines with Magic Markers.

Eve gestured to the scripts. "Looks like he's a reader for a production company, synopsizing and criticizing screenplay submissions for executives who have no time to read themselves. It pays about fifty dollars a script."

"And he's an aspiring writer, which pays nothing." Gus picked up another script off the kitchen counter and read the title page aloud. "*Thrack of Oberon* by Gregory Nagy. Sounds thrilling."

Eve started taking pictures. Duncan opened up the desk drawer and sorted through Greg's bills and papers.

"How do you know about readers?" Duncan asked.

"I made extra cash working as a reader when I was in college. It was easy to do in my spare time," Eve said. "My mom had a boyfriend who was in development."

"You mean he was an adolescent?" Duncan said, grinning.

"I mean his job was to give writers creative suggestions on rewriting their scripts until they were good enough to never get produced."

Gus slid open the built-in closet. It was clean and well organized. Nagy's clothes were hung and neatly folded. His shoes were lined up in rows on the floor. On the top shelf there were several shoeboxes. Gus pulled one down and lifted the lid.

"I guess he didn't want any of his houseguests stumbling on these." He held out the box to Eve and Duncan. It contained loose bullets, a Patek Philippe watch, and a few rings.

"He's got the same kind of goodies as Dalander and Colter," Duncan said. "They all seem to have kept some loot for themselves."

"Insurance for a rainy day?" Gus asked.

"I don't know," Eve said, "but it does make me wonder where the bulk of their money was going. None of these guys was living large. In fact, they all seemed to be just scraping by."

"Maybe there are more accomplices out there," Gus said. "Meaning a bigger split of the pot after each job."

"If so, we haven't got a lead on any of them yet," Eve said. "Nor do we know what ties the three men together."

"They are all in the morgue." Duncan closed the desk drawer. "Let's seal the place up. CSU will come by later to take the computer, watches, and shells."

Gus gestured to the shoes on the closet floor. "The shoes might give you something. I once cracked a murder case because a piece of gravel stuck in the treads of the suspect's Nikes was unique to the victim's garden. The suspect had claimed that he'd never been to the house, so how did the gravel get there?"

"Good idea," Duncan said. "We'll bag the shoes at all three homes. Thanks for the tip."

Eve didn't think it was a useful tip and assumed Duncan was just being polite to his friend.

Gus put his arm around Duncan's shoulders. "I want you to finish your career on a win."

"Finishing alive is a win," Duncan said.

Gus laughed. "Ain't that the truth."

Eve and Duncan stopped in at the Bay Cities Italian Deli up the street for two of their famous Godmother sandwiches-to-go, then ate their dinner as they drove up Pacific Coast Highway, their windows rolled down so they could smell the ocean even if they couldn't see it in the darkness.

They rode in silence. The violence of the morning felt to Eve like it had happened years ago. She'd been constantly busy and on the move since the shootings, so she'd easily avoided thinking much about them, except for her interview with the Officer-Involved team.

But now, as she drove up Malibu Canyon toward Calabasas, the gruesome images were coming back to her. Twice in the last few weeks she'd seen a man's brains blown out in front of her and she knew from painful experience that if she didn't find some other aspect of the case to obsess over, for the next week or so the gore would play on an endless loop in her mind whenever she slowed down, particularly when she tried to go to bed.

The sheriff's black Expedition was parked in the station's back lot when they arrived, his driver sitting behind the wheel, the engine running and wearing sunglasses in case, Eve supposed, the glare of the moon was too hard on his eyes. The deputy's name was Rondo and she'd never heard him speak.

Eve parked and the first thing Duncan did when he got out was knock on the driver's side window of the Expedition and wave at Rondo.

"How do you drive with those sunglasses on at night?" Duncan asked. "Are they infrared so you can see in total darkness? Are they computerized to display some kind of cool digital readout?"

Rondo remained still and expressionless, which seemed to please Duncan as they continued on into the station.

"Why do you go out of your way to irritate that man?" Eve said.

"I want to remind him that he's not invisible."

"It's his job to be invisible." The sheriff had lots of confidential conversations in the back seat of that Expedition, on the phone and with guests, and Eve figured Rondo didn't want to make his boss self-conscious about the deputy who was overhearing it all.

They went inside and walked down the hall toward the squad room. The door to Captain Moffett's office was open as they passed and he called out to them.

"Ronin, Pavone, could we have a moment?"

The "we" meant Moffett and the sheriff, who sat in one of the two chairs in front of the captain's desk.

Sheriff Richard Lansing was in uniform, which he wore the way his father, a preacher, wore his faith. He was in his fifties and, in Eve's view, more of a politician than a cop, using his badge as a stepping-stone to higher office. But those aspirations were in doubt. The department had been embroiled in one scandal after another since the day he took office, a situation Eve had leveraged to her benefit to get to Lost Hills.

The sheriff was both Eve's benefactor and her adversary, and she knew his support for her depended entirely on whether it helped him or not. The angry expression on his face tonight, though, suggested that his support had evaporated.

"Come in, close the door, and sit down," he said.

Eve and Duncan did as they were told, settling on the couch.

Lansing stood up, walked around to the back of his chair, and leaned on it as if it were the pulpit in his father's church. Eve felt a speech full of fire and brimstone coming and braced herself for it.

"On the strength of your experience, and your record of producing results, Captain Moffett approved a costly sting operation to arrest the gang responsible for a series of home invasion robberies. But what we got was a shoot-out in a home that left two suspects dead and another on the run, leading to a carjacking and subsequent pursuit that caused a multivehicle crash that sent two civilians to the hospital." Lansing glared at Eve. "The chase became an active shooter situation in a crowded grocery store that ended when a civilian gunned down the third suspect."

He stared at them, using the silence as a bludgeon for a long minute before continuing.

"Three men dead, two people injured, and a civilian traumatized by having to kill a man. The department is probably facing tens of millions of dollars in lawsuit settlements. Tell me why I shouldn't walk out of here with somebody's badge in my pocket for this?"

Moffett stared at her, too, but there was also a glint of pleasure in his eyes. He was happy to see Eve getting reprimanded. But Lansing's speech, rather than intimidating her, sparked her anger.

"You should absolutely take a badge," Eve said.

"Are you offering me yours?"

"I'm demanding that you take Deputy Collier's. This is entirely his fault."

Moffett leaned forward on his desk and stabbed his finger in her direction. "You're *demanding*? Does your arrogance, disrespect, and insubordination have any boundaries, Ronin? This was your operation, not Collier's. You and Duncan were in the field, not him. You two were responsible for the situation. Don't try to lay the blame on Collier for your catastrophic failures."

"Collier's job was to watch the video feed and send backup to the house the instant the invasion went down," she said. "He didn't do it."

Moffett sat back in his chair. "He did fumble the ball due to circumstances beyond his control, but I've seen the video. You both let things go too far before you took action. You allowed the situation to spiral out of control."

Duncan sighed, a dramatic exhalation that expressed his weariness and his frustration, then said, "We were playing for time, waiting for backup to arrive and catch the perpetrators in the act. But if I'd known the deputy you assigned to watch our backs was taking a shit instead, I would have pulled my weapon on those three assholes before they'd walked in the door."

Moffett waved away Duncan's criticism. "Even if Collier had acted immediately, I'm convinced backup wouldn't have arrived in time to change anything that happened in that house."

Lansing watched the back-and-forth as if he were a spectator at a tennis match. The ball was in Duncan's court.

Duncan said, "What about the carjacking, chase, and the shooting in the grocery store? Are you convinced it wouldn't have prevented that?"

That elicited another wave from Moffett. "Who can say? But I know it should have ended in the house with the two of you."

"Dead," Eve said.

Lansing looked at her now. "Excuse me?"

"I'm finishing the captain's sentence," she said. "*It should have ended in the house with the two of you dead.* That's what Collier was hoping for when he went to the bathroom instead of calling for backup. If he actually left his post. I think he just waited to see how things played out for us."

Moffett pointed his finger at her again. "You're accusing a deputy of attempted murder."

"I sure am. He's got a Great White tattoo on his calf, just like the deputies I sent to prison."

"So do dozens of other deputies who've served here over the years," Moffett said. "It doesn't make them all criminals or put their integrity in doubt."

Eve knew that it was true. Deputy Tom Ross had the tattoo and he was a good cop. There were certainly more like him out there among the deputies in the clique. At least she hoped there were. But that wasn't the point here.

"Collier saw an opportunity for payback and he took it."

"You have no evidence to support that charge," Moffett said.

"I have the three corpses in the morgue and the wound on Duncan's face."

Lansing turned to Duncan. "Do you agree with her?"

"I only slugged Collier when I saw him," Duncan said. "But, in retrospect, I should have arrested him, too."

Moffett rose from behind his desk. "You struck a deputy?"

"I also kneed him in the balls, not that he has any."

"Unbelievable. This is a hell of a way to end your career, Duncan."

Lansing nodded. "It certainly is. A lesser man would have shot the son of a bitch."

Moffett gave him an incredulous look. "You're congratulating Duncan for his self-control?"

"That's right. I don't think I would have been so gentle if I'd been in his position. Collier is fired, effective immediately. I'm going to tell him that if he fights me on this, I'll order Eve and Duncan to arrest him for attempted murder and he can go to prison instead. That's not the only personnel change I'm making. Tomorrow morning, you start your new assignment at the Men's Central Jail."

Moffett was startled. "What?"

"As captain of Lost Hills station, you are ultimately responsible for every operation and the safety of your officers. Collier's fuckup is entirely on you. I'd hoped you'd step up and say that. I'd have respected that and might even have kept you in that seat. But no, you took the coward's way out. You're done here. Pack up."

Moffett started to walk around the desk to the sheriff. "Sir, could we discuss this in private?"

"No, we can't. You're lucky you still have your badge and bars. Say another word and you might lose those, too." Lansing faced Eve and Duncan, his back to Moffett. "I wanted you to hear this for yourselves so you'd know that while Captain Moffett doesn't have your back, I do."

Duncan stood up and offered Lansing his hand. "Thank you, sir."

Lansing shook it. "Step outside with me for a moment."

He opened the door and walked out of the office. Eve and Duncan followed him, without taking another look at Moffett. Lansing led them outside into the parking lot and stopped beside his Expedition before he spoke again.

"I heard from the Officer-Involved unit. The videos at the house and supermarket conclusively clear you both. Your actions were entirely justified." Lansing shifted his gaze to Eve. "Though I wish you could have been gentler on the confiscated Rolls-Royce. It wasn't insured."

Duncan pointed across the parking lot. "I'll swap you my Buick for the Rolls to make up for it."

"I appreciate the selflessness of your offer, Duncan, but I'll pass. Sometime in the next day or two, the mayor of Calabasas and I are going to give that security guard an award for his heroism. I'll let you know when and where. I'm sure you'll both want to be there." His gaze settled on Eve for emphasis.

"Of course," she said. "I wouldn't miss it."

"Good. I want this case wrapped up fast. I'll tell the watch commander to give you a couple of deputies tomorrow to help you with the final grunt work."

"That would be very helpful, sir," Duncan said. "Thank you."

"Now both of you go home. It may not feel like it right now, but this was your lucky day. It could have been you two in the morgue instead of those three assholes."

Lansing got into the back of the Expedition. Eve and Duncan remained in place, like two soldiers at attention, until the sheriff drove off. Duncan watched him go. "Hell of a thing Lansing just did for us."

Eve wasn't impressed. She knew Lansing too well.

"He was protecting himself and the department. Somebody had to take the fall for this mess and it just as easily could have been me instead of Collier and Moffett."

"What about me?"

"You were always in the clear because you're retiring. It's like a temporary superpower. You're invincible to reprimand."

Duncan shook his head and started walking to his Buick. "How can you be so cynical?"

Eve walked beside him. "Lansing knew if he didn't fire Collier, I'd probably go public with my beef and resurrect an embarrassing scandal that he'd like to see remain buried."

"Which one?"

"The corrupt deputies," she said.

"That doesn't really narrow it down," Duncan said. "All of his scandals involve corruption."

"I've only been involved in one. He still could have used this disaster to demote or transfer me, but he knows that the public likes me, even if most of his rank-and-file deputies don't, and there's the possibility of that TV series, which would be good PR for the department. Moffett is largely unknown to the public, at least outside of Calabasas and Malibu, so sacrificing him was an easy call. Besides, the last scandal happened under Moffett's watch. Now Lansing can use me and the security guard's heroism to turn this mess into positive publicity. For Lansing, it always comes down to politics and public perception."

"Or the sheriff simply did the right thing," Duncan said as they reached his car.

"How can you be so naive?"

Duncan started to say something, but she surprised him and herself by pulling him into a long, tight hug. It had just dawned on her how close she came that day to losing him.

He gently patted her back, as if she were one of his daughters, silently reassuring her that everything would be all right.

And then, without a word, she let go of him. They gave each other warm smiles, and she turned and went to her car, wiping the tears from her eyes.

# CHAPTER EIGHT

The Hilton Garden Inn was next door to Calabasas city hall, which was so seamlessly connected to the Commons that the seat of local government seemed like just another place to shop. The two-story hotel was also around the corner from the front gates of Vista Grande. It occurred to Eve, as she trudged to her room, that her temporary home was walking distance from the day's two crime scenes, three if she counted the car crashes in the intersection.

The first thing she did when she got into her room was remove her blouse, peel off the boob tape, and toss it in the trash. She made a mental note to donate the rest of the roll to her sister, Lisa.

Eve didn't like her reflection in the bathroom mirror. Her once flat tummy was getting chubby.

She used to ride her bike through the Santa Monica Mountains every weekend and to Lost Hills station each day. But because of two bone-breaking work-related injuries happening nearly back-to-back, Eve had been on her bike just twice in the last ten weeks.

It felt like she'd gained twenty pounds in that time. Eating every morning at the Hilton's breakfast buffet didn't help, certainly not on top of the fast-food lunches she usually grabbed with Duncan. She made another mental note to pick up her bike from her condo and start getting some exercise.

The problem with all of her mental notes was they somehow got erased the moment after she made them. She supposed she could start writing them down on actual paper, but she was afraid if anybody saw them, they'd think she was fighting early Alzheimer's.

She got onto the bed, propped herself up on her pillows, and, against her better judgment, turned on the TV and was shocked to see her own face staring back at her.

The shootings in Calabasas were the top story on the KTLA 10:00 p.m. news. The reporting was mostly accurate and there were a few shots of her in the Chanel jacket, showing her cleavage and talking on her phone, the smashed Rolls-Royce behind her. She thought she looked like the least-endowed Kardashian pretending to be a cop. The report ended with a clip of Sheriff Lansing facing the press at LASD headquarters, where he gave a short statement.

"A sting operation in Calabasas snared the three assailants who were responsible for a string of violent home invasions. Two of the assailants were killed in a confrontation with undercover detectives, the third was shot by a security guard in the grocery store behind me. Thanks to the heroic actions of two law enforcement professionals and a brave civilian, a brutal crime spree has been put to an end."

Eve thought Lansing was taking a premature victory lap. She had no idea if the spree of home invasions was over, so how could he be so certain? And she wondered what conclusion the media would draw tomorrow when they learned that Captain Moffett was reassigned in the wake of what Lansing had just hailed as a success.

Her iPhone rang. The caller ID read GODZILLA. Eve took a deep breath, clicked off the TV, and answered the phone.

"Hello, Mom."

"You looked great on TV," Jen said. Her voice was smoky and rough from smoking a lot of cigarettes. Men found her voice sexy but Eve worried it was a symptom of future lung cancer. "That's the way you should dress every day."

"I was undercover."

"And now you've been outed as an attractive woman. No need to hide it anymore."

Her mom usually criticized how she looked on TV, and that irritated Eve. But now her mom was calling to tell her she looked great, and that irritated her, too. It seemed to Eve that they were destined to always be caught in this irritation loop. That was why they rarely saw each other, even though her mother lived up the coast in Ventura, only about forty minutes away.

"I told you before, Mom, it's not appropriate attire for a homicide detective."

"Make it appropriate. You've come a long way already, making history in the department."

"Which is why turning myself into a sex object now would be taking a big step backwards for me and all women in the department."

"I don't see how."

*Of course you don't.*

Her mom liked to show off her curves, which had both embarrassed and infuriated Eve when she was a teenager. Because whenever her mom, a single mother, dressed that way, it often meant that Eve, her younger sister, Lisa, and her little brother, Kenny, would wake up the next morning to find another strange man in their kitchen eating their frosted cinnamon Pop-Tarts.

"I want to be seen by my colleagues as a detective," Eve said, "not as a woman."

"That will never happen, so use the advantages that you have."

"You want me to use my sex appeal to get my job done."

"You're lucky you've got it," Jen said. "You can thank me for that. My genes kicked the shit out of your father's. The women in his family looked like turtles who'd lost their shells."

"I'll have to take your word for that." She knew her mom's genes were strong. Both she and her sister had her mom's vibrant blue eyes and her tenacity.

Eve had never met anyone on Vince Nyby's side of the family. She barely knew him. Her father was an episodic TV director who'd seduced Jen, a nonspeaking background player on one of his shows, with promises of big acting jobs that never came. He got her pregnant and then immediately dumped her. His idea of paying child support was sporadically showing up on Eve's birthday to give her a Barbie doll. He'd fathered a lot of children with a lot of women and Eve imagined he'd kept a box of Barbie dolls for the girls and a box of Hot Wheels cars for the boys, so he never ran out of meaningless, generic birthday presents for his unsupported offspring. Vince was in his seventies now, hoping to come out of retirement to direct the pilot of her TV series, which was being written by a woman he'd briefly worked with years ago when she was "a baby writer" and not the top showrunner she was today. Eve hated that he'd found a way to wriggle back into her life just to enrich himself.

Jen said, "If you change your look, you could be as successful as the women investigators I met when I worked in the top forensic unit in the country."

"You were a corpse on *CSI*," Eve said. "I have shocking news for you. You weren't really dead and that wasn't a real forensic unit."

"There's nothing wrong with using your natural gifts to your advantage. Natalia Boa Vista did."

"Who is that?"

"I'm surprised you don't know," Jen said. "She's a top investigator with Miami-Dade Police Department's CSI unit. She has terrific cleavage and an amazing arrest rate."

"In other words, she's a fictional character."

Jen ignored the statement and pressed on. "Catherine Willows was a stripper before she was a Vegas CSI. She's hot and everyone takes her very seriously."

"Again, because she's *fictional*."

Eve felt her shoulder muscles tightening up the way they always did when she argued with her mom.

Jen sighed. "You've heard of the CSI effect, haven't you?"

"It's the unrealistic expectation, particularly among juries, that forensics results will be as quickly obtained and as irrefutable as they are on TV."

"Well, Hardnose, the same goes for how they want their detectives to look. Don't you want to win the confidence and the admiration of the public and your colleagues?"

Hardnose was what Vince called her when she was a child, supposedly because of her stubbornness and her "cute little nose," though she often wondered if the real reason was that he saw her so rarely that he had trouble remembering her name. It was a low blow for her mom to call her that.

"And you think I can do that by showing a little cleavage," Eve said.

"It couldn't hurt. But that's definitely how your character on the series should dress."

That was Eve's nightmare of what the TV series would be, if it ever happened. It was a big reason why she wanted Duncan to become the show's technical adviser when he retired from the LASD.

"Hell no," Eve said.

"Why not? She's fictional."

"She's me."

"People know the difference between fiction and reality."

Eve felt the tightness in her shoulders rise up her neck to the base of her skull. "You just argued that they don't."

"No I didn't. Where did you get that idea? If you want to look drab and sexless and never get laid, fine. But why shouldn't your character be a knockout?"

Eve kept her voice even so her reply wouldn't come across as patronizing. She really, really wanted her mom to understand her reasons.

"Because if the TV show happens, I have to live with how I am portrayed, and it's not going to be as a detective with terrific cleavage and a great arrest rate."

"Why not? *That* should be your real-life goal. Why wouldn't you want to be a great-looking, successful cop? Are you striving to be a drab failure? I don't understand you at all."

Eve felt the spike of pain jamming into her head, so she massaged the back of her neck with her free hand. It was like trying to massage granite. "I can't have this conversation now."

"Why not? What else do you have to do?"

"You just saw the news," Eve said, gesturing to her TV, even though it was off and she was the only one in the room. "I have *that* to do."

"You want to close your case fast? Use your undercover wardrobe and the boob tape. You'll thank me later. Sweet dreams, honeybunch."

Jen hung up and Eve thought her head might explode.

Eve took a scorching-hot shower to loosen her muscles, dried herself off, put on her bathrobe, then got on the bed again and opened her laptop. She checked her emails and found links to download all the video footage she'd asked for that day from both the supermarket and the Vista Grande guard gate.

She started by watching the video from the supermarket again, from the moment that Paul Colter burst in, holding the gun, and headed for the liquor aisle. Panicked customers and employees fled or took cover behind checkout counters or food displays. Grayson Mumford headed straight for Colter, ducking into an aisle at the last moment to avoid being seen by the gunman, who was only a few feet away.

Eve saw and heard Colter demand that she show herself, and when she did, he turned to her, his gun not quite raised but not quite loose at his side, either. Grayson stepped out of hiding and shot him. It was a brave thing for Grayson to do, she had to give him that.

Her iPhone rang again. She checked the caller ID. It was her agent, Linwood Taggert. She ignored it and he gave up after a few rings. Then the phone started to ring again, but this time it was her brother, Kenny, who was five years younger than her. She debated not answering but then remembered the hell she got from her family for not returning their calls for days after her last violent, widely reported incident on the job.

"Hey," Eve said.

"I saw you on the news. I love the new look."

"Have you been talking to Mom?"

"No," he said. "But she came by yesterday and gave Rachel and Cassie each a roll of boob tape."

"Cassidy is five."

"It's for playing dress-up. Mom says it's never too early for a girl to embrace her feminine power."

"And what was Rachel's reaction?" Eve said. Rachel was his wife. They'd met as students at Cal State, Northridge. She got pregnant, so they dropped out, got married, and he started what became a fairly successful pool-cleaning business.

"She says she might use the tape if we ever go to a restaurant again that doesn't have a drive-through window."

Eve laughed. That was Kenny, always upbeat. Maybe taking calls from her family was a healthy thing to do after a rough experience.

Kenny said, "It's good to hear you laugh. I guess that means you're okay."

"Yeah, I'm fine." There was a beep on the line. Eve looked at her phone and saw she had an incoming call from Lisa. She put the phone back to her ear. "Lisa is calling. Thanks for the call. Give my love to Rachel and Cassie."

"I will."

Eve clicked off on him and answered Lisa's call. Her sister was three years younger than her and an ER nurse at West Hills Hospital, just a few miles north of Calabasas.

"You're up late," Eve said. "Or are you working?"

"I'm off. I just saw the news online about the shooting. How are you feeling?"

"I'm fine. I wasn't hurt at all."

"The article says you'd be dead if it wasn't for that security guard. I'd like to give him a big hug. I hope you did."

"I'm not a hugger," she said, then remembered that she'd hugged Duncan that night, but she told herself that it was just an aberration, a one-off reaction to nearly losing him, because it embarrassed her. "Besides, he didn't exactly save my life."

"He shot the guy before he could shoot you, didn't he?"

"Yes, but I could've handled it."

"You're always so sure of yourself," Lisa said, like confidence was a bad thing. Eve was proud of it. "Have you ever had to shoot anyone?"

"Not yet."

"But that poor security guard did. That deserves a hug. You deserve one, too. Want me to come over? I'll bring ice cream."

If Eve had ice cream every time she felt some stress, she was sure that she'd be morbidly obese in a month, but it did explain Lisa's persistent pudginess. "That sounds nice, but I'm fine, really."

"You could have been killed."

"That's part of my job," Eve said. "Like getting puked and bled on is part of yours."

"You saw some men die in front of you today."

"It's not the first time." She thought of the two heads she'd seen explode as they were pierced by bullets and suddenly she could smell the fresh, wet brain matter as if it were on the wall, like it had been in her condo, or in the aisle at the supermarket.

*It's just your imagination.*

"Have you talked to anybody about it?" Lisa asked.

"I'm talking to you right now." And it wasn't helping. In fact, she was sure that it was making things worse, even though her sister meant well. Eve didn't dwell on her pain, she worked through it until it was gone.

"I mean *really* talked."

"You see patients die in the ER all the time. Do you talk about it?"

"Yes, I do. I'm part of a support group of nurses. We meet each week and share our experiences. We shed a lot of tears, give a lot of hugs."

Tears and hugs. It was Eve's idea of hell. "That's not something cops do."

*Liar. You just did it.*

"What do they do instead?" Lisa asked.

*They drink, do drugs, sleep around, get divorced, eat themselves up inside.*

"I ride my bike," Eve said.

"When was the last time you did that?"

She pinched her belly fat. "It's been way too long."

"Take a ride this weekend. Want some company?"

"You couldn't keep up with me."

"Nobody can," Lisa said. "Maybe you should slow down and give somebody a chance. What about that forensic anthropologist?"

"Daniel Brooks. He's on Tarawa, in the South Pacific, digging up old bones. I don't know when he'll be back." They'd hooked up while working together on a case. She liked him a lot and missed him when he left, though he'd invited her to come join him if she wanted to get away for a while. "Besides, I'm not sure that what we had is a thing."

"You could make it a thing."

"I'm too busy for a thing."

"A thing is something you should always make time for," Lisa said. "Things can be very relaxing. You could get a battery-operated thing."

Eve laughed. "I think the thing we're talking about just changed into a different thing."

"It's kind of the same thing."

"Good night, Lisa."

"Good night, Eve."

Eve disconnected, tossed her phone on the bed beside her, and instead of going to sleep, and facing that endless loop of death, she opened her laptop again and watched some of the Vista Grande gate video, starting a list of the vehicles that came and went. She got bored after a while, so she switched to searching the web for Sherry Simms' It's A Steal business.

She found accounts for It's A Steal on eBay and Poshmark. Joel Dalander's girlfriend was selling designer handbags, accessories, and jewelry, basically all the things Eve had seen in their home office during her initial search. A telling clue was that the It's A Steal accounts on the two sites were opened a few weeks before the spree of home invasions. Eve made a mental note of that.

That was the last thought Eve had before she fell asleep sitting on top of the bed, her laptop still open on her lap.

# CHAPTER NINE

Eve overslept by an hour. So she dressed quickly without showering first, which she told herself was okay since she'd showered the night before, and rushed down to the lobby for the breakfast buffet.

She was serving herself a modest portion of scrambled eggs and four strips of bacon when Duncan showed up, took two plates off the stack of dishes, and joined her in line. Most of the Hilton staff knew that he wasn't staying there, but they didn't mind him mooching off their buffet since he was Eve's guest and she'd been a resident for several weeks. She'd more than paid for his meals as part of her rent during her extended stay.

Duncan heaped bacon and sausage onto one of the plates. "I hope you don't leave this hotel until I retire."

Eve said, "That reminds me, I need to check on the work at my condo today. The renovation is taking forever."

He loaded his second plate with pancakes and scrambled eggs, then covered the food with maple syrup. "I told you to go with a real contractor instead of a crime scene cleaner doing it as a side gig. But you wanted to save a buck."

It wasn't just that. It was also more convenient and she wanted to do a favor for the crime scene cleaner, who was an ex-cop. But she knew he was right.

Eve gestured to his breakfast. "I've been meaning to ask you this for a couple of weeks now. Why do you take two plates of food at once?"

"I don't want to get maple syrup on my meat." He picked up a plate in each hand and they headed for one of the tables.

"Have you thought about taking smaller portions or finishing one plate before starting on another?"

"I don't want to make extra trips to the buffet."

"Of course not," Eve said. "God forbid you should get more exercise."

They sat down. He tucked a napkin into his collar in a futile attempt to protect his tie, already a historical mosaic of everything he'd eaten in the last month, from getting stained. They began to eat. Duncan started with his plate of syrup-slathered pancakes and eggs.

"What did your wife say about your face?"

"Since you and I were possibly going to be undercover at the sting house all week, Gracie went down to Palm Springs to start fixing up our condo to be our primary residence. Don't ask me what that involves, because I don't know. I'll join her there for the weekend."

"Did you tell her that you got hurt?"

"Why spoil her trip? She'll get all worried and rush back. I'm fine and enjoying my quality time with Marshal Dillon and Colonel Sanders."

"She's going to notice the injury and be mad at you for keeping it from her. Your daughters will be, too."

"Who did you call from your hospital bed a few weeks ago?"

Just him. "I'm learning from my mistakes and trying to share my wisdom."

"You're not old enough to have wisdom. Have you read your email?" Duncan asked, abruptly changing the subject.

"Not since last night."

"I was up early this morning. Lots of info has come in. For instance, we got the lab report on the contents of the shredder at Joel Dalander's house. It's credit cards. Probably from the wallets they stole during the home invasions. They probably jotted down the numbers, expiration dates, and security codes and then shredded them."

"I wonder how much stuff they were able to buy, or cash advances they were able to get, before the cards were reported stolen and the account numbers deactivated."

"I don't know, but the take from the cards might have been worth more than the merch they took."

"It would be great if we could match the designer bags and other bling we found in our searches, and on Sherry Simms' eBay and Poshmark pages, to items stolen in earlier home invasions."

Duncan shrugged. "I don't see how. A handbag is a handbag."

"It couldn't hurt to show some of the bags and wallets we found to the victims. Maybe they'll recognize a scratch or stain. Wouldn't you recognize your wallet if you saw it?"

Duncan took out his canvas Velcro-sealed wallet, a bulging binder of receipts, credit cards, and cash that looked like it might burst. "Who'd steal this?"

"Nobody, but you get my point."

"I do. That's time-consuming grunt work our two deputies can do for us."

"Speaking of deputies, do we know if patrol found any of the cars belonging to the three assailants?"

Duncan set aside his empty plate, sticky with maple syrup, and pulled the plate of bacon and sausage in front of him. "Nope. They've checked every street in the vicinity, including the two adjacent gated communities, and the parking lots at the two shopping centers that are within walking distance. Also, there's no record of cars of their make, model, and year being towed since yesterday."

"So we still don't know how those three got into Vista Grande or how they planned to get out."

Duncan shook his head. "We're going to have to go through the gate log and the entrance and exit videos and match every guest and license plate."

"I started last night. Oh, the glamour of police work."

"That's what gets the job done, not boob tape and car chases in Rolls-Royces. Be sure to tell the writers that if your TV series ever happens."

"You tell them. I'll still be right here, doing the job in the real world."

Duncan wrapped a piece of sausage in bacon and popped it in his mouth. "I didn't say I'd be the show's technical consultant."

"You didn't say you wouldn't."

Eve's phone buzzed. She glanced at the caller ID. It was her agent again, right on cue, as if he'd overheard them talking about the show. She ignored the call, but looking at her phone gave her an idea.

"The only phones on the perps were burners. But we know Paul Colter definitely had his own phone. His mom gave us the number. And I saw iPhone chargers, but no phone, at his place and in Nagy's studio."

"Everybody has a phone." Duncan was nearly finished with his meat and his gaze drifted back toward the buffet, where the hostess was putting out a platter of fresh cinnamon rolls. "What are you getting at?"

"Let's reach out to the cellular providers for the tracking data on their real phones and see where the three guys were when their devices were last switched on. It could lead us to where their cars are parked now. The locations might give us some idea how they got here and planned to get away." If they learned that, Eve believed they'd know if there were others involved in the home invasions who were still at large.

"Good idea. I'll write up the warrant requests. We also need to find out how these three men are connected. Did they come together on their own or are they working for someone?"

Eve was stuffed, but the smell of the cinnamon rolls was intoxicating. "And we need to find Sherry Simms. She was selling stolen goods."

"We don't know that. It could be stuff she found legitimately at swap meets, estate sales, or garage sales." Duncan got up and made a run for the rolls before they were all gone. Eve got up, too, telling herself it was just so they could continue the conversation.

"So why did she run?"

Duncan took a plate and gingerly picked up two hot, sticky rolls. "Hey, I'm on your side. I'm just thinking like the judge who is going to deny any warrant involving her. Not being home when the police come knocking isn't a crime."

That was true, and such a depressing thought, that Eve decided to console herself with a cinnamon roll. They headed back to their table and sat down.

Eve began to delicately unfurl her roll, exposing the cinnamon inside. It was how she'd eaten them since she was a child and the ritual had become part of the pleasure. "Let's make a list of things we need to do and divvy it up."

They discussed the tasks ahead, then Duncan said, "You can go through all the videos and security logs, since you've already started and watching it would put me to sleep."

"You can't stay awake watching anything unless everybody is wearing cowboy hats. I'm surprised you don't wear one."

"You've never seen me off duty. I've even got spurs," Duncan said. "They're hell on my recliner, though. I'll get the warrants, do the background checks, and go through the interviews from the canvass of Vista Grande. We'll meet at lunch, share what we've learned, and if I'm caught up, I can jump in on the videos with you."

"Works for me," she said. "Let's giddyup."

They got up, Duncan stole a cinnamon roll for the road, and they took their separate cars to the station.

Detectives Wally Biddle and Stan Garvey, known within the station as Crockett and Tubbs, were in the squad room when Eve and Duncan came in. Biddle and Garvey both wheeled around in their chairs to face them in such perfect synchronicity that they reminded Eve of the Pips, minus Gladys Knight and one Pip.

Biddle was white, in his forties, a lifelong surfer who parted his sun-and-salt-water-bleached blond hair down the middle, single-handedly keeping the eighties alive. She was sure that he longed to wear board shorts and flip-flops to work instead of a suit.

His partner, Garvey, was black, also in his forties, and struck Eve as far more interested in sucking up to celebrities, of which there were many in their jurisdiction, than fairly enforcing the law. The famous always got preferential treatment from him compared to ordinary civilians. His cubicle was covered with selfies with the actors, singers, and athletes he'd helped out of embarrassing legal jams over the years.

Garvey said, "We were in court all day yesterday and missed the excitement."

Biddle looked at Duncan. "I heard you punched a deputy and got him fired."

Duncan dropped into his seat, which squealed like an injured animal under the strain. "He had it coming."

"The other deputies don't think so," Biddle said. "It's a good thing you're retiring, Donuts. You're not too popular with the uniforms here anymore."

Garvey swiveled to face Eve. "But he's a hell of a lot more popular with them than you, Deathfist. I heard you got Moffett exiled to Siberia."

Eve said, "That was the sheriff's decision, not mine."

"The same sheriff who bumped you up overnight from a deputy in Lancaster to Lost Hills homicide," Garvey said. "Are you fucking him or what?"

"Yes, that's it, Tubbs. So you better watch yourself, or I might roll over in bed tonight and tell Lansing to fire you." Eve went to her desk and sat down, her back to the three of them.

Biddle addressed her back. "Moffett started as a uniform and worked his way up to the captain's chair. It took a lot of long, hard years to get here and now he's down at stinking Men's Central Jail. You think that's fair?"

Duncan said, "At least Moffett still has his job and his bars. He's just got a different desk."

"It's not right," Biddle said. "Moffett was well liked and highly respected around here."

"So was Captain Mendoza," Eve said as she logged in to her computer. Mendoza was fired for sexually harassing a female Lost Hills deputy. The woman ended up leaving the department with a fat seven-figure legal settlement. Captain Moffett took Mendoza's place. It all happened long before Eve showed up at the station.

"That was wrong, too," Biddle said. "Everybody here knew that relationship was totally consensual."

"It can't be truly consensual when there's a power disparity," Eve said.

"So how's that different for you and Lansing?" Garvey asked. "Or did he have you agree to sex in writing, and have it notarized, before you went to bed?"

The discussion might have continued, and become a lot more heated, but deputies Tom Ross and Eddie Clayton came in, and that shut everybody up. The deputies approached Duncan and Eve.

Like Lansing's driver Rondo, Clayton always wore sunglasses, earning him the nickname Shades. Unlike Rondo, Clayton was gregarious and not the least bit invisible. He was also the one other Lost Hills deputy who Eve completely trusted.

Tom took a seat at the cubicle beside Eve's. "The captain says me and Eddie are deployed to you and Duncan this shift."

"Which captain?" Duncan asked.

"Captain Roje Shaw. He just transferred over from Compton. Some friends of mine down there say he's a good man, comes from a family of cops in Jamaica."

Eddie leaned against the cubicle where Tom sat. "I heard that he was in here at five a.m. I sure hope he's not gonna make that a regular thing."

"Why?" Eve asked.

"Because then everybody else will start coming in early for their shifts so they don't look like laggards."

Duncan smiled. "Laggard. There's a word I haven't heard in a while."

Eddie shrugged. "My dad called me that so often when I was a kid that I thought it was my first name."

Eve assigned the two deputies the task of trying to match the recovered goods with items stolen from homes, and just as they were all about to get to work, the new captain came in. Shaw was black, tall, broad shouldered, and bald. A linebacker in a captain's uniform.

Everyone stood up to show their respect, which made him smile. "Please, sit down, this isn't the military. I wanted to introduce myself. I'm Captain Roje Shaw. There will be time later for us to get to know one another but right now"—he pointed to Biddle and Garvey—"you two need to go. There's been a hit-and-run on Pacific Coast Highway. One man is dead. Dispatch has the details."

"Yes, sir," Biddle said. He and Garvey got up and rushed out of the squad room.

Shaw looked back at Eve and Duncan. "I read up on the home invasion case. Where are we, Detectives?"

"No further than last night, sir," Duncan said. "Give us until lunch and we may know a lot more."

Shaw nodded. "I'm buying. Pizza work for you?"

"Always," Duncan said.

"If you need extra manpower, or a push with any warrants, let me know. The sheriff wants this closed yesterday."

"Will do," Eve said. "Thank you, sir."

"See you at lunch," he said and walked out.

Once the door closed, Duncan looked at Eve. "I think I'm going to like him."

"You're a dog," Eve said. "You love anyone who gives you food."

"Woof, woof," Duncan said, then swiveled to face his desk and get to work.

# CHAPTER TEN

Captain Shaw came back into the squad room at 1:00 p.m. with two large thin-crust sheet pizzas from Barone's in Westlake Village. He set the boxes on the conference table and opened them up. The smell immediately drew Eve, Duncan, Ross, and Clayton away from their cubicles to eat. The pizzas, a Meat Lovers and a Fire Roasted Veggie, were sliced into rectangular pieces and rested on plastic screens that kept the crust from touching the bottom of the cardboard boxes and the dripping grease.

Duncan took a slice of the Meat Lovers. "I'm impressed, Captain. This is the good stuff. Frankly, I was expecting a delivery from Domino's."

Shaw took a slice of Fire Roasted Veggie. "My first priority when assuming a new post is to find the best pizza in the vicinity."

"You succeeded," Eve said and took the smallest slice of the Meat Lovers she could find and then got as far away from the boxes as she could without leaving the room. Her fear was that if she stayed within reach of the boxes, she'd eat half the pizza herself.

The two deputies went out to the break room and brought back paper plates, napkins, and soft drinks. Everyone spent a moment eating in comfortable silence, then Duncan grabbed another slice and went over to the dry-erase board, where he'd filled in more details on the three assailants and had added a new column under the DMV photo of Sherry Simms.

"I did a deep dive into Joel Dalander, Paul Colter, and Greg Nagy," he said. "But here's the executive summary: They all are from the West Valley. They are all the same age. And they are all white."

"So they definitely wouldn't have drawn any attention in Calablackless," Deputy Clayton said, then seemed to remember that Shaw was black, and added, "No offense intended, sir."

"None taken, Deputy. Facts are facts. I'm aware of the racial makeup of this community and I think you're right—being lily-white and clean-cut served these home invaders well."

Duncan used the interruption as an opportunity to eat two more big bites of pizza. When he spoke again, it was with his mouth half-full.

"The guy who acted as ringleader of the crew and took a swan dive onto the patio was Joel Dalander. He grew up in Woodland Hills, went to Taft High School, and spent two years at Pierce College, where he got an associate degree in business administration and became night-shift manager at a Burger King in Reseda."

Duncan tapped Sherry Simms' picture. "Dalander's girlfriend, Sherry, is from Santa Clarita and also went to Pierce, which is where I assume they met and when they moved in together. Her parents wouldn't talk to me."

"They are protecting her," Eve said.

"That's a parent's job," Duncan said. "Sherry left Pierce with a skills certificate in small business entrepreneurship, which she put to use to create her online store It's A Steal to sell stolen goods."

"Can we prove that they're stolen?" Shaw asked.

Deputy Ross answered. "We're still reaching out to the robbery victims with photos of the merchandise that has been recovered from the homes of Dalander, Colter, and Nagy. Nothing has been ID'd yet."

"But CSU determined that the shredder at Dalander's place was full of credit card smithereens," Eve said. "That strikes me as highly suspicious."

"Agreed," Shaw said, and gestured to Duncan to continue.

"Greg Nagy, the guy I shot, grew up in Canoga Park, went to Canoga Park High School, then on to Cal State, Northridge, where he studied creative writing. He was working as a freelance script reader for Pinnacle Studios and was an aspiring writer. I read one of his screenplays to see if there might be a clue in it. All I learned is that he was better at robbery than he was at writing."

"He got killed robbing a house," Clayton said.

"That's true," Duncan said. "I stand corrected. He sucked at both. His family also refuses to talk to me and suggested that I submit any questions we have in writing to their lawyer so he can refuse to answer them."

Shaw said, "Did you get anything from his computer?"

Eve answered his question. She'd been watching videos all morning, the monotony broken only by the calls she fielded from CSU.

"Not yet, sir. CSU is taking the MacBook to the morgue so they can unlock it biometrically with his fingerprint. They'll do the same with Colter's laptop."

Duncan continued: "Colter is the assailant who led Eve on a merry chase and was shot by the security guard at the Commons. He grew up in Sherman Oaks and somehow his parents finagled him into Reseda High School, which is on the other side of the 405 from where they live."

Eve went to Reseda High School, too, and just realized that she and Colter were students there at the same time. They might have passed each other in the hall a hundred times, never knowing that their paths would cross again on his last day alive.

"Colter barely graduated and has had a string of odd jobs ever since," Duncan went on. "Waiting tables, phone sales, clerking at a shoe store, that kind of thing. He lived with his parents and, when he wasn't robbing homes or watching porn, was driving for Uber and Lyft."

Shaw dabbed at his lips with a napkin. "Have you found out how they all met or what brought them together to form this crew?"

"Nope," Duncan said. "The lack of cooperation from their families isn't helping, either."

"I can't really blame them for refusing to help us prove their sons were criminals," Shaw said.

"They are probably busy with their lawyers trying to prove we are responsible for their sons' deaths," Duncan said.

"Did you get anything from their burner phones?"

"Another dead end," Eve said. "CSU says they were just activated and no calls were made."

"How about their guns?" Shaw asked.

Eve said, "CSU says the serial numbers were removed and they haven't been able to raise them. The lab also test fired the weapons, ran the expelled bullets through the national ballistic database, and got no hits."

"Okay," Shaw said. "Did anything come up in the canvass of Vista Grande after it was locked down?"

"Nope," Duncan said. "Deputies interviewed everyone in the community. The residents didn't see anything unusual. Same goes for the guests, most of whom are regulars, like maids, gardeners, pool men, et cetera, who come and go every week. The rest were contractors, electricians, plumbers, painters, or delivery and utilities, like the telephone company, the electric company, United Parcel Service, Spectrum Cable, FedEx, Lightning Delivery, Sparkletts Water, and Amazon."

Shaw frowned, his frustration beginning to show. "What about video from home security cameras? Did they catch anything?"

Eve answered. "No, sir. The majority of home security cameras in the community are motion activated. So, naturally, none of the cameras are pointed at the street or they'd be recording constantly. I didn't get anything from them so far, but I'm still slogging through the footage, hoping to see one of the guys climbing over a backyard fence so at least we'd know how they got inside."

"Tell me about the front gates and how the security system works," Shaw said.

Eve did, and finished by detailing how guest passes were issued and controlled.

"Homeowners can put anybody they want on their permanent guest list and can order individual day passes by using an app or calling the guard at the front gate," Eve said. "Either way, the guard keeps a log of every pass issued. On top of that, the license plates of every vehicle that enters the community, resident or guest, are automatically photographed by a camera and logged. I've checked the logs and videos. Every nonresident who came in through the Vista Grande gate yesterday also left the same way."

Shaw thought about that for a moment. "So we don't know how the three men got into the community or how they planned to get away."

"That's right," Eve said. Not knowing that frustrated her. She was sure the answer to those questions was the key to truly solving the case.

"Have you compared the list of visitors at Vista Grande yesterday to the lists at the other gated communities on the days when they had home invasions?"

"I haven't had a chance to do that yet, but we did it among the other communities that were hit and there was a lot of overlap. I'm sure there will be with Vista Grande, too."

"It's not surprising, sir," Duncan added. "The same gardeners, pool men, delivery trucks, et cetera, serve all the adjacent communities along Parkway Calabasas. It didn't really narrow the suspect pool down for us."

"That's why we did the sting house," Eve said.

Shaw looked at Eve. "That was your idea?"

Duncan raised his hand. "It was mine. My grandfather always said, 'You can't catch fish with your line in the boat.' So we put out a line."

"He was a wise man." Shaw got up and paced in front of the whiteboard, looking at the photos of the three men. "Where are you with warrants to track their phones?"

"The judge granted them," Duncan said. "I emailed the warrants to the cellular providers, and now I'm just waiting for them to comply.

I know the people over there and they know me. They're usually pretty fast. We'll get the information today."

There was a long moment of silence as everyone digested the information and their pizza. Eve assumed they were all coming to the same conclusion—that they'd eaten too much and knew no more today about the home invasions than they did yesterday. Sherry Simms was the one person who might be able to tell them more, but she was in the wind. They hadn't heard from her neighbor or the LAPD, which was sending patrol cars past her home on a regular basis to check for activity. Eve thought finding her should be their next move.

But before Eve could voice that opinion, Duncan's phone rang. He answered it, listened for a moment, made some notes on a pad, and tore the sheet off as he hung up.

"That was the watch commander," Duncan said. "The fire department and a deputy responded to an emergency call in Oakdale, one of the gated communities on Parkway Calabasas, from a woman giving birth in her home. The baby was dead when they got there, apparently a stillbirth."

Shaw nodded. It was standard procedure for homicide detectives to initially investigate those deaths, which 99.9 percent of the time were quickly determined to be by natural causes. Even so, Duncan and Eve would have to go.

"While you're out handling that, I'll keep the train moving down the tracks," the captain said. "The deputies will continue trying to match the goods recovered with the home invasion victims. And I'll cross-reference the Vista Grande visitor list with the ones at the other communities on the days they had robberies."

Eve gave him the Vista Grande list as she left the squad room with Duncan. They went outside to one of the plain-wrap Explorers in the parking lot.

"I'll drive," Duncan said.

That was fine with her.

They got onto the Ventura Freeway at Las Virgenes and headed east, around the northern edge of the ridge that Vista Grande and Oakdale were atop and that divided the east and west side of Calabasas geographically and socioeconomically. The east side had the Commons, city hall, the Hilton Garden Inn, Mercedes and BMW dealerships, and most of the homes and high-end gated communities. The west side had low-rise office parks, gas stations, fast-food restaurants, a cheap hotel, the Lost Hills station, and lots of condos. The freeway was the easiest and fastest way to cross from one side of the small city to the other.

"The new captain is very hands-on," Eve said.

"Feet-on, too. Hopefully, it will only be with this case, the one that got his predecessor booted, or your life is going to be a living hell when I'm gone."

"I was thinking the same thing," she said. "I don't want him looking over my shoulder all the time."

"You don't even like me doing it," Duncan said. "And I'm adorable."

# CHAPTER ELEVEN

The fountains in the center of the road leading to Oakdale reminded Eve of champagne being poured over stacked glasses. Past the fountain was a guardhouse so tiny that it appeared that the heavy uniformed Hispanic woman inside was wearing the guardhouse like a large stucco overcoat.

Duncan and Eve waited in the guest lane behind two other cars that were lined up to get their passes from the guard and be allowed through the gate.

"The afternoon guard is Ruthie Ortega," Duncan said. "She's been here for twenty-five years."

"I can't imagine spending two decades in that little shack," Eve said as one car went up the hill and the car in front of them moved forward to the guardhouse. "Aren't there rules against that kind of confinement in the Geneva Conventions?"

"She loves it. She treats this place like she's the guard to the Emerald City. I call her the Oracle. Nothing goes on behind those gates that she doesn't know about. Bring her donuts once in a while when I'm gone and chat her up. It'll pay off for you."

The car in front of them departed. Duncan pulled up to the guardhouse and rolled down his window. "Afternoon, Ruthie."

She sat at her desk and smiled at him through her half-open window. "Hello, Duncan. I heard about your adventure yesterday. I see it was a close shave."

"When did you become a comedienne?"

"I've always been renowned for my wit. Ellen DeGeneres is lucky I chose the security profession or I'd have her show." Ruthie looked past Duncan to Eve. "And you owe me your life, Deathfist."

Well, Eve thought, at least there was no need for introductions. "How do you figure that?"

"I trained Grayson," she said proudly. "I taught him everything he knows."

"You taught him how to shoot?" Duncan asked.

"Except for that. More importantly, I instilled in him the values, integrity, and courage behind the Big Valley Security badge." She tapped her badge for emphasis. "That's why everybody who works in Calabasas for Big Valley Security trains with me first. He was in here with me for three months." Eve had a hard time imagining how the two of them could fit inside the guardhouse. "Now he floats among the different guard gates, mostly substituting for sick or vacationing guards, when he isn't working down at the Commons." Ruthie narrowed her eyes at Duncan. "I suppose you're here about sweet Mrs. McCaig and her baby."

"Yes, we are," he said. "What can you tell us about Anna McCaig?"

Ruthie leaned toward her open window and lowered her voice, though there was nobody around who could possibly hear them.

"It's so sad. She and Jeff McCaig have been trying to have a child ever since they got married. I think this is her third miscarriage."

"How long have they been married?"

"Three years. Anna is his second wife, fifteen years younger than he is, from Romania. He told me that he was attracted by her energy, youth, and great birthing hips."

"What a compliment," Eve said.

Duncan gestured to the gate and the steep hill of homes in front of them. "Is he home?"

"Oh no, he's on a business trip in Europe somewhere, selling movies internationally for one of the studios. That's how he met Anna. In Berlin, during a film market. She was a hostess at his hotel. He had an affair with her for months while he was still married to the first Mrs. McCaig."

Eve leaned forward so Ruthie could see her. "How do you know all of that?"

"The first Mrs. McCaig told me when she moved out. She said they tried forever to have kids, and when she couldn't, he dropped her for a fertile Romanian slut."

"What does the second Mrs. McCaig do?"

"She's overseeing the remodel of their house," Ruthie said. "I suppose to make the place her own and so she has something to do when he's away. They're doing the kitchen now."

"How far along was her pregnancy?" Eve asked.

"She was just about to pop," Ruthie said. "That's what makes it so sad. She must be devastated."

"Thanks, Ruthie," Duncan said. "I appreciate the briefing."

"All of us who protect and serve have to stick together." Ruthie hit a button on her desk, opening the gate. Duncan waved goodbye, then drove through the gate and up the hill.

The homes were architecturally similar to the ones in Vista Grande, but they were much smaller, bunched closer together, and had tiny front yards. The one-story McCaig house was easy to spot—a fire truck, a paramedic unit, an LASD patrol car, and an ambulance were parked out front. There was a large walk-in dumpster in the driveway and a porta-potty on the front lawn.

Duncan parked in the open half of the driveway. He and Eve got out and went inside the house, where the temperature dropped by about thirty degrees. It was like stepping into the cold room at Costco to buy vegetables, Eve thought.

The dining room was to the right and was being used as a temporary kitchen, with a microwave, coffee machine, paper plates, plastic cups, and disposable utensils on the table and boxes of food and drinks stacked against the walls. A couple of firemen with nothing to do stood there, out of everybody's way.

Straight ahead of Duncan and Eve was a large family room, and that's where the paramedics and the deputy were, and where a woman, crying inconsolably, was being lifted by two ambulance attendants onto a gurney. She was a petite bottle-blonde, with collagen-injected lips and augmented breasts.

Duncan and Eve were met by a crew-cutted deputy in his thirties who didn't seem very happy to see either one of them. Perhaps, Eve thought, he was a friend of Collier's.

"What's the story, Joe?" Duncan asked him.

The deputy barely looked up from his notepad as he relayed the details in a robotic monotone. "The woman is Anna McCaig, age twenty-four. She reports that she was upstairs, taking a shower, when she felt pain in her abdomen and noticed that she was bleeding from her groinal vicinity."

*Groinal vicinity?* Eve wondered if that bizarre terminology reflected his lack of familiarity with female anatomy or was an attempt to avoid saying something that could be construed as crude in front of a woman.

He cleared his throat and continued. "She put on a bathrobe, and was walking to the living room, when the pain got worse. She sat down on the couch and delivered the baby on the floor. She went to get a towel, came back, and saw the baby wasn't breathing. She called 911 and started CPR, following instructions from the operator. She was still on the line, and performing CPR, when the paramedics arrived and determined that the baby was dead."

Eve glanced at Anna, sobbing on the gurney, and saw past her to the bloodstained couch, where a paramedic stood over a blanket-wrapped bundle that she presumed was the baby.

"What was the sex of the baby?" Eve asked.

"A boy," said the deputy.

"Wait outside for me," Duncan told the deputy, then turned to Eve, his face pale. "I've seen enough dead children for one lifetime without seeing one more before I retire. Do you mind waiting here for the ME's office to come collect the body? I'll go to the hospital with Mrs. McCaig, get her official statement, and catch a ride back to the station with the deputy."

"Sure," Eve said, with the confidence of someone who'd handled a dozen cases like this before. But this was the first time she'd ever been called on a stillbirth and her inexperience made her uncomfortable.

Duncan approached the gurney as it was being wheeled toward them by the two ambulance attendants. He gestured to the attendants to stop and he leaned over Anna McCaig, who was covered up to her neck with a sheet and was still crying, though with less fervor, exhaustion or weakness calming her down.

"I'm Detective Pavone, Mrs. McCaig. I'll be going with you to the hospital. Can I grab your purse and clothes for you?"

Anna nodded, sniffled, and said in a heavily accented voice, "My purse is in the dining room."

Eve grabbed the purse from a dining room chair and set it on the gurney at Anna's feet while Duncan went to get her clothes. She knew he didn't make the offer just as a courtesy. It was also a sneaky way to get her permission to go to her bedroom, open a few drawers, and look in the closet. She wondered what he was looking for. Illegal drugs that might have provoked the stillbirth? Or perhaps he was just generally snoopy. She certainly was.

The ambulance attendants continued out with the gurney and Eve went into the family room. The tiny baby was on the couch, swaddled in the blanket, like he was sleeping, only he was far too still. His skin was grayish blue and the blood and amniotic fluid had been wiped away from his face. There was some blood on a seat cushion and a little more on the hardwood floor.

The blanket around the baby bothered her.

She looked over her shoulder and saw Duncan leaving the bedroom, carrying some women's clothing. He shook his head to indicate that he didn't see anything unusual and went outside to the waiting deputy. The firefighters started to clear out, too. One of the paramedics was still by the couch, putting away his equipment. Eve approached him.

"Excuse me. I'm Detective Eve Ronin. Could I talk to you for a minute?"

"Yeah, sure." He turned and wiped tears from his cheeks. "Sorry. I'm not usually so emotional. Stillbirths are always hard to take but my wife is pregnant and, well, this time it really got to me."

"Is that why you wrapped the baby in a blanket?"

The paramedic looked over at the baby for a long moment. "I know we're not supposed to do that, but the mother was a total wreck. I didn't want her to have to see all that blood, the umbilical cord, and everything. I wanted her last memory of her baby to be . . . peaceful, you know? He looks peaceful now, doesn't he?"

He did, Eve thought. Ordinarily, at an unattended death, it was wrong to cover the body or to unnecessarily disturb the scene in any way. But she could see that it was an emotionally charged situation and, judging from the paramedic's reaction, not a crime scene, so preserving evidence wasn't going to be an issue. Even so, it irritated her.

"Is there anything we need to know? Anything out of the ordinary?"

"No, she did all she possibly could to save her baby. She was still doing CPR and sobbing when we got here. We had to pull her away. I can't imagine how horrible this must be for her."

"Can I get your name for my report?"

"Rick Gage."

"Thank you, Rick."

He closed up his equipment case and started to leave, the last man out, when he paused for a moment in the entry hall. "I usually tell my wife everything about my day, but I'm not going to tell her about this."

Rick looked back at Eve, as if seeking her permission. So she nodded. He gave her a half smile of thanks and left her alone with the baby's body.

Eve had goose bumps, not from the situation, but from the cold air in the room. She thought about waiting outside in the warm sunshine for the attendant from the ME's office, but instead she went through the motions of documenting the scene by taking photos of the baby, the couch, and everything else in the room.

When she was done, she wandered into the dining room and looked at the stacks of food. It was mostly cookies, sugary cereals, candy, and a wide assortment of pastries, along with some jumbo bags of potato chips. Obviously, Anna McCaig had some strong cravings for junk food during her pregnancy. Eve decided it was a good thing Duncan wasn't the one who'd been left alone in the house. He might have eaten everything.

The doorway to the kitchen was open, the door removed, and she could see the remodel was nearly done, so she went in to check it out.

There was dust everywhere. The drywall was up, and the cabinets and the stone countertops were installed. A few of the backsplash subway tiles, arranged in a herringbone pattern, were up, and she liked it. She'd also picked subway tiles for her backsplash, but a herringbone design hadn't occurred to her, nor was it suggested by her contractor, whose expertise was cleaning crime scenes, not interior design. Was it too late to make a change?

The kitchen island, like the one in the sting house, was absolutely enormous, a second kitchen unto itself. There was no room for one like that in Eve's kitchen and she felt a pang of island envy.

She walked to the french doors at the end of the kitchen, which opened up to a patio with a built-in barbecue grill, a small refrigerator, and a Jacuzzi. The yard overlooked the Volvo dealership on Calabasas Road and the Ventura Freeway. It wasn't Eve's idea of a million-dollar view.

Eve left the kitchen through an open doorway to the family room just as the attendant from the medical examiner's office came in. He was black with salt-and-pepper hair, wearing a white jumpsuit with the office emblem on the chest and holding a clipboard and a small black body bag in his gloved hands.

"It's colder than the morgue in here," he said. "Are you the detective in charge?"

"Yes. Eve Ronin. LASD."

He handed her the clipboard. "I've got some paperwork for you to fill out."

While she did that, he carefully picked up the blanket-swaddled baby, slipped him into the body bag, and zipped it up.

"You don't remove the blanket?" she asked.

He looked at her like she was the stupidest person on the planet. "I don't remove anything. That's all done at the morgue."

"Right," Eve said and, trying not to look embarrassed, handed him the completed paperwork. "Just double-checking."

"Uh-huh." He tore off the bottom sheet, handed it to her, then picked up the body bag, holding it like a football player on the run with the ball. "I've been doing this for fifteen years. How about you?"

"Not as long."

"I hope you kept the training wheels," he said and walked out.

# CHAPTER TWELVE

Duncan was already at his desk when Eve got back. Biddle and Garvey were telling him about the case they were investigating.

"The surfer was crossing PCH," Garvey said, "which is like playing Russian roulette, and was hit by a new red Ferrari going southbound at about a hundred miles per hour."

"Just mowed over him and kept on going," Biddle said. "Dozens of people saw it."

"Anybody get a plate?" Duncan asked.

Garvey shook his head. "He was going too fast. He was a red blur, like the Flash."

Eve asked, "So how do you know it's a new Ferrari and not an older one, or even an entirely different sports car?"

Biddle looked at her. "A couple of the witnesses are car nuts and identified it as a Ferrari F8 Tributo. It has very distinctive lines."

"I googled it," Garvey said. "The car has a 3.9-liter V-8 that gives it 710 horsepower and a top speed of over 200 miles per hour. The base price is $275,000, or about $1,300 per mile of speed."

"Not many people can afford that," Duncan said.

"You'd be surprised," Biddle said. "There are fifty-seven registered owners in Southern California."

"So, we're doing this old school," Garvey said, grabbing his jacket and getting up from his desk. "We're going to personally visit the owner of every red Ferrari F8 Tributo in the area and see if their cars are damaged."

"Good plan," Duncan said.

It sounded to Eve like an excuse for Garvey to suck up to celebrities and studio executives, who were likely to be among the owners of the expensive sports car.

"Don't forget to take selfies," Eve said.

Garvey flipped her off and walked out with Biddle.

Eve went over to Duncan's desk. "How did it go with Mrs. McCaig?"

"She was a mess, but I got the same story from her that we heard from the deputy," Duncan said. "I ran into your sister as I was leaving the ER. She wanted to have a doctor look at my cut, so I scrammed."

"Are you afraid of doctors?"

"I'm afraid of deductibles. The captain left us the list of common guests in each community in the hours immediately before and after each home invasion. There's an overlap of about a dozen guests." He handed her the paper.

Eve scanned the list and saw a lot of familiar gardeners, utilities, pool cleaners, and delivery services. "I might not mind him looking over my shoulder if he's also going to do my legwork."

"He's just in a hurry to put this case in his rearview mirror. CSU called. They've unlocked the laptops belonging to Paul Colter and Greg Nagy and have mirrored the contents for us on encrypted virtual drives in the cloud. I've emailed you the links."

"Okay," she said.

"We also got access to the tracking data on the phones. But don't get excited." He pointed to three open windows on his computer. Each one showed a red pinpoint on a map. "These are the last pings for each of their phones. And they're right outside each man's front door, two hours before the invasion went down. My guess is that they turned off their phones when they got in their cars and then stowed them in their glove boxes."

"These guys are smarter than we thought. They knew we'd track their phones if they got caught. They didn't want us following the trail back to the staging area where their cars are parked or, more importantly, where the rest of their crew may also be."

"How selfless of them."

Eve had a sudden realization. "Maybe more than they thought. They may have unintentionally incriminated themselves in more crimes."

"How do you figure that?"

"Where were their phones when the other home invasions went down?"

"Read me the dates and times," Duncan said.

Eve went back to her desk, opened up her notes on her computer, and called out the information to Duncan, who entered the data.

"I'll be damned," he said.

She swiveled in her seat to face his cubicle. "Let me guess. They turned off their phones at their homes a couple of hours before each of those crimes, too."

"They did," he said. "This ties them to all the other robberies."

"Circumstantially, anyway."

"It'd convince a jury . . . if these guys were still alive to be tried."

"Out of curiosity," she said, "after the other robberies, when and where did they turn their phones back on?"

Duncan typed in some commands and checked the results on his screen. "A few hours later, when they got back home."

"Smart guys," she said.

"Not as smart as you," he said. "They didn't see how the cover-up would nail them, assuming they'd been caught instead of killed."

"It doesn't do us much good now."

"It tells us they were the bad guys."

That was true. At least they'd solved *something*. It helped take the sting off her embarrassing conversation with the guy from the ME's office.

Captain Shaw came in. "I have good news. While you two were in the field, the victim in the Calabasas Estates home invasion told the deputies about a stain in her purse and they matched it to a bag recovered at Dalander's. That ties the three guys to at least one other robbery."

"We can tie them to the rest," Duncan said, then explained what they'd learned from the phone tracking information.

Shaw broke into a big smile. "Exceptional work. You've closed the case in one day. The sheriff will be very pleased."

"It's not closed, sir," Eve said. "The tracking information suggests they had accomplices out there they didn't want to incriminate."

"*Suggests* being the key word," Shaw said.

"There's more. We still don't know how they got into Vista Grande, or any of the other communities, or how they planned to leave, and Sherry Simms is on the run. We know she's guilty of selling stolen goods."

Shaw waved off her concern. "You can't always tie up everything in a neat bow. This is good enough. Write up your reports." He started to go, then turned back, something occurring to him. "The awards ceremony for Grayson Mumford will be at city hall on Thursday at eight a.m. The sheriff wants you both to be there."

The captain walked out. As soon as he was gone, Eve faced Duncan. *"Good enough?"* Eve repeated Shaw's words. "That's a pretty low bar."

"Look at the bright side—if there were others involved in the invasions, they were probably scared straight when their three friends got killed."

"What about Sherry Simms?"

Duncan shrugged. "She could be in Paris, Texas, or Paris, France, by now. Besides, we don't have enough evidence to convict her of anything. She'll claim she had no idea that what her boyfriend gave her to sell was stolen goods."

"Do you believe that?"

"No, but I also don't believe she's worth chasing across the country or around the globe."

Eve wasn't satisfied. "We have enough grounds to get an arrest warrant on her and I want to go for it. That way, if she's ever pulled over for speeding, she'll be dragged back here to answer for her crimes."

Duncan sighed. "Go ahead."

"You're giving up," Eve said.

"No, Eve. I'm retiring."

They spent the rest of the day on paperwork, writing up their reports on the home invasion case and Anna McCaig's stillbirth.

Afterward, Eve drove to her condo on Las Virgenes, across the freeway, a half block north of the overpass. It was a very short trip, but even so, she rolled down all the windows and tried to breathe only through her mouth. Her car had been completely cleaned, but it still reeked of dog shit. Or was it her imagination? She wasn't sure.

She parked in front of her place, a two-story, two-bedroom townhouse, and saw three weeks' worth of yellowed, soggy issues of the *Acorn*, the local newspaper, piled on her front steps.

Eve stepped over the newspapers, unlocked her door, and went inside. The air was hot, stuffy, and still. There was a fine layer of dust on everything, despite the huge sheets of plastic that were taped between her open-concept kitchen and her living room. Her bike, propped behind her IKEA couch, was covered in white powder.

The plastic barrier, white dust clinging to it on the kitchen side, was attached to a temporary wooden frame of two-by-fours wedged between the ceiling and floor. There was a vertical zippered seam in the plastic to allow entry and exit to the kitchen. Eve unzipped the opening and stepped inside.

It was even dustier in the kitchen. The cabinets were up, and the marble countertops installed, but work still hadn't begun on the backsplash, which would have made her angry before she saw the herringbone pattern at the McCaigs'. Now she had the opportunity to make a design change without causing a problem or added expense.

The drywall was in place, but Eve could see that the corner pieces had angled screws that popped out a bit. That prompted her to take a closer look. She also noticed a slight tear where the edges of two adjoining pieces didn't quite fit and a few instances where the screws were in too deep, puncturing the paper. The holes cut for electrical outlets and switches were rough and not quite square. Clearly, her contractor was better at washing away blood than installing drywall.

Eve made a punch list on her phone of changes and fixes she wanted her contractor to make, took a few pictures, and stepped out, zipping up the plastic behind her. Despite the problems, she was pleased with how the kitchen was shaping up, mainly because it was totally different than it was before the death that had happened there. Her hope was if the kitchen didn't look the same, she wouldn't relive the horrible incident every time she made herself a cup of coffee. It would be like living in a new place. Then again, she thought she'd cleaned the smell of dog poop out of her car, too.

There was another sheet of zippered plastic in front of the stairs. She unzipped the opening and went up to her bedroom to get her cycling wear and helmet. There was dust everywhere upstairs, making Eve wonder why the workers bothered with the plastic at all. She got her stuff, came back down, zipped up the house behind her, and left with her dusty bike, which she loaded into the back of her Subaru.

She went back across the Las Virgenes overpass to the Taco Bell, picked up some Cheesy Gorditas at the drive-through for dinner, then got back on the freeway to her hotel on the east side of town.

But when she pulled into the parking lot of the Hilton, she saw a golden Bentley parked near the lobby and almost turned around to avoid the man she knew was waiting inside for her.

That would be cowardly, and she liked to think of herself as someone who bravely confronted every conflict that she faced, so she parked and went inside.

Linwood Taggert sat on a couch in the lobby. Her agent was in his fifties, wearing a perfectly tailored Italian suit and a handmade shirt with his initials monogrammed on the cuffs. His tan rivaled George Hamilton's and his straight white teeth were so bright, she was sure he could stand on a cliff during a storm as a beacon to guide ships at sea. He was one of the most powerful men in Hollywood, so it amused her to see him sitting on a cloth couch in a hotel for families and business-people traveling on a tight budget.

"You've been ignoring my calls," he said.

Eve sat down in a chair across from him and set her Taco Bell bag on the coffee table. "You're not a man who sits and waits for anyone. How did you know when I'd be here?"

"I called the station and they said you were gone for the day. Since your entire life is the job, I knew you'd be back here soon."

"I could have gone shopping or to the movies, hung out with friends, or spent the night with a boyfriend."

"A normal person could have. You? No. Your life is the job. So I was willing to give it an hour on my way home." He lived in Hidden Hills, a gated community of 568 homes across the freeway that was so rich and exclusive, they got themselves granted cityhood. The LASD was the law there, too. "I saw the news the other night and I love your new look. You should stick with it."

"That's what you wanted to tell me? Now you know why I ignored your calls." She started to get up, but Linwood dropped a thick manila envelope on the table.

"Actually, I came to give you this."

She sat down again and looked at the envelope. "What is it?"

"The first-draft pilot script for *Ronin*."

"Already?" It had only been a week since she'd spent a few hours being interviewed by Simone Harper, the Emmy Award–winning writer and producer who'd optioned the rights to her story.

"Simone was so inspired by you that she had to get your story out of her system. It was demanding to be told," Linwood said. "That raw energy comes out in the scenes. I think the script is terrific. She really captures your character."

"You don't know my character. This is the third conversation we've ever had. Why did she show the script to you before me?"

"She wanted to make sure it was ready for prime time," he said. "And it is."

"Your opinion isn't the one that matters. I'm the one with final approval."

Linwood held up his hands in surrender. "I know, I know. But you have zero experience in television. You're looking for authenticity but you can't see the elements that make for a hit show. I can. My clients are the biggest showrunners in the business."

"Good for you. I need to go, my dinner is getting cold." Eve reached for the Taco Bell bag and the envelope.

"Here's an idea. Toss that bag in the trash and let me take you to dinner at Mastro's in Malibu. They make a great steak and a lemon-drop martini that will change your life."

"No thanks." She stood up.

He stood, too. "I'm on your side, Eve. Why do you treat me like the enemy?"

"Because I hate everything about this." She shook the envelope at him. "I feel like I've been forced into it."

She'd only accepted the deal because she knew that a series, or a movie, could be made with or without her because she was arguably a public figure. But by agreeing to participate, it gave her a measure of control over how she was portrayed and her story was dramatized. And, eventually, it would give her a nice paycheck. Even so, she wished it would all go away.

"Having a TV series? That's the cross you have to bear?"

"Yes, it is."

Linwood laughed. "There are thousands of people in this town who've spent their entire lives desperately struggling to get where you are right now and they've never come close."

She knew that. Her mom and dad were two of those people, and they'd both managed to strong-arm their way into the deal. It was Vince who'd brought in Simone and then reached out to Jen to arrange a meeting with Eve. Vince wanted to direct the pilot and Jen wanted a regular speaking role. The possibility of getting some work off of Eve was enough for her mother to set aside her decades of justified bitterness toward Vince for being an absentee, deadbeat father . . . and enough for him to finally make an effort to be in their lives. It made her angry at both of them.

"The difference is, it's their dream, not mine," Eve said. "All I ever wanted was to be a good cop."

"Dreams can change."

Eve walked away.

Linwood called after her. "Read it tonight and call me."

If her hands weren't full, Eve would have given him the finger.

Eve ate her greasy, cold dinner and stared at the envelope the whole time like it contained a rattlesnake waiting to strike.

To distract herself, she turned on the TV and watched the Property Brothers renovate an entire house for what it cost her just to install a kitchen countertop. The show was about as realistic as an episode of *Star Trek*. She turned off the TV in disgust and her gaze landed on the envelope again.

Her curiosity got the better of her. She took out the script, flipped to the first page, and began reading:

EXT. LOS ANGELES—DAY

From above, the city is a big, flat swath of urban sprawl that smacks up against the Santa Monica Mountains, which look like an island of dry, green wilderness in a sea of bleak concrete and asphalt.

                    EVE'S VOICE
        The law in the City of Los Angeles is
        enforced by the police department.

As we get closer, heading northwest, we can see that the Santa Monica Mountains are bordered by the city to the south, Pacific Coast Highway to the west, the San Fernando Valley to the north, and the Sepulveda Pass to the east.

                    EVE'S VOICE
        But here in the Santa Monica Mountains
        and the surrounding communities, the
        law is enforced by the Los Angeles
        County Sheriff and his deputies.

                              WE PUSH IN ON:

EXT. MULHOLLAND HIGHWAY—DAY

The winding two-lane road snakes along the razor's edge of the mountains and dips into the canyons. The farther northwest we go, the more perilous and empty the road becomes.

WE FIND:

A FEMALE BICYCLIST

speeding down the sharp curves. She's in her late twenties, lean-bodied and totally focused, clad in razor-slim sunglasses, an aerodynamic helmet, and skintight, sculpted spandex, all worn for efficiency and practicality, not fashion. Though she wears it very well. She is one with her bike and the road, lost in the speed. This is EVE RONIN.

She couldn't read any further. There was nothing about what she'd read that was particularly objectionable, but it still made her nauseous.

Or perhaps it was her dinner. Or the combination of both.

So she tossed the script aside, opened her laptop, and found the email from CSU with the links to the encrypted virtual drives created from Colter's and Nagy's laptops. She started with Colter's computer and it didn't take long for her to discover that Duncan's guess was right: it was full of porn. Colter had downloaded hundreds of porn movies from the internet. She opened some of the files, watched a few minutes, and saw it was generic XXX stuff, nothing illegal, at least not in California.

There didn't seem to be any personal photos or documents on the computer and she wasn't able to access his Gmail account without his password. He seemed to use the device primarily as a porn delivery system. She opened his web browser and checked his history. It was, as she expected, a long list of porn sites.

Disgusted, Eve switched to the virtual drive of Greg Nagy's computer. His laptop was filled with drafts of his own screenplays and the withering critiques he'd written of the scripts he was hired to read for various studios. The only scripts that he seemed to like were period dramas and historical films that were totally outside the action-adventure genre that he was writing in.

She opened a couple of his scripts to see if his own writing lived up to the high critical standards he used to judge other writers. They didn't. His work was formulaic crap, mechanically rehashing the clichés and tropes of the genre without any originality or cleverness. It was as if they were written by a software application rather than a person.

The rest of his drive was stuffed with pirated movies, mostly AVI and MP4 files of recent superhero fare, and thousands of personal photos, the bulk of which were automatically downloaded from his phone each day and stored on iCloud. His pictures went back a decade. She randomly scanned through hundreds of photos from the last year, hoping to spot Dalander, Colter, or Simms in one of them, but she had no luck. She saw a lot of Nagy's family, their dogs, selfies of Nagy, and pictures of food that he'd eaten, which she assumed he'd also uploaded to his social media accounts.

Eve logged on to Facebook and Instagram, searched for his accounts, but found they were all private.

By this time, it was after 2:00 a.m. and she felt tired and queasy.

She dropped two Alka-Seltzer tablets into a glass of water, guzzled it down as a nightcap, and went to bed, falling to sleep instantly.

# CHAPTER THIRTEEN

Eve was awakened by her phone, which wasn't unusual. It was how she was awakened every morning. But it was ringing at 6:00 a.m., ninety minutes early. The caller ID read: MEDICAL EXAMINER'S OFFICE.

Her mouth was dry, so she quickly swallowed a few times, licked the inside of her cheeks and around her teeth to generate some saliva, and answered the call, trying to sound alert instead of half-asleep.

"Ronin."

"This is Emilia Lopez. I'm the deputy medical examiner handling the autopsy of the McCaig baby."

There was a strange urgency in Lopez's voice. Had Eve, in her inexperience, made some horrible procedural error? She felt a stab of anxiety in her chest. "What can I do for you?"

"You need to get to Anna McCaig's house right away, with some paramedics, though she's probably bled to death by now."

"What?" Eve sat up in bed, fully alert now, and whipped away the sheets.

"I found a portion of her ovaries and uterus still attached to her baby's placenta. I called the hospital to check on the mother's condition and learned that she left the ER yesterday before she was examined," Lopez said. "If she's still alive, she's unconscious and bleeding out. Don't wait for her to answer the door. Break it down."

*How could the paramedic have missed such a serious injury?*

There was no time for Eve to ask Lopez that now. The answer could wait.

"I will."

Eve dressed quickly in yesterday's clothes, grabbed her gun, her badge, and her keys, and hurried out the door, calling the dispatcher on the run to send paramedics and an ambulance to Anna McCaig's house.

But she knew she'd get there first. She lived less than two minutes away from Oakdale and she sped up to the gate, where a male guard was on duty.

Eve rolled down her window, held up her badge, and yelled, "Sheriff's Department! Open the gate and keep it open. Paramedics are right behind me."

As if on cue, they could hear the sirens coming. The fire station was at the corner of Parkway Calabasas and Calabasas Road, nearly as close to Oakdale as her hotel.

The guard opened the gate and Eve tore up the road to the house, came to a skidding stop at the curb, put the car in park, and left the engine running as she rushed to the door. It was mostly glass, like the one at the sting house. She pounded on the door with her fist.

"Mrs. McCaig! This is the police."

There was no answer.

Following the ME's advice, Eve kicked out one of the glass panes, then reached inside and opened the door. The paramedic unit pulled up behind her car. A man and a woman spilled out and grabbed their equipment from the back of the truck.

Eve rushed into the freezing house and ran down the hall to the bedroom, where she found Anna in bed, lying on her side, the comforter pulled up to her neck, a bottle of pills open on the nightstand beside an empty glass.

She whipped back the sheets, revealing Anna in her pajamas on clean sheets, just as the paramedics rushed in. The female paramedic pushed Eve aside.

"Mrs. McCaig," the paramedic said, shaking Anna. "Do you hear me?"

Anna rolled over, groggy and disoriented. "Who are you? What are you doing here?"

Eve picked up the bottle of pills. It was Ambien. Sleeping pills.

"Have you been bleeding?" the paramedic asked.

"No," Anna said. "I mean . . . not much."

Eve spoke up before the paramedic could. "You need to go to the hospital right away."

"But I feel fine," Anna said.

"You aren't fine. The medical examiner doing the autopsy on your baby says you suffered serious internal injuries during childbirth. You need to go to the ER right now or you will die."

Eve said that to Anna but also for the benefit of the two paramedics, who were giving her questioning looks. Her fear was that Anna would refuse to go to the hospital. So she wanted to get Anna so caught up in the urgency of the situation, and Eve's authority, that it wouldn't occur to her that she had the right to say no.

The female paramedic knew something was up but went along with it, turning to the ambulance attendants. "Let's get her onto a gurney."

Eve gestured to the male paramedic, put the lid back on the bottle of sleeping pills, and tossed it to him.

He looked at the bottle, then at Anna on the gurney, who was being covered with a sheet and strapped in. "How many sleeping pills did you take?"

"One. Maybe two. I don't know. I couldn't sleep. I kept seeing . . . my baby."

"When?"

"Tonight." Anna was confused and Eve wanted to keep her that way, at least until she got to the hospital and the doctors could look at her. "My clothes, my things . . ."

"I'll get everything," Eve said. "Go! Go!"

The ambulance team and the male paramedic rushed Anna out. The female paramedic lingered behind, put her hands on her hips, and gave Eve a hard look.

"What the hell is going on here?"

"What's your name?"

"Jamie Dundas."

Eve handed her a card. "I'm Eve Ronin. If you get any blowback for this, Jamie, I'll take full responsibility and say I forced you into it. The woman gave birth to a dead baby yesterday. This morning the ME found parts of the uterus and an ovary attached to the placenta."

Dundas was shocked. "There should be blood all over the place."

Eve checked the bathroom. There was no sign of blood and it smelled of cleansers, bringing back troubling memories of her first homicide scene. She pushed them to the back of her mind. They had nothing to do with this.

"Maybe she bled in the bathroom and cleaned it up."

"I suppose it's possible," Dundas said, "because it's already a miracle that she's still alive."

Eve quickly gathered some clothes from the closet and the dresser drawers. "What about grogginess? Could that be a symptom of her injuries?"

"Any woman would be groggy if she gave birth yesterday, took some sleeping pills, and was awakened only a few hours later. This woman should be dead."

"Thanks for taking a risk on me. I owe you one. I've got to get to the hospital," Eve said, holding the clothes. "Close the front door, will you?"

Eve rushed out, grabbed Anna's purse in the dining room, and ran to her car, hopped in, made a screeching U-turn, and sped off to catch up to the ambulance.

She waited until she hit Parkway Calabasas to call the ME while, at the same time, leaning on the horn and weaving through traffic.

"We got her. She's still alive."

"Oh, thank God," Lopez said. "I was in a panic. It's not often we get a chance to save a life down here. It's a miracle she didn't bleed out."

That was the second time someone had said that to Eve and she didn't believe in miracles.

"Actually, there was no blood at all. We found her asleep in a clean bed."

She got onto the eastbound Ventura Freeway and soon saw the ambulance ahead of her, getting off at the Valley Circle/Mulholland exit.

"Was there blood anywhere else?"

"Not that I saw." She sped up behind the ambulance as it turned onto Valley Circle and stopped leaning on her horn, letting the ambulance and its siren clear the traffic ahead for them.

"That doesn't make any sense," Lopez said.

"That's what I thought, given what you told me. How did the paramedics miss the bits of the uterus and ovary in the placenta?"

"Their focus is saving lives and stabilizing patients until they can get to a hospital. They had no reason to examine the placenta, and even if they did, they wouldn't have known what they were looking at. They don't deliver many babies and they don't have much experience identifying partial organs outside the body."

Eve stayed glued to the ambulance, riding in its wake, north to West Hills Hospital. "There wouldn't have been other signs that something was wrong?"

"This kind of injury during birth should have resulted in enormous blood loss at the scene, and there wasn't. It appeared to the paramedics to be an ordinary stillbirth in all respects."

"What does it appear to be now?"

"I'll let you know after I finish the autopsy." Lopez ended the call.

Eve was sure Lopez knew or suspected more than she was saying.

A few minutes later, the ambulance arrived at West Hills Hospital and the attendants wheeled Anna in, where they were met by an ER doctor and several nurses. One of the nurses was Lisa, Eve's sister.

Lisa spotted Eve coming in and approached her. "I was afraid we'd see her back."

"Why?" Eve asked, watching as the medical team wheeled Anna into an exam room.

"She wouldn't give us the name of her obstetrician yesterday and she refused to be examined. She checked herself out right after Duncan left and took an Uber home."

"Why didn't you call me?"

"It's not a crime to refuse an examination after giving birth," Lisa said.

"In a situation like hers, is it unusual for a mother to walk out of the ER before an exam?"

"A woman who has experienced the trauma of giving birth at home to a stillborn baby isn't in a position to make sound decisions, especially without a spouse, loved one, or friend with them to act as an advocate. They are all emotion, pain, and raging hormones. I don't blame her for wanting to get out of here."

Eve handed her Anna's clothes and purse. "Here are some fresh clothes and her purse."

Lisa took them. "Thanks. Wait here and I'll let you know if she's okay."

Lisa went back to the exam room. Eve stepped to a quiet corner of the corridor to call Duncan.

He answered on the second ring. "Oversleep again? I need you down here. I'm at the breakfast buffet, but without you with me, I'm getting lots of dirty looks for filling my plate."

"I'm at the ER with Mrs. McCaig." Eve told him about the call from the deputy medical examiner and what happened at McCaig's house. "I'll be back as soon as I know what's what."

"I'll let the captain know. Hold on a second." Duncan spoke to someone else. "This isn't for me. I'm taking this up to Eve Ronin in room 306. She's having her period. Terrible cramps."

"Who are you talking to?"

"Nobody," he said. "Bye."

Eve pocketed her phone and turned to see Lisa escorting Anna, now in a hospital gown, to a restroom by gently holding her forearm.

Anna yanked her arm away from Lisa. "I can walk on my own."

Lisa paused at the door. "I'll be right out here if you need me."

"I can piss on my own, too." Anna went into the restroom and closed the door.

Lisa saw Eve watching and walked over to her. "Doctor Bradford from obstetrics is coming down to examine her."

"She doesn't look critically ill to me," Eve said. "But I didn't go to medical school."

"Appearances can be tricky. We once had a lady calmly walk in here with an arrow in her head and she seemed just fine, too."

"Except for the arrow," Eve said.

"That was the giveaway," Lisa said. "Not every patient has one."

The door to the bathroom opened and Anna came staggering out, bleeding down her legs. Lisa and Eve rushed over to her.

Lisa held her firmly by one arm, Eve by the other, and called out to some orderlies for help.

"What happened?" Lisa asked Anna.

"I don't know . . . something just burst inside."

The orderlies rushed over with a gurney, lifted Anna onto it, and wheeled her back into the ER, Lisa hurrying alongside them.

Eve snatched a pair of plastic gloves from a box at the nurse's station and went into the bathroom. There was blood on the toilet seat and on the linoleum floor. She crouched to get a closer look and spotted a bloody ballpoint pen on the floor beside the toilet.

She took out her phone, snapped several pictures of the scene, then picked up the pen and left the bathroom.

A nurse passed by and Eve stopped her. "Do you have a baggie of some kind?"

The nurse slipped into an unoccupied exam room and came out with a baggie marked HAZARDOUS WASTE.

"Will this do?"

"Yes, thank you." Eve took the baggie, dropped the pen inside, and found herself a seat in the waiting room.

While she sat there, a custodian with a surgical mask and gloves rolled his cleaning cart up to the women's room, dropped a yellow caution cone on the floor, grabbed a mop, and went inside to clean up.

Twenty minutes later, the bathroom was clean and Lisa emerged from the exam area with a doctor in tow and they headed for Eve. She stood up to meet them. Lisa gestured to Eve.

"Dr. Bradford, this is my sister, Eve, the detective who brought Mrs. McCaig in for treatment."

Bradford appeared to be about fifty and somehow wore his stethoscope around his neck as if it was a tie, a fashion accessory that fit into his personal style statement, rather than a tool of his profession.

He stuffed his hands into the pockets of his lab coat and gave Eve a grim look. "Anna McCaig's uterus and ovaries are intact and her cervix is fully closed."

"Which means what, exactly?"

"She hasn't given birth and she injured herself in a crude attempt to make it look like she did."

"I found this in the bathroom." Eve held out the hazardous waste bag to him and opened it so he could see the bloody pen inside. "Would this do it?"

He peered in and nodded. "I spoke to the deputy medical examiner this morning. My concern right now is for the actual birth mother. If she didn't get immediate medical care, then she's likely dead."

"And Mrs. McCaig?"

"She'll be fine," Bradford said. "She can go home today."

Eve did some quick thinking. "I'd say that a woman who'd mutilate herself to make it appear like she was seriously injured during childbirth is clearly a danger to herself, especially now that she knows her lie has been exposed. Don't you agree?"

"Are you angling for a 5150?" Bradford asked, referring to the section of the state welfare and institutions code that empowered a doctor to detain an individual, against their will, for psychiatric evaluation if their mental state posed a risk of harm to themselves or others.

"I need to figure out where that baby came from, what happened to the birth mother, and keep Anna McCaig from hurting herself or disappearing on me while I do it."

"The 5150 will only give you a seventy-two-hour hold," Bradford said.

"I'll take whatever I can get."

While Bradford mulled that over, Lisa asked, "Can't you arrest her?"

"I have nothing to charge her with yet," Eve said. "And when I do, I want it to stick."

Bradford nodded to himself, telegraphing his decision. "I'll issue the order but we don't have the psychiatric facilities here to hold her. She'll have to be transported to Northridge Medical Center."

"Do whatever you have to do," Eve said.

"I'll go make the arrangements." Bradford walked away.

Eve turned to Lisa. "Where is Mrs. McCaig? I need to talk with her."

"Exam room four."

Eve went to the exam room, knocked on the door to announce her arrival, then went in without waiting for an invite. Anna sat on the edge of her gurney in a fresh gown.

"What do you want?" Anna said, angry.

"I need to read you your rights," Eve said, and then did so. "Do you understand your rights as I've explained them to you?"

"Yes, I do. Are you arresting me?"

"Not yet."

"Then what was the point of all that?"

"We know that you didn't give birth to that baby and that you mutilated yourself with a pen to make it look like you did." Eve held up the bag. "I have it right here."

"That's an outrageous and unspeakably cruel thing to say. I just lost my son. You were there. You know what happened."

"I know your DNA doesn't match the baby's. The tests just came back. They aren't even close."

It was a lie, but Eve's mom was right—thanks to TV, everybody believed in instant DNA results.

Anna certainly did. She lowered her head and cried, big sobs that racked her whole body.

Eve stood there, waiting, knowing that Anna was stalling for time, trying to figure out what story to tell. That was fine. She wanted to hear it.

After a few moments, Anna got a hold of herself, or at least settled on her story, and looked up at Eve.

"My husband, Jeff, wants a family so much and if I can't have a child, he'll leave me. That's why he left his first wife. We keep trying to get pregnant, but it's not working. I love him. I don't want to lose him or our wonderful life together."

Including, perhaps, her right to stay in the United States, Eve thought. A divorce without a child might mean a one-way plane ticket back to Germany or Romania.

"I saw all the junk food in your dining room. You were fattening yourself up to fake a pregnancy, weren't you?"

"I had to. If I wasn't showing, even a little, he'd suspect something. I just wanted more time to get pregnant for real. But it didn't happen, and he was traveling so much . . ."

"Time was running out, so you found another solution. You got a baby from someone else."

Anna shook her head. "No, no. You've got it all wrong."

"Who is the mother?"

"I don't know—"

Eve stepped closer to her, invading her space. "Where is she?"

Anna leaned away. "I never saw her."

"Then where did the baby come from?"

"It was a gift from God!" Anna yelled, loud enough for people to hear outside the room.

Eve took a step back and regarded her with undisguised skepticism. "You're saying it just magically appeared in your living room?"

"I took some garbage out to the dumpster . . . and the baby was there, wrapped in the blanket . . . a little boy, just like Jeff wanted . . . it was like a miracle . . . like God had answered my prayers. I brought the baby inside, cleaned him up . . . but he wasn't breathing. He was dead."

"But you called 911 and went through the charade of doing CPR anyway," Eve said. "Why?"

"I thought about putting the baby back in the dumpster and saying nothing, but I couldn't treat him like he was trash. What if the contractor found the baby? What would he think? I was afraid nobody would believe I had nothing to do with it."

Eve certainly didn't. "More importantly, you also realized that faking a stillbirth would get you off the hook with your husband, at least for a while."

Anna nodded and gave Eve a heartfelt, pleading look. "Does Jeff have to know the baby wasn't mine?"

Eve took the pair of handcuffs off her belt and snapped one loop on Anna's left wrist and the other to the rail of the gurney.

"What are you doing?" Anna stared at the cuffs in disbelief. "You said I wasn't under arrest."

"You aren't. I'm restraining you."

"What for? Do you think I want to hurt you?"

"It's so you can't hurt yourself again. You're being held for psychiatric evaluation."

"I told you the truth. I haven't done anything wrong. I'm not the one who threw a baby in my trash."

"You'll be out in three days," Eve said, "unless they decide to commit you for treatment."

Anna yanked at her cuffs. "You can't do this to me."

Eve walked out of the room. Lisa was waiting outside the door and had clearly heard every word.

Lisa asked, "What happens if she calls a lawyer?"

"She won't. She wants to keep this from her husband. But even if she does bring in a lawyer, the 5150 will hold."

Eve had no experience to justify that certainty and hoped that her sister couldn't see through her false confidence.

# CHAPTER FOURTEEN

Eve's phone rang as she got into her car. It was Emilia Lopez.

"I've discovered some irregularities that raise questions about the circumstances of the baby's death," Lopez said. "I've suspended my autopsy until you're present and a crime scene technician arrives to collect evidence."

"I've discovered some irregularities, too," Eve said, and shared with her everything that had happened and what she'd learned.

"That makes a lot of sense and is consistent with my initial findings."

"Which are?"

"I'll see you soon, Detective." Lopez ended the call.

Soon was optimistic, Eve thought. The county medical examiner-coroner's office was in Boyle Heights, on the grounds of the LAC-USC Medical Center, a few miles northeast of downtown Los Angeles, and getting there now, right in the middle of rush hour, could take her ninety minutes or more if there were no accidents along the way.

She called Duncan as she drove out of the hospital parking lot, repeated what she'd told Lopez, and added that she was heading downtown to observe the autopsy. What she didn't say was that she'd never observed an autopsy before and was worried about making a fool of herself.

"You've had a busy morning," Duncan said. "I'll check if there are any missing person reports involving pregnant women and I'll call area hospitals to see if they've treated any women in the last twenty-four hours who've lost vital lady parts."

"Have you ever come across anything like this before?"

"I had a case where a woman stole a baby from a hospital nursery, but we caught her an hour later, walking down the street. She'd been faking a pregnancy, too, and had run out of time. Do you believe Anna McCaig found the baby in her dumpster?"

"It's a mighty big coincidence, given the timing."

"Or it's not a coincidence at all. Whoever left the baby could have known how desperately Anna wanted a child."

"That's a stretch."

"Ruthie the Oracle knew. It follows that others in the neighborhood did, too. Remember what I told you," Duncan said. "You have to keep an open mind."

Within reason, she thought, and she wasn't sure if Anna's story, or Duncan's theory, qualified. "In that case, we shouldn't rule out a gift from God."

"If it is," Duncan said, "he's a cruel bastard."

Eve knew Hollywood touched everything in Los Angeles. So it was no surprise to her that the Los Angeles County Coroner-Medical Examiner's office was the only one in the nation with a gift shop and its own line of souvenirs, from beach towels to toe tags. The store was in the lobby of a stately 1909 Italianate building that was once Los Angeles County General Hospital and was often used as a police precinct in cop shows and movies.

But only administrative work was done in there now. The autopsies and scientific work were conducted in the buildings behind it, structures so generic and unremarkable that their facades would never be reproduced on the souvenir shot glasses.

Eve arrived and parked in front of one of the generic buildings. But she didn't get out right away. She sat there for a long moment, trying to collect herself, even though she'd already spent two hours parked in traffic. She was afraid of how she might react to seeing a dead baby being cut open and examined.

There was a knock on the window, startling her. She turned to see Nan Baker, the head of the CSU unit, standing outside her driver's side door.

Nan was an African American woman in her forties who looked like she could wrestle a bear to the ground without breaking a sweat. She was in her usual Tyvek suit and gloves, a camera around her neck, and holding her evidence processing kit.

"Are you coming?" Nan asked. "I don't have all day."

Eve opened the door and got out. "Could I ask your professional opinion on something?"

"That's what I'm here for."

"Could you take a whiff inside my car and tell me what you smell?"

"You're joking," she said.

"Please. Pretend it's a crime scene. Give me your first impressions."

Nan opened the back door and sniffed. "French fries, sweat, old socks, formaldehyde, and dog shit."

"I knew it," Eve said and kicked the driver's side door shut. "It's a relief to know I'm not crazy."

"I'm not qualified to give you a professional opinion on that." Nan closed the back door and they headed into the building together.

The baby was on his back on the aluminum exam table and his blanket was in an evidence bag on a nearby cart.

Emilia Lopez, a short woman in scrubs, stood across the table from Eve and Nan. She wore thick glasses behind her protective goggles that made her eyes seem unnaturally large.

"The subject is male, approximately thirty-eight weeks old, and weighs six pounds, two ounces. I began my autopsy by examining the placenta." Lopez pointed to a bloody organ in a metal tray on another cart. Eve wouldn't have known what she was looking at if Lopez hadn't identified it. "I observed that part of a uterus and ovary were still attached."

Nan stood over the tray and took pictures.

Eve asked, "Is that something that can normally happen during childbirth?"

"It is if the mother has a prolapsed uterus with very thin lining."

"I have no idea what that means." The words came out of Eve's mouth before she had a chance to think about the consequences. But she didn't regret it. She decided that she'd rather look foolish than make a critical mistake because she was ashamed of her ignorance. Besides, the morgue attendant probably already told Lopez about her dumb question at McCaig's house. Eve figured she might as well double down on her inexperience.

"The uterus can slip down and protrude from the vagina if the muscles and ligaments that hold it are weakened and stretched," Lopez said without any apparent condescension or judgment in her voice or expression. Eve was thankful for that. "And that could cause the uterine lining, particularly if it's thin, to tear during childbirth. There can be considerable blood loss as a result. That was my initial concern, which is why I called you to check on the welfare of the mother."

Nan lowered her camera for a moment. "Isn't a prolapsed uterus something that affects older women who've given birth before?"

"It can happen at any age," Lopez said, "regardless of whether or not the woman has given birth."

"Is there any other explanation for what you found?" Eve asked.

"Yes. The placenta could have adhered to the uterus, a condition which, if previously undetected, could be fatal for the mother and baby during a vaginal delivery," Lopez said. "In that case, doctors would perform an emergency C-section and perhaps an immediate hysterectomy after the birth. But that's not the case here, though it is a relevant example."

"Relevant in what way?"

"When I resumed my autopsy, I noticed this . . ." She pointed at two very tiny cuts on the top of the baby's head. "Two nicks. The baby supposedly was born naturally, without any medical equipment, so where did these cuts come from? That's when I halted the autopsy and called both of you."

Nan leaned over the baby's head and took more pictures. "Could the cuts have come from being tossed in the dumpster?"

"No, there would be other, more extreme trauma to the body from that. These nicks are straight, like they came from the edge of a sharp object, the sort of damage you might accidentally do to a product while cutting open the box. That observation prompted me to go back and reexamine the uterus and ovaries more closely."

She walked over to the tray containing the placenta. "What I observed first is jagged tearing here that could be consistent with a prolapsed uterus." She pointed to one spot, and then to another. "But not here. Or here. These tears are straight."

Nan got in close, taking pictures.

Eve didn't need to see the cuts for herself because she understood the point Lopez was making. "Straight cuts don't occur naturally."

"No, they don't, Detective. I think the nicks on the baby's head came from the same knife or other sharp object that did this."

The autopsy continued. It was clinical and detailed and that helped distance Eve from what she was seeing and keep her emotions in check. When Lopez finished her work, she peeled off her gloves and said, "I can conclude, with a reasonable degree of medical certainty, that the baby was not the product of a natural birth and died of asphyxiation in utero, likely as a result of the mother's death."

Eve wanted to be sure she correctly understood Lopez's conclusion. "You're saying the mother and baby died during a botched C-section?"

"I wouldn't put it so nicely. This baby was torn out of the womb. And I can tell you if the mother's body is out there, nobody in Los Angeles County has reported it yet."

◆ ◆ ◆

Eve called Duncan as soon as she stepped outside and told him everything.

"You're saying Anna McCaig cut this baby out of a pregnant woman's body and pretended it was her own child?" he asked.

"That's right," Eve said, trying to keep her voice even and unemotional, to choose her words carefully and not betray her rage. "The actual term for it is 'fetal abduction' and it's an extremely rare occurrence."

"Thank God for that."

"The deputy medical examiner has read about such cases but has never dealt with one until now."

"That makes two of us. I would have liked to retire without ever having heard of or investigated a fetal abduction case, but here we are. But we don't know for certain that Anna McCaig did it."

"Did you find reports of any missing pregnant women in Los Angeles?"

"Not in the county or even in the state of California," Duncan said. "And no women have come into any ERs in Los Angeles or Ventura Counties with injuries consistent with what you described to me before."

"So it had to be Anna McCaig."

"Don't get locked into one theory of the case. It has got you into trouble before."

That was true, but she knew in her bones that she was right. What other possibilities were there? That someone in the neighborhood just happened to toss a baby in Anna's dumpster? Anna's cruel "gift from God"? Eve didn't believe it. There was a desperate look in Anna's eyes, like a cornered animal, when Eve confronted her at the hospital with her inconsistencies. It was the look of a guilty woman.

Eve walked around the parking lot, trying to calm herself down so she could think clearly. But the crime that Anna McCaig committed was so barbaric that it was hard to remain calm and reasonable, to resist the urge to hunt her down and strangle her to death.

She spoke to Duncan with a forced, measured tone. "I don't know why there hasn't been a missing person's report filed, but I know the real birth mother is dead and her body is at Anna McCaig's house."

"How do you figure that?"

"Because the baby was still warm, still covered with blood and other fluids, when the paramedics got there."

"Okay, assuming you're right, that Anna McCaig abducted a pregnant woman and hacked a baby out of her uterus, that doesn't mean the body is still on the property. Anna came home from the hospital yesterday. She could have waited until nightfall and disposed of the body somewhere else."

"That's easy enough to check by reviewing the front gate videos. If she came or went, we'll see it. But whether she moved the body or not, the murder happened in the house."

She saw a family of four, the parents and their two children, emerge from the old administration building. The father carried a black Los Angeles Coroner body bag–style sleeping bag, the mother had on a cap with the department logo, and the kids were wearing matching T-shirts adorned with the chalk outline of a dead body. Eve turned away, disgusted, and walked back to her car. This wasn't an amusement park and there was nothing fun about death.

"I'll start writing up a search warrant request for her property, the dumpster, the porta-potty, and her car," Duncan said.

"How long do you think it will take a judge to grant the warrant?"

"You'll probably hear a sonic boom before you get back to the station."

Anna McCaig's cold house was full of crime scene technicians in white Tyvek, led by Nan Baker, who'd spent three hours checking every room, every surface, and every drain for signs of flesh and blood.

Eve and Duncan stood in the dining room, watching the search unfold. Eve's arms were crossed under her chest, mostly to retain her warmth, and she tapped her right foot nervously on the floor. Neither the two of them, nor anybody in the CSU, had discovered any evidence yet.

Duncan nodded to the wall of food. "Somebody should search that box of Ding Dongs."

"You think a murder weapon might be in there?"

His stomach growled. "Or in the bag of Doritos."

It would be nice if it were, Eve thought. She was half tempted to search them out of desperation, and to keep herself busy, when Nan approached them.

"There's blood and other bodily fluids on the couch," she said, "but I can already say nobody bled out there or, as far as we can determine, anywhere else in the house, garage, or backyard."

"What about in the bathrooms?" Eve asked. "Could the murder have taken place in a bathtub or shower?"

"She obviously did some cleaning in the master bathroom. We detected the presence of cleansers, but we'd still expect to find some traces of blood or flesh after the gutting the medical examiner described," Nan said. "But we didn't. And, it goes without saying, but we haven't found a body anywhere, either."

Eve, Duncan, and the CSU searched every closet, under every bed, and up in the rafters. The house was built on a flat foundation, so there was no place under the house to stash a body. The garage was full of stacked drywall, two-by-fours, toolboxes, tile-cutting equipment, and other materials for the kitchen renovation, including the new appliances, still in cardboard boxes. They opened every box in the garage and found nothing.

"I know the murder was committed here," Eve said. "Maybe it was done on a rug, and then Anna rolled up the body in it and took it away."

Duncan shook his head. "I checked with the guard. Anna McCaig's car didn't leave the property last night."

"We also thoroughly examined her car," Nan said. "There's no sign of blood or other bodily fluids inside."

"Maybe she got someone else in the community to help her dispose of the body."

Duncan said, "We can talk to every resident and vendor who left the community after Anna returned from the hospital, but I doubt she talked the Amazon delivery guy or Sparkletts guy into helping her out."

"Maybe a gardener or pool man, though. We should talk to other vendors, too," Eve said, then turned to Nan. "Did you find anything in the backyard?"

Nan sighed. "Ninety percent of the backyard is hardscape and what dirt there is hasn't been disturbed. So I can safely say nothing was buried. We also thoroughly checked the dumpster and found nothing bloody or suspicious. I even had Noomis check the contents of the porta-potty. All he found was human waste."

Duncan looked at Eve. "You're going to owe him a terrific Christmas gift."

Nan waved off Duncan's comment. "It's not necessary. Noomis specializes in urine and feces. He was in his comfort zone."

"No wonder he's single," Duncan said.

Eve was so frustrated, she could cry. She knew Anna McCaig was guilty. The evidence had to be here—they just weren't seeing it.

"Do you have any potential leads at all?"

"Well, there were rags in the dryer and it's possible she used them to clean the bathroom. We'll take them back for analysis," Nan said. "We're also taking all the sharp objects that could have been used to remove the baby, like kitchen knives, scissors, drywall cutters, garden shears, and retractable blade utility knives, back for testing."

"She didn't find that baby in the dumpster," Eve stated.

"I know how you feel, Eve. I want to see justice for that baby and his mother, too," Nan said. "But we haven't found any evidence consistent with a fetal abduction or murder occurring in this house."

"I understand," Eve said. "Thank you, Nan."

Nan walked away and started gathering her crew. They were finished here.

Duncan opened the box of Ding Dongs, peered inside, and took one of the packages out. "No sharp objects hidden in here. It would have been remiss for me not to check."

"You don't want to be remiss." Eve noticed a grocery store receipt flutter to the floor and figured that it must have been under the box of Ding Dongs. She picked it up.

The receipt was a scroll of junk food, sugary fruit juices, and soft drinks, with the exception of some bananas and a few miscellaneous things, like paper plates, air freshener, baking soda, paper towels, and laundry detergent. Eve put the receipt on the dining room table, the wood so polished she could almost see her reflection in the finish.

"But now that I've touched this Ding Dong," Duncan said, "I can't really put it back."

"It might be contaminated."

"Exactly, it'd be a health risk, so I will confiscate it out of an abundance of caution," Duncan said and began to unwrap the Ding Dong. "Maybe we've approached this case from the wrong direction."

"What other direction is there?"

He took a bite out of the chocolate-coated cake. "Let's find the birth mother."

"You mean her body."

"I mean find out who she was and how her path crossed with Anna McCaig's." Duncan took another bite. "That might lead us to the scene of the crime."

Eve saw the last CSU tech leave. "Okay, but I still think it's right here."

"Duly noted for the record."

"I'd like to put a deputy on the house. I don't want to release the scene, and invalidate the warrant, until the last possible moment."

If they left, it would mean the search was completed, and they would have to get a second warrant to go through the property again, and Eve knew it would be very hard to convince a judge to give them a second bite without new evidence to justify it. By stationing an officer there, it technically kept the search active and the warrant valid.

Duncan finished the Ding Dong and looked at the box, clearly contemplating a second one. "I think I can talk the captain into that."

Eve stepped between him and the Ding Dongs. "We need to know if there are any pregnant women in this community and confirm they are still alive."

"Let's talk to the Oracle," he said.

# CHAPTER FIFTEEN

Eve drove them down to the gate in Duncan's plain-wrap Explorer. They got out of the car and walked to the guardhouse to talk with Ruthie, who stood up and opened the door to greet them.

"Lots of excitement up at the McCaig house today . . ." Ruthie let her voice trail off, an invitation for them to fill in the blanks.

Duncan held up his hands. "I'm afraid we can't share any details, Ruthie. We're going to need all the security camera footage and visitor logs from yesterday."

"I don't have the authority to give them to you. You'll have to talk to the HOA about that. They can give you a link to watch it online."

Duncan gave Eve a glance. One more warrant to write up.

Eve asked, "Are there many pregnant women in the community?"

"There's Tara Bowers on Park Naples. Naomi Eng on Park Umbria. And the Schnitzers' daughter Claire on Park Positano," Ruthie said. "Claire and her husband are living at home while they go to graduate school for their MBAs."

"Could we have their addresses and phone numbers, please?"

Ruthie thought about that for a minute. "I suppose that's okay. But if any residents raise a stink, you didn't get the information from me."

"Deal," Eve said and Ruthie started writing down the information on a sheet of paper. "What about home care workers, like housekeepers and nurses? Are any of them pregnant?"

Ruthie answered while continuing to write. "Most of the maids arrive in the morning, at the bus stop over there, and walk up." She pointed her pen to a bench at the corner. "And they are usually gone before I arrive so they can catch the bus home before their kids return from school, so I really don't know any of them."

Duncan looked at the bus stop, then up at the hill behind them, and shook his head. "I can't imagine a homeowner who'd make a pregnant woman schlep up that hill to their house."

"You'd be surprised, though a few will meet their maid down here with their car." Ruthie tore the sheet of paper from her pad and handed it to Eve. "Nobody takes them downhill."

"Thanks," Eve said, pocketing the list. "Would the coming and going of the maids be in the log?"

"Honestly, no, the walk-ins get waved through. The morning guard knows them by their faces. He sees them every day."

"And what about the maids and nurses who drive in?"

"They get waved in, too, but the camera will catch their license plates." Ruthie narrowed her eyes at them. "Why are you so interested in all the pregnant women in Oakdale?"

"Can't say," Duncan said. "Thanks for your help, Ruthie. I owe you a baker's dozen."

"If you buy a dozen," Ruthie said, "it'll be a half dozen by the time you get the box here."

He smiled at her. "You know me too well."

Eve and Duncan got back into the Explorer and she started the engine.

"I'd like to visit the Bowers, Engs, and Schnitzers and see if all is well," Eve said.

"You do that," Duncan said. "I'll go back to the station and get the warrant for the visitor logs and videos."

Eve pulled out and made a U-turn around the guardhouse, and Ruthie opened the gate for them.

"Okay, but please sweet-talk the captain first." Eve sped up the hill. "I won't leave Oakdale until a deputy is stationed at the house, even if it means I'm the one who has to spend the night."

"I admire your tenacity," Duncan said. "But I'm afraid it's going to kill you."

Eve visited the women on Ruthie's list and they were all fine. She asked each woman if they knew Anna McCaig but none of them did. The steep hills in the neighborhood, she was told, prevented a lot of walking and that cut down on kids playing in the street or the parents socializing.

After visiting the women, Eve parked in front of the McCaig house in her Subaru, rolled down the windows for the fresh air, and noticed half a dozen landscapers mowing and blowing at the home across the street. A box van and pickup truck emblazoned with the words GREEN'S GREENERY were parked out front. She was familiar with the trucks. They worked all the gated communities in Calabasas.

Eve got out of the car and crossed the street. As she did, one of the landscapers set down his Weedwacker, peeled away from the group, and met her, a smile on his face. He was lanky, with a day's growth of beard on his ruddy face, his khaki shirt stained with sweat and dirt.

"I saw you a few times at Vista Grande," he said. "But you looked very different."

"Better car," she said. "And more cleavage."

He snapped his fingers and pointed at her. "That's it. I'm Michael Green. I own this landscaping company."

"Eve Ronin." She showed him her badge. "Since you're so obser-vant, I wonder if you've noticed anything unusual at the house across the street over the last two days."

"You mean besides all the cop cars, forensic vans, and morgue wag-ons today? No, I haven't, but we weren't here yesterday. Was somebody murdered?"

"That's what we're trying to figure out."

"Does it have anything to do with all the excitement at Vista Grande?"

"They're unrelated."

"Except for you."

"Luck of the draw. Were you in Vista Grande that day?" Eve knew his crews were working at each gated community on the days they were hit. She'd seen the vehicles in the security videos and in the gate logs.

"I wasn't, but one of my crews was. That was some pretty wild shit. Ironic, isn't it?"

"What is?"

"The people who live in these places think the gates protect them from all the crime and misery that's out there, but it doesn't. It just locks them in with it."

"You think whatever happened came from within the gates?"

"I don't know where it came from, that's your job. But I'm sure there's as much evil inside these gates as there is outside of them. Maybe more."

Eve couldn't argue with that, not after what she believed hap-pened inside Anna McCaig's house. That was pure evil. She noticed an LASD patrol car coming up the hill and reached into her pocket for her card.

"If you or anyone in your crew ever sees any of that evil, please give me a call." Eve gave Green her card.

He stuck it in his shirt pocket and handed her one of his. It was glossy and featured a picture of his trucks. "And if you ever need yard work, keep me in mind. Green keeps you green, that's our motto."

"Catchy," she said and went back across the street. The patrol car had pulled up behind her Subaru and Tom Ross was at the wheel. He rolled down the window.

"I've been assigned to watch the house," Tom said.

"That's my fault," she said. "Sorry for the dull shift."

"I don't mind dull."

"What's the feeling at the station about all the personnel changes?" Eve had only heard what Biddle and Garvey had to say, but she didn't trust them or their take on things. She trusted Tom's.

"Deathfist took down two more of us."

Biddle and Garvey were right. "I guess I shouldn't count on any backup for a while."

"You can count on me," Tom said. "Eddie Clayton is on the next shift."

"Are you two watching out for me?"

"And your cases," he said. "When we can."

"I wish there were more deputies like you."

"There are more than you think. We just don't send out press releases."

Eve's phone rang. She pulled it out of her pocket. It was Duncan. She answered the call with, "Thanks for sweet-talking Shaw."

"I really didn't have to," Duncan said. "Once he learned we're working a fetal abduction, he was glad to give us whatever I asked for. He wants to keep this case under the radar, and away from the media, as long as possible, ideally until it's solved. He doesn't want to see the press exploit the lurid aspects."

"So it remains a stillbirth on the blotter?" Eve asked, referring to the daily log of crime and incident reports that was available to the media.

"Yeah, and the incident at the McCaig house this morning is listed as a medical emergency with no elaboration. But word is going to get out that a crime scene unit was in Oakdale today. It won't be long until the media gets curious. Even the reporters at *The Acorn* can put two and two together," Duncan said, referring to the small local newspaper. "We may have a day, tops, before they start sniffing around."

Now they had two ticking clocks, Eve thought: the 5150 hold running out on Anna McCaig and the media learning about the fetal abduction.

"Hopefully it will all be over by then," she said.

"I got the warrants for Oakdale's gate videos and visitor logs. Ruthie can print out or email the logs for you and the HOA will email you the link to stream the video."

"Me? What about you?"

"I'm calling it a day. I'll jump in first thing tomorrow."

Eve checked the time on the phone. It was almost 6:00 p.m. "How can you quit now? We only have about sixty-six hours left until our 5150 hold on Anna McCaig expires."

"Statistics show that if we can't solve a case in the first forty-eight hours, it's not going to get solved. So we have about twelve hours to spare," Duncan said. "I'm going to use mine for dinner and sleep. You should, too. But I know you won't."

She didn't have to tell him that he was right.

Eve stopped at the gate on her way out, picked up a hard copy of the log for the last forty-eight hours from Ruthie, and also asked the guard to email it to her.

Although Eve was only a few blocks from the Hilton, she realized she hadn't eaten all day and was ravenous. So she called ahead to Barone's in Woodland Hills and ordered a pizza. It was ready for her when she got there. She brought the pizza back to her hotel room and settled down to eat while she fast-forwarded through the Oakdale gate videos, starting the playback at sunrise the day before and comparing what she saw to the logs as she went along.

She hit pay dirt almost immediately. Two pregnant women were among the dozen people who walked into Oakdale from the bus stop between 7:30 a.m. and 9:00 a.m. None of their names were listed in the logs.

Over the course of fast-forwarding through all twenty-four hours' worth of footage, Eve counted two hundred guests visiting Oakdale in a vehicle and only two dozen on foot. It was in the final hour of footage, though, that Eve made a striking discovery. One of the pregnant women who came in on foot at 7:30 a.m. the previous day never walked out.

Eve scrubbed the timeline needle back to the woman's arrival and froze the image. The woman was Hispanic, perhaps in her thirties, and had a huge belly.

Eve felt a wave of sadness as she looked at the woman, arriving for work, unaware of the horrific fate that awaited her and her unborn child.

*I promise I will get you justice.*

She zoomed in on the woman's face, snapped a screenshot on her laptop, and AirDropped the photo to her phone so she could ask the Oakdale guard about her first thing in the morning . . .

. . . which it already was.

At first, Eve thought she was looking at the video's time code on her phone and then realized to her shock that no, it was also seven thirty in the morning now. And that's when she also realized that the sheriff's award ceremony at Calabasas Civic Center for Grayson Mumford was happening in thirty minutes.

*Thank God it's next door.*

Eve brushed her teeth and, because she smelled like sweat and pizza, took a very fast shower. She dried herself off, got into fresh clothes, and grabbed a Red Bull from her mini-fridge for breakfast as she dashed out of her hotel room.

She ran from the hotel next door to the civic center, a Spanish Colonial–style set of buildings that included city hall and the library. A crowd of about fifty people, a dozen uniformed deputies, and half a dozen reporters and their photographers milled in the front plaza, where a small stage and podium had been set up. The sheriff stood in front of the stage, introducing Captain Shaw to members of the Calabasas City Council as a city photographer snapped some pictures. Ethan Dryer, the head of Big Valley Security, hovered nearby, waiting for a chance to insert himself into the discussion.

She spotted Duncan pacing in the shade of the city hall arcade and walked over to him, catching her breath on the way. He was dressed in a clean suit and a new tie.

"I was about to call you," Duncan said. "Lansing was worried you weren't going to show. Now he might be terrified that you did."

Eve took the last sip from her can of Red Bull and dropped it into a nearby trash can. "Why? What's wrong?"

"You look like you rose from the grave."

So much for the shower and fresh clothes, she thought.

"I was up all night watching the Oakdale videos."

"Of course you were."

"It paid off. Two pregnant women walked through the gates in the morning but only one left," Eve said, showing him the photo on her phone. "We need to find out who she is and not waste our time here on this PR crap."

"You're doing it again," Duncan said.

"Doing what?"

"Obsessing over your case to the point of exhaustion. You need a life and some sleep. You can't physically, mentally, or emotionally sustain being relentless."

"I'm only doing it now because we've got a ticking clock on this one."

"You've done it on every case we've had."

"You make it seem like years. We've only been working together for a few months. It hasn't been that long."

"Exactly. If you keep up this pace much longer, you'll burn out, one way or another. Your body will quit on you, or you'll make a big mistake or take a foolish risk that either kills you, kills your career, kills somebody else, or all of the above. You've come pretty damn close to that twice already."

Just the mention of those incidents made her chest and right wrist ache, which she dismissed as imaginary pain, mentally induced reminders of her past injuries. She blamed Duncan for that. She didn't need those distractions right now.

"Instead of giving me a lecture, how about congratulating me on making a huge discovery that breaks open our case?"

"If you'd slept last night, you still would have made the same discovery today, except you'd be rested and a lot more healthy."

"It also would have cost us precious hours we don't have." Eve looked past Duncan and spotted Grayson Mumford, wearing an ill-fitting suit and talking to a group of people outside the library.

"Who are they?" she asked, just to change the subject.

He followed her gaze. "That's Grayson Mumford. The security guard who saved your life."

"Yes, I know. Who is that with him?"

"His parents, Bill and Karen, and his twelve-year-old sister, Emily, and Maureen Stoker, the mayor of Calabasas," he said. "You should go say hello."

"How do you know all their names?"

"Because I went and said hello."

"And you remember their names?"

"I also remember where I parked my car," he said, "and that was even longer ago."

"I've already forgotten their names," Eve said, wishing she had another Red Bull within reach.

"Good, then you'll appear genuinely unprepared when you go and say hello. Quick, you have an opening now that the mayor is leaving." He gave her a shove and she reluctantly straggled over to Grayson and his family.

"Pardon me for intruding, I just wanted to say hello," Eve said, catching Grayson's eye, "and to thank you again for what you did."

"I was just doing my job," Grayson said. There was something stiff and rote about the line now. Eve wondered how many times he'd said it over the past seventy-two hours.

"He keeps saying that," his mother, Karen, said, as if reading Eve's mind. "But he went above and beyond. Too far, if you ask me."

Eve felt the same way. She wasn't convinced that Paul Colter had to be shot, that she wouldn't have been able to talk him down.

Bill Mumford turned to his son. "They better give you a fat bonus or a promotion to a command position."

Eve nodded toward Ethan Dryer, who was sucking up to Sheriff Lansing, who was smiling but clearly scanning the crowd for someone more important to talk to. "You should talk to the guy who is with the sheriff. He runs the security company and writes the checks."

"I'll do that." Bill offered his hand. "I'm Bill Mumford, this is my wife, Karen, and daughter, Emily."

Eve shook hands all around. "I'm pleased to meet all of you. I'm Detective Eve Ronin. I was in the store that day."

Emily didn't let go of her hand. Instead, she drew Eve close. "I know who you are. I've seen all your videos. I'm a big fan."

The compliment made Eve uncomfortable. Emily talked about the videos like they were episodes of a show, or advertisements, that Eve had produced. But they were neither. Eve had nothing to do with the production or posting of the videos.

Having a fan also bothered Eve, who believed that real cops didn't have fans. Only the fictional ones did. But then she remembered the *Ronin* script sitting in her hotel room and realized that soon she might be real and fictional, which only made her more uncomfortable.

Bill Mumford took out his phone and gestured to Eve and his son. "Could I get a picture of the two heroes together?"

Eve moved beside Grayson and they turned to face Bill. But before he could take the picture, Karen stepped up to Eve, blocking his view. "When I said I wished Grayson hadn't done what he did, I didn't mean to imply I'd be happier if you'd been shot."

"I didn't take it that way," Eve said. "I also wish he'd run out with the customers and employees."

"But you would have been killed."

"I *could* have been," Eve said. "But I'm paid to take those risks. Grayson isn't. If one of us was going to risk their life, it should have been me."

"Move, Karen," Bill said. She did, and he gave Eve and Grayson some direction. "Smile and look this way."

He took a few pictures, then Emily handed her dad her phone.

"Can I get a picture, too?" She didn't wait for an answer—instead she stood beside Eve and took her hand.

Bill took some more pictures, and then Emily whispered to Eve, "I'm going to crop Grayson out."

Eve turned to Grayson. "Could I talk to you alone for a minute?"

"Sure," Grayson said.

Eve smiled at his family. "Please excuse me, I'm going to steal your son for a minute."

She led him into the library, where they'd have some privacy. As soon as the door was closed, and she was sure nobody was around, she said, "I want to apologize for not reaching out to you after the shooting. I got swept up working some cases. How are you feeling?"

"It's been kind of a whirlwind for me, too, no time to stop and think. I've been on all the local news shows, plus a bunch of radio interviews," Grayson said. "I've been reliving what happened, but not dwelling on it, if you know what I mean."

It had become a story that he told, not an experience that he'd lived, and with each telling, he distanced himself from the reality of it even more. Or, as he'd put it, the horror. Perhaps it was a good thing, she thought.

"Are you sleeping?" Eve asked.

"Not much, mostly because of all the interviews. They leave me pretty cranked up afterwards."

"I know the feeling," she said. "I also know what comes later. When the whirlwind dies down, and it will, and it's just you and your thoughts, it can be tough. If you need to talk to someone, you have my card. I meant what I said. Call any time."

"Thanks," Grayson said. "What about you?"

"What do you mean?"

He looked her in the eye. "You saw him die, too."

Eve met his gaze. "I wasn't the one who pulled the trigger."

"But still, you must feel something."

She didn't. She'd been in a different whirlwind, one of constant work. There was no time to think about spattered brains or butchered wombs. Perhaps that was intentional, Eve thought. She was avoiding the gruesome loop.

But he deserved an answer, so Eve gave him one. "I feel grateful to be alive."

Grayson nodded. "So do I."

She realized now that they would always have this private bond, a moment of violence they'd shared that would shape the rest of his life in subtle and, perhaps, profound ways. Maybe hers, too.

Sheriff Lansing came through the door. "I wondered where you two were hiding. We're ready to get started."

Eve smiled at Grayson. "It's showtime."

# CHAPTER SIXTEEN

Eve and Duncan stood on the stage with Grayson Mumford, the Calabasas City Council, Ethan Dryer, Captain Shaw, and the sheriff as the backdrop for Mayor Maureen Stoker, the mother of six children and former president of the local PTA, as she spoke at the podium.

"We expect our law enforcement professionals to put their lives on the line for our safety, to run towards danger, not away from it, to protect us. We deeply appreciate that service and sacrifice, which they do every day. But it's truly extraordinary when a civilian, someone who doesn't wear a badge, does the same thing."

Stoker looked over her shoulder and gave Grayson a smile, then continued with her speech.

"Three days ago, an armed, desperate man ran into a grocery store in the Commons with a detective in hot pursuit. Grayson Mumford was the security guard on duty that day. His job ordinarily consists of removing unruly customers and nabbing shoplifters. But Monday he faced a new challenge—an armed felon. Instead of fleeing or taking cover, he confronted the active shooter, risking his life to take him down. For that act of exceptional courage, on behalf of the City of Calabasas, I'm proud to honor Grayson Mumford with our Meritorious Citizen Award."

Stoker reached into a shelf in the podium, brought out a plaque, and waved to Grayson to step forward. She handed him the plaque to the applause of everyone in the audience. Stoker and Grayson then posed for photos for the city photographer, a few press photographers, and Grayson's very proud father. After everyone got their shot, Stoker quietly told him to stay where he was and then she went back to the microphone.

"Now I'd like to present Los Angeles County sheriff Richard Lansing, who has a few words he'd like to say."

Eve knew it would be a lot more than a few words. Lansing loved a podium and a microphone.

"Thank you, Mayor Stoker. Grayson, your actions in the supermarket not only protected the employees and customers in the store but saved the life of one of our officers. You were in a uniform, wearing a security company patch, and yet you embodied all the qualities I expect from the men and women who wear this badge." Lansing reverently touched his own badge. "That's why I am proud to award you the Medal of Valor, the highest honor we can bestow upon an officer in the Los Angeles County Sheriff's Department."

He reached into the shelf, pulled out a medallion that dangled from a lanyard, and draped the award around Grayson's neck.

"I believe this is the first time it has ever been given to a civilian," Lansing said. "Making this a truly historic moment."

Eve wanted to gag. Lansing was degrading the medal by giving it to a civilian purely as a publicity stunt to distract everybody from the monumental disaster that the grocery store shooting really was. If backup for Eve and Duncan had arrived at the sting house, Grayson wouldn't have had to fire his gun and all three men might still be alive. But the public would never know about that, about Deputy Collier's intentional dereliction of duty and his motive for it. That was a scandal that Lansing wanted to avoid at all costs.

*Look over here at this bright, shiny medal,* Eve thought, *not at the smelly, disgusting corruption over there.*

"You're grimacing," Duncan whispered. "Try smiling."

But nobody was watching her. All eyes were on Lansing and Grayson, posing for photos.

"He shouldn't be getting the Medal of Valor," Eve whispered back.

"Now you know how everybody in the department felt when you got promoted to homicide."

"It's not Grayson I'm mad at."

"It's the sheriff, I know," Duncan whispered. "You're objecting to the cheapening of the award for the sake of the department."

"That's right," Eve said.

"The same goes for your badge," Duncan said.

When the photographers were done, Lansing shook Grayson's hand. "Have you ever thought about a career in law enforcement?"

"It's crossed my mind, sir," Grayson said.

"Well, if that's what you decide to do, I hope you'll consider the Los Angeles County Sheriff's Department. We could use a man like you."

"Would you write me a letter of recommendation?"

The crowd roared with laughter and Lansing clapped Grayson warmly on the back.

"Just wear that medal when you apply. It says it all." Lansing returned to the podium again.

"Oh God," Eve whispered to Duncan. "He's not done."

Lansing said, "Before we go, I am pleased to announce that the spree of home invasion robberies that terrorized Calabasas is over, thanks to the exceptional work by Detectives Eve Ronin and Duncan Pavone, who have conclusively linked the three dead assailants to those crimes." He looked back at Eve and Duncan and gave them a thumbs-up. Eve forced herself to smile. The crime wasn't solved yet, not as far as she was concerned. Lansing turned back to the audience, shifting his gaze to the handful of reporters. "Now I'll be glad to take a few questions."

The first person he pointed to was Scott Peck, the reporter for *The Acorn*. He was Eve's age and eager to get on to the staff of a major newspaper. "Thank you, Sheriff. You're presenting this investigation as a success, and yet within hours of the Calabasas shootings, you reassigned Captain Moffett from Lost Hills station to the Men's Central Jail and replaced him with Captain Shaw from Compton, effective immediately. That seems punitive."

Lansing smiled. "Not at all, Scott. The realigning of personnel was in the works for weeks and, unfortunately, it just happened to fall on the same day as these events unfolded."

That was a lie, Eve thought, and Lansing wasn't fooling anyone. It was a game he and the press played.

Beside Peck was Zena Faust, a heavily tattooed blogger for *Malibu Beat*, and the last person Lansing would ever call on for a question, so she immediately shouted out, "So you'd planned to demote Moffett before this happened? If so, why? Was it because of the Great White scandal?"

*Gotcha*, Eve thought.

Lansing's smile wavered. "It's not a demotion, it's a lateral move that better utilizes the unique talents of both of these fine captains. Shaw is a terrific leader who will build on the strong foundation left by Moffett, who will make operations at the jail even more efficient, while following through on my commitment to the safety and security of individuals in our care." He quickly pointed to Kate Darrow, a TV reporter who looked like a supermodel, a quality she often used to disarm her prey into thinking she wasn't tough and smart. "Yes, Kate?"

"Does that mean deputies won't be putting rival gang members in the same cell anymore and betting money on who survives?"

"That's all for today, thank you, everybody, for coming," Lansing said and turned his back to the audience.

Eve couldn't blame Darrow for baiting Lansing with that last question. He deserved it for shoveling so much bullshit on them.

She tugged Duncan's sleeve. "Let's go before we get dragged into any more PR stunts or a reporter tries to ask us a question."

Duncan and Eve hopped off the stage and walked toward the parking lot, which was between city hall and the Hilton. He checked his watch and smiled. "There's still time to catch the breakfast buffet at the Hilton before it closes."

"No, there isn't. We need to get to Oakdale right away and follow up on the pregnant maid. We've wasted enough time already."

"Fine, but if I pass out from low blood sugar, it's on you."

"Stop whining," Eve said. "You already had a big breakfast. I can see it on your tie."

He checked his tie and saw an egg yolk stain. "Damn."

They took Duncan's Buick, since it was parked at city hall, and he drove them up to Oakdale's guard gate. The same guard Eve had seen the previous morning was on duty again. He was young and looked like he'd slept in his uniform and combed his hair with a swipe of his hand. His name tag read HARVEY MAPES. Duncan badged him.

"I'm Duncan Pavone, and this is my partner, Eve Ronin. We're detectives with the Los Angeles County Sheriff's Department."

Mapes said, "Everybody wants to know why you've had a patrol car parked in front of the McCaig place all night."

"It's a speed trap. Tell everyone to slow down or they'll get a ticket."

Eve took out her phone and found the screengrab of the pregnant woman. "Do you know who this woman is?"

Duncan took the phone from her and held it up to Mapes, who nodded.

"That's Priscilla. She's a cleaning lady."

"Do you know her last name?" Eve asked. Mapes shook his head. "Is she here today?"

"No, she only works here once a week, on Tuesdays, for the Grayles up on Park Positano."

Duncan took out his notebook and pen. "What are their full names?"

"Lester and Daphne Grayle."

Duncan wrote it down. "Are they home?"

"Mr. Grayle left for work a few hours ago. Mrs. Grayle is home."

"Can we have their address and phone number?"

Mapes looked it up on his computer and gave Duncan the information, which he wrote down in his pad.

"Thanks. You can open up the gate and lower the drawbridge over the moat. We'd like to go up and see them now."

Mapes hit the button, and as the gate started to roll open, he said, "Do you want me to call ahead? We're a gated community. People here don't usually open their doors if they don't know who is coming, especially after all the home invasions."

"Sure, give her a call."

Duncan thanked Mapes and they drove up to the Grayle house, which was the same model as the McCaigs', only flipped and with a southwestern-style facade.

They walked up to the front door, careful not to sting themselves on one of the cacti in the rock garden along the path, and rang the bell. The door was answered by Daphne Grayle, an athletic-looking woman in her thirties, wearing a paint-spattered white T-shirt and torn, paint-spattered jeans. Her long brown hair was pinned up in a bun to keep it from getting in the paint.

"Please forgive how I look. I'm repainting the family room. What can I do for you?"

Duncan glanced at Eve, once again handing her the baton, as he often did with women. Eve introduced them.

"We'd like to ask you some questions. May we come in?"

Daphne stepped aside. "Of course."

They walked in. The dining room and kitchen were to their left, but the family room was still in front of them. All the furniture in the family room was pushed into the center of the room and covered with bedsheets. The walls were mostly beige with white trim. But now half of the walls in the living room were mocha. Canisters of paint, a roller pan, roller, and brushes were on one of many tarps laid down to protect the hardwood floors.

"What prompted the redecorating?" Eve asked.

"I'm bored with beige. I thought a new color might liven things up."

Duncan said, "Wouldn't it have made more sense to begin before Priscilla came to clean and not the day after?"

"I didn't have the epiphany until she left," Daphne said. "It drives my husband nuts that I'm always redecorating. But he's not the one cooped up here all day. Is this about Priscilla? Is she in some kind of trouble?"

"Not at all," Eve said. "We'd just like to talk with her. Do you have her number?"

"Sure, it's on my phone." Daphne led them through the dining room and into the kitchen, giving Eve the chance to see what the McCaigs' kitchen layout was like before their remodel, and in reverse. There weren't as many cabinets in this kitchen and the appliances were in different locations.

Daphne picked up her phone off the kitchen island, which was half the size of the McCaigs' new one, and scrolled through her numbers until she found the one she wanted. "Here you go."

She held out the phone to them. Duncan entered the number on his phone, excused himself, and walked away.

Eve and Daphne settled into spots across the island from one another. "What's Priscilla's last name?"

"Alvarez."

She took out her pad and started taking notes. "When did you last see her?"

"She left here on Tuesday, at one thirty, like she always does, so she could catch the two p.m. bus and be home when her kids get out of school," Daphne said. "One of her kids is twelve but I think the other one is five or six, so she doesn't like to leave them alone."

Eve made notes, looking at her pad as she casually asked, "When do your kids get out of school?"

"I don't have kids, not yet anyway. I've repainted the nursery three times, a fresh start each time we've tried in vitro."

The comment startled Eve. Daphne was another woman in Oakdale who was struggling to have a child . . . and she just happened to be repainting her walls shortly after the day her pregnant maid entered the community and didn't leave. Could Daphne be painting over the bloody evidence of a crime?

Eve willed herself to appear indifferent so she wouldn't reveal how significant that revelation was to her. "It must be hard on you."

Daphne went over to the subzero refrigerator and opened it. "It's disappointing, that's for sure. My husband is also getting tired of having sex in a cup and I've got to admit that getting clumsily stabbed in the butt with a syringeful of hormones is not my idea of foreplay, so we may give up and do a private adoption."

"What's a private adoption?"

Daphne took out three bottles of fruit-flavored vitamin water and set them on the island. "It's when a lawyer finds a pregnant woman who doesn't want her child and arranges in advance for you to adopt it."

Eve made some more notes and kept her eyes on the page. "Did you think about approaching Priscilla?"

"Our cleaning lady? Of course not. That would be inappropriate and extremely offensive. Why would I dare to assume she didn't want her baby? The thought never crossed my mind and, frankly, I'm surprised it crossed yours."

Eve looked up as Duncan came back in.

"No answer. Not even voice mail."

"Help yourselves to some vitamin water," Daphne said. "Would you like some melon to go with that?"

"Do you have any cookies?" Duncan asked.

"Will Oreos work?"

"Oreos always work," Duncan said.

Daphne went to the pantry, took out a package of Oreos, peeled it open, and set it on the counter.

"Thank you." Duncan took out six cookies and stacked them in front of him like poker chips. "I firmly believe it was an Oreo, not an apple, that tempted Adam in the Garden of Eden."

Just to be sociable, and to maintain the nonconfrontational atmosphere, Eve plucked a cookie from the package and asked Daphne, "What else do you know about Priscilla?"

"Nothing, I'm ashamed to say. We didn't really talk. She's only here a few hours and doesn't want to fall behind and miss her bus. And there's a language barrier."

Eve took a bite of her cookie. "She doesn't speak English?"

Daphne took a drink from her bottle of water before answering. "Only enough to get by, the broad strokes, but not the nitty-gritty, if that makes sense."

"It does. How long has she worked for you?"

"About two years."

Eve finished her cookie and opened her water bottle. "Does it bother you having a pregnant woman in the house when you're trying so hard to have a child of your own?"

That question caught Duncan's interest. He hadn't been around for the discussion about Daphne's failed attempts to get pregnant. And now that he was down to one cookie in his poker stack, he wasn't distracted. He suddenly saw Daphne in a whole new light. Possible murderer.

"No, not really," Daphne said. "I'm not the jealous type."

"There's something I don't understand," Duncan said, holding the last cookie in his hand. "You know Priscilla's pregnant, right?"

"It's hard to miss."

"And you still make her walk up and down the hill? That'd kill me and I'm not carrying a child, though it may look like it."

Daphne gave Duncan a cold glare and moved the carton of Oreos out of his reach. "I've offered many times to drive her, but she says she likes the walk. Besides, I'm half-asleep and still in my pajamas at seven thirty. It's not a convenient time to get in my car. What is this about? Are you working with INS?"

Eve cocked her head. "Why do you ask that? Is she illegal?"

"I don't know. I just assumed since you're so interested in her, that's what it must be. She's certainly no criminal."

Duncan said, "How would you know if you two never really talked?"

"Because she's so sweet and caring and trustworthy," Daphne said. "I've left plenty of jewelry and cash lying around and she's never touched it, except to move out of the way to dust."

"She'd have to be more dumb than dishonest to fall for that," Duncan said.

Eve asked, "Do you know if she has any friends in the community?"

"She usually walks down to the bus stop with the lady who works at the Greenbergs' house."

"Where do they live?"

"23780 Park Venice. Sheryl Greenberg and I do Pilates together. It was her maid who recommended Priscilla to me."

Duncan finished his cookie and asked, "Do you know Anna McCaig?"

Daphne still glared at him. "No, who is she?"

"One of your neighbors, over on Park Ronda."

"Where the patrol car is parked?" she asked.

"Yeah," he said.

"Never met her. There's a couple of hundred houses here and people don't talk much," Daphne said. "What happened? People are saying it's a murder."

"Really?" Duncan said. "I thought you and your neighbors didn't talk much."

"We do when there's a murder."

Eve closed her notebook and smiled at Daphne. "Thank you so much for your help and the snack. We appreciate it."

She and Duncan walked out of the kitchen, Daphne behind them. "You never mentioned why you want to talk with Priscilla."

Duncan looked back at her as they reached the front door. "I'm looking for someone to clean my house."

Eve and Duncan were silent until they got into his car, then he turned to her and said, "Remember what I said about keeping an open mind?"

"Yeah."

"Don't you find it odd that she's struggling to have a kid and she's picked today to repaint, two days after her pregnant maid never left Oakdale and Anna McCaig found a baby in her dumpster?"

"You think Anna was telling the truth and that Daphne Grayle killed Priscilla for her baby, it went bad, so she tossed the baby in Anna McCaig's dumpster?"

"I think after meeting Daphne Grayle," he said, "it's a much stronger possibility."

"It crossed my mind, too, but there's too much that doesn't track. Why not dispose of the baby with the mother's body?"

"To shift suspicion to Anna McCaig, who Daphne Grayle knew was even more desperate than her to have a baby."

It seemed far-fetched to Eve. How could Daphne know that Anna wouldn't immediately call the police when she found the baby in her dumpster rather than try to pretend it was her own? Eve didn't believe the killer was Daphne and they were running out of time to hold Anna on the 5150. "I still think Anna McCaig did it."

"We searched her place and it was clean. I want to search Grayle's property," Duncan said. "But to convince a judge to give us a warrant, we're going to need more evidence."

"Like confirming that Priscilla Alvarez is actually missing and not safe at home or cleaning someone else's house today," Eve said. "We should check if there are any new reports of missing pregnant women."

"I checked this morning. There weren't any. But we can check again."

"We could also reach out to the cellular provider for Priscilla's phone and ask them to track her movements."

"We don't have enough grounds for that warrant, either. But there might be a faster way to find out where she lives."

# CHAPTER SEVENTEEN

Duncan drove around the corner and two streets over to 23780 Park Venice, the home where Daphne Grayle told them that Priscilla's friend worked for the Greenberg family.

They parked in front of the two-story house, went to the door, and knocked, provoking what sounded like a pack of wild dogs to start barking and shrieking. Eve heard the scratching of dog claws on a tiled floor, a woman saying "shut the fuck up," and a door slamming, slightly muffling the barks.

The front door opened and they were greeted by a woman who was as young and fit as Daphne Grayle, but her hair was completely gray.

"Who are you? I didn't get a call from the gate," the woman said.

Duncan flashed his badge. "Mrs. Greenberg? I'm Duncan Pavone with the sheriff's department. Could we have a word with your cleaning lady?"

"Fernanda? What has she done?"

"Nothing, ma'am. We're trying to reach one of her friends."

Greenberg looked over her shoulder and yelled, "Fernanda, could you please come here? Be careful not to let the dogs out of the kitchen." She looked back at Duncan and Eve. "If the dogs get out, don't run or they will chase you."

Fernanda opened the kitchen door a crack and squeezed herself out, the dogs trying to nose their way through, too. But she managed to get out without the dogs escaping and nervously approached the door, obviously picking up their cop vibe.

*She's illegal,* Eve thought. Fernanda was round faced and round bodied, wearing a T-shirt and floral leggings, her hands in rubber gloves. Eve recognized her immediately as one of the women she saw in the gate video.

Duncan smiled warmly and addressed her in Spanish and she answered. The only word Eve understood was "Priscilla." They exchanged a few more words, then Duncan thanked her and turned to go. Eve followed him to the car.

"I didn't know that you speak Spanish," Eve said.

"There's a lot you don't know about me. For instance, did you know I'm a magnificent ballroom dancer?"

"You are?"

"No, but I could be, because I'm a mystery to you. Fernanda doesn't know where Priscilla lives, but she knows it's in a motel and what bus stop she gets off at each day." Duncan gave Eve the address on the valley stretch of Sepulveda Boulevard that ran parallel to the 405 freeway north of Burbank Boulevard.

Eve knew the area. A lot of undocumented immigrants lived in the many cheap motels and low-end apartments that lined that end of Sepulveda. It was also a hot spot for drugs and prostitution.

"If Priscilla and her family are here illegally," Eve said, "that would explain why nobody reported her missing. We better call the LAPD and let them know we'll be in their backyard again."

"Not this time," Duncan said. "If they send a black-and-white and some uniforms to the motels, people will scram or clam up."

"You don't think the same thing will happen when we start flashing our badges?"

"I'll win them over with my charm."

On their way out of Oakdale, they had to pass Anna McCaig's place, where Deputy Clayton was parked out front. Eve told Duncan to pull up alongside the patrol car and roll down his window so she could speak across him to the deputy.

"How is it going, Eddie?"

"Dandy." Clayton held up a Jack Reacher paperback. "I'm getting paid to catch up on my reading."

"Could I ask you to do us a favor?"

"As long as it's police work and not picking up your dry cleaning."

"Has anybody ever asked you to do that?"

"I choose to remain silent on that," he said. "I don't need more enemies."

"I'd like you to run the plates of every vehicle that left Oakdale between Tuesday at one thirty p.m. and Wednesday at seven a.m. and let me know who owns them. I'd do it myself, but we're going to be tied up in the field for a few hours and we're racing the clock on this case."

"What are you looking for?"

"A pregnant maid who walked into this community on Tuesday morning and never walked out."

"I'm on it," he said. "You have the plates?"

Eve asked for his email address, then forwarded him the Oakdale gate log. "I owe you one."

"You owe me a lot more than one."

"I'll pick up your dry cleaning," she said.

He laughed and they drove off.

Duncan gave her a look. "Do you really think Priscilla got a ride out or that her body was in somebody's trunk?"

"You're the one who said to keep an open mind."

"I'm glad to see you're taking my hard-earned wisdom to heart."

"Besides, if Anna McCaig got a dead body out of her house, she didn't do it in her car. It would have to be in one of the vehicles on the list."

"I'm also glad to see you don't give up easily."

"I don't give up at all," she said.

They hit one dreary motel after another for two hours. The places were low-slung cinder-block motor courts with rusty window air conditioners that whined in mechanical agony as they desperately sucked in air and wheezed it out again. The instant Duncan and Eve arrived at each place, the tenants would rush away or dash inside their rooms. Drapes would close and cars would peel out. None of the resident managers recognized the photo of Priscilla, or at least they claimed they didn't. But on the eighth or ninth motel, the half-drunk desk clerk's eyes widened with recognition and he told them where they could find her distraught husband, Alejandro Alvarez, in his room.

"He hasn't left in days," the manager said. "In case she comes back."

Duncan and Eve walked back outside to the last unit in the building, where a dazed, unshaven man sat in a chair outside his door, wrapped in a blanket. Eve wondered how long he'd been sitting there, waiting. He looked up with bloodshot eyes as they approached. Eve's heart ached for him.

"Alejandro Alvarez?" Duncan asked.

He nodded. "Who is asking?"

"We're detectives with the Los Angeles sheriff's department. We're looking for Priscilla."

Alejandro sat up a little straighter in his chair and drew the blanket tighter around himself. "Why are you looking for her?"

Eve said, "We think she might be able to help us with a case we're working on in Calabasas. Do you know where she is?"

Alejandro shook his head and began to softly cry. Duncan found another chair, pulled it over, and sat down facing him. Eve had to look away, afraid his tears would provoke her own.

"How long has she been missing?"

"She went to work on Tuesday and didn't come back. I tried calling her but got no answer." Alejandro looked pleadingly at Duncan, then up at Eve. "I don't know what to do. My children, they are crying for their mother. So am I."

"Did you try calling the Grayles? The people she works for?"

"I don't have their number. It's on Priscilla's phone. I don't even know where the house is in Calabasas. Do you know what happened to her? Is she all right?"

"That's what we are trying to find out," Duncan said. "But first, we'll need to file a formal missing person report."

Alejandro hesitated and Eve had a good idea why.

"We don't care whether you are here legally or not," she said. "All we care about is finding your wife. Could you get us a better photo of her?"

Alejandro nodded, got up from the chair, and went inside the motel room. Duncan got up, too, and stepped into the motor court with Eve, who said, "This is heartbreaking."

"You will get calluses on your heart working homicide," he said. "But the moment you begin to feel them, Eve, you've got to get the hell out."

"How do you feel them?"

"It's what you don't feel." He tipped his head toward the empty chair. "It's when you stop feeling their pain."

She didn't ask him if that's why he was retiring because she was afraid of the answer. Instead, she said, "We need to get her toothbrush, or her hairbrush, so we can compare her DNA to the baby's."

Duncan waved that off. "That's almost irrelevant at this point. Our priority right now is getting CSU to the Grayles'. Daphne can paint the whole damn house and it won't hide any blood on the walls."

"Do you think we have enough for a warrant?"

"Now that we know Priscilla is truly missing, and that the Grayles' house was the last place she was before her baby ended up in Anna McCaig's dumpster, and that Daphne Grayle, who is aching for a kid, suddenly had the urge to repaint, yes, I'd say we do."

"You make a compelling but entirely circumstantial case," Eve said.

"That's why I'm going to call the ADA and ask her to get the warrant," Duncan said. "This is going to take some fancy legal footwork to dazzle a judge."

While Duncan made the call, Eve got some basic information about Priscilla from Alejandro, along with her hairbrush and a photo of her in a park, sitting on a blanket. The picture was taken before she was pregnant, or at least before she was showing. Priscilla was unsmiling, eyeing the camera warily, her black hair tied in a severe bun. She was in her thirties, round faced and a little chubby, wearing a Lakers hoodie and jeans. She seemed tired to Eve, but more than just physically. It was her whole being, body and soul.

Eve promised Alejandro that they'd get in touch with him as soon as they had any information. But Eve sensed that he knew they were holding something back and that it wasn't good.

Before heading to Lost Hills, Duncan insisted that they have lunch at Dr. Hogly Wogly's Tyler Texas BBQ, which was only a few blocks away, and since he was driving, Eve had no choice in the matter.

The ribs came drenched in watery sauce. Duncan was tempted to take off his jacket, tie, and shirt to protect them from stains but instead covered himself in napkins from his chin to his knees. Eve ordered a pulled pork sandwich, to cut the risk of staining her clothes, and a large Coke, hoping the sugar and caffeine would keep her alert.

Rebecca Burnside, their go-to ADA, called Duncan while they were eating to let him know they got their warrant to search the Grayles' house for evidence of murder and for Priscilla Alvarez's body. She also strongly advised Duncan to buy a lottery ticket today, because he was a very lucky man. The grounds for the search warrant were very thin.

But Duncan already knew he was lucky. He'd finished lunch without getting a single spot on his clothes.

The first thing Duncan and Eve did when they got back to Lost Hills station was to bring Captain Shaw up to date on the case. When they were done, he stared at them from across his desk. He didn't look pleased.

"This will make two homes you've searched in two days."

Since Duncan was the one leading the charge on the Grayles' house, Eve let him answer the captain.

"The investigation has evolved," Duncan said.

"That's not the way it looks to me. You seem to be scrambling."

"We're trying to keep up with fast-moving events," Duncan said. "This began as a stillbirth but then the autopsy revealed that we're actually dealing with a fetal abduction. That changed everything. We know the baby doesn't belong to Anna McCaig. We also know that Priscilla Alvarez, a pregnant woman who works in Oakdale, came through the gate the same day and didn't leave, at least not alive."

"We're confident that DNA taken from hairs on Priscilla's brush will confirm that the baby was hers," Eve added, trying to bolster Duncan's argument. "But we can't wait for that or vital evidence at the crime scene could be lost in the meantime."

"Which crime scene?" Shaw asked.

*Oh crap,* Eve thought. She'd reminded him that they were still holding the scene at McCaig's place.

Duncan spoke up before she could create more problems. "McCaig says she found the baby in her dumpster and the last person to see Priscilla alive was Daphne Grayle, who is desperately trying to have a kid. If what McCaig says is true, then the murder happened at the Grayles'."

Shaw looked at Eve. He wasn't so easily distracted. "What about the McCaig house? Do you still want to hold the scene?"

"At least until we have something definitive on Priscilla Alvarez."

"Uh-huh." Shaw leaned back in his chair, steepled his hands on his chest, and regarded the two detectives. "I'm sensing a difference of opinion between you two. You think it's McCaig and he thinks it's Grayle."

Duncan said, "We're keeping an open mind and exploring all avenues of investigation."

"While tying up a lot of department resources," Shaw said.

"Someone ripped a baby from a mother's womb," Eve said. "Getting the monster who did that is worth all of our resources."

She'd surprised herself by saying that, more by the vehemence behind it than the words themselves. Shaw and Duncan both looked at her. After a moment, Shaw leaned forward and put his hands on his desk.

"You'd better find what you are looking for at the Grayles' house," Shaw said. "Because if you're wrong, the weather forecast for tomorrow is a category five shitstorm."

# CHAPTER EIGHTEEN

Duncan and Eve rode in a plain-wrap Explorer that led a caravan of two CSU vehicles and two patrol cars past the Oakdale guardhouse in the resident's lane. Ruthie sensed their urgency and immediately opened the gate without waiting for anybody to wave at her.

As they headed up to Daphne Grayle's house, Duncan said, "I'm going to go at her hard, see if she cracks."

"What do you want me to do?" Eve asked.

"Pick up the pieces."

"I don't think Grayle did it."

"We'll know soon," he said. "One way or the other."

They parked out front and got out of the car. Daphne Grayle already had her front door open and marched out to meet them.

"What the hell is going on?"

Duncan handed her the warrant. "This is a search warrant for your home and vehicles."

Daphne snatched the paper from him but didn't look at it. "What are you searching for?"

"Priscilla Alvarez."

"I haven't seen her since she left here on Tuesday."

"Nobody has," Duncan said. "Please step aside."

She took a step back, careful to avoid the cacti, and so did Duncan and Eve, making room for Nan and four of her technicians to pass. The CSU team were all wearing their white Tyvek suits, gloves, and booties and carrying toolboxes containing their forensic equipment. The two uniformed deputies remained on the street, securing the scene and keeping back the four curious neighbors drawn outdoors by the arrival of the vehicles.

Daphne stared at the CSU team as they went into her house. "I don't understand. Why are you searching for her here? And what do you need them for? Those are CSI people. They investigate murders."

Duncan glanced at Eve, who answered, "An hour after you say that Priscilla left here, Anna McCaig found a dead baby in her dumpster."

Daphne seemed bewildered. "You think Priscilla gave birth to the baby here . . . and threw it away?"

Eve shook her head. "The medical examiner determined that someone tried to perform an amateur C-section on Priscilla, an operation she couldn't have survived."

Daphne gasped and covered her mouth in horror. "Oh my God. No."

Duncan stepped forward, invading her personal space. "You told us how much you wanted a child. The question is, just how desperate are you?"

The question transformed Daphne. Her horror and confusion evaporated, overtaken by rage. Eve thought it was like watching a person morph into a werewolf.

"Let me get this straight," Daphne said, unconsciously taking a defensive stance with her body, planting her feet on the ground and tensing her fingers. She was a fighter at heart. "You think that I gutted my maid, tossed her unborn baby into somebody's garbage, and what else? You think her body is in my closet or buried under my roses?"

"Is that a question or a confession?" Duncan said. "Because if it's a confession, we need to read you your rights first."

Daphne took a step forward so she and Duncan were almost nose to nose, defying his attempt at intimidation. He stood firm.

"You're a fucking monster," she said. "How could you think that about me?"

"You're desperate for a baby and you chose the day Priscilla disappeared to paint your living room," he said. "Was it the beige you couldn't stand to look at anymore or the blood spatter?"

"You're sick." Daphne reached into her back pocket for her iPhone. "I'm calling my husband. He's a senior partner at the law firm of Lappin, Guillerman, and Boze. He'll have your badge for this."

"You're welcome to it. I'm retiring in three months and I have all the paperweights I need."

Daphne shouldered past them and out to the street to make her call. Eve studied Duncan. This was not the man she knew.

"I can't tell if this asshole is a role you play," Eve said, "or if it's actually a side of your personality."

He met her gaze. "Does it matter?"

"Only if you enjoy it."

Duncan didn't answer. He turned his back to her and went inside the house, leaving Eve to decide for herself.

Two hours later, the lack of sleep was beginning to get to Eve. She wasn't feeling particularly tired, nor was she fighting to stay awake. It felt more like she was trapped between dimensions, not entirely occupying the space she was in or moving at the same speed as the world around her.

Perhaps, she thought, the infrared camera that Nan Baker was using to photograph Daphne Grayle's recently painted family room walls could also capture the dissonance Eve was feeling. Would she show up in the image as crisp, while the world around her was a blur?

"Do you see anything behind the paint?" Eve asked.

Nan studied the image on her camera. "Just more paint."

"How many layers can that camera see through?"

"A lot," Nan said. "There's no blood here or anywhere else. This house is almost as clean as the McCaig place."

"Almost?"

"I'm not including Mrs. McCaig's couch," Nan said. "The Grayles have old dog pee they haven't been able to clean out of the hallway carpet. Could have been there for years. Probably has been, since there's no dog around. But dog pee persists. That's a fact."

"Good to know."

Eve walked through the family room to the french doors that opened out to the backyard. The Grayles had a small lawn and a lap pool, the yard bordered with roses, bushes, and small trees. Duncan stood under the retractable awning watching CSU technicians poking at the dirt with poles. She stepped outside and joined him.

"How's it going?" she asked, though she already knew the answer. If anything had been found, word would have spread immediately.

"The dirt up here is as hard as concrete. Nothing is buried here, not even acorns."

"The house is clean," Eve said, though he had to know that, too.

"We're both screwed," he said. "You more than me."

"How do you figure that?"

"My career as a sheriff's detective is already over," he said. "But you still cling to the ridiculous hope that you can have one."

"We've got the TV show to fall back on."

"In other words, if you can't make it as a cop in the real world, try make-believe instead."

"At least on TV, we can decide how the case ends," she said.

"Perhaps we need to explore other avenues of investigation, one that isn't Daphne Grayle Boulevard or Anna McCaig Street."

Eve could only think of one remaining option. "I asked Deputy Clayton to run the license plates of all the cars that left Oakdale between the time Grayle says Priscilla left here and when McCaig called 911."

"Get the list," Duncan said. "That's where we should look next before—"

"Anna's 5150 runs out," Eve interrupted.

"I was thinking before the captain gives Crockett and Tubbs our case, sidelines me until retirement, and the sheriff reassigns you to patrol Metrolink trains."

With that possible future hanging over her head, Eve left the Grayles' house, carefully avoiding Daphne, her angry husband, and their lawyer, and walked around the corner and down the street to Anna McCaig's place.

She saw Deputy Clayton leaning against his patrol car, arms crossed under his chest, his eyes hidden behind his wraparound sunglasses.

He tilted his head toward her. "How's it going over at the other house?"

"Same as this one," she said. "Did you get a chance to run those plates?"

He opened the driver's side door of his car, leaned inside, and came out with several sheets of paper.

"Here you go." Eddie handed her the sheets.

She thanked him and glanced at the paper. His handwriting was neat and precise, almost as if it had been typewritten.

He said, "Catholic school."

"Excuse me?"

"You were puzzling over my handwriting. Catholic school is the answer. Good penmanship is a reflection of your character. That's what the teachers used to say, right before they smacked your knuckles with a wooden ruler."

"You're right," she said. "Maybe you should be a detective."

"I like being in the field," he said. "Where the action is."

"Seeing lots of action today?"

"I also like the fresh air."

Eve started to go, then glanced back at the house, the dumpster, and the porta-potty. This was where the murder happened, she was convinced of that. Even if Anna managed to remove the body from Oakdale, with the help of one of the people on Eddie's list, the blood was still spilled here.

*So why isn't there any evidence to prove it?*

She stuck the papers in her inside jacket pocket and went to the front door. The glass was still broken where she'd kicked in a pane. She reached inside, unlocked the door, and went inside.

The house was cold and empty. The McCaigs were going to get a huge electric bill, Eve thought, but they were probably used to that. Shards of broken glass crunched under her feet as she walked inside. Nobody had been here to clean up the mess she'd left. And that would probably irritate Anna, too, since the house was impeccably clean.

*Good. Screw her.*

Eve wandered over to the dining room table and picked up the grocery store receipt. She scanned the list of all that junk food, then she looked at the purchases stacked against the wall, seeing the potato chips, cookies, pastries, and candy from a different perspective this time.

It was evidence of Anna's fraudulent pregnancy.

Eve set the receipt down and noticed again the smooth finish on the table. Not a speck of dust.

She looked up and into the kitchen, the remodeling nearly finished, and she got a chill. But it wasn't from the cold air in the room. Fatigue, probably. She knew that thirty-some hours without sleep had to be taking a toll on her mind and body.

Eve went into the kitchen and admired the stone countertops. The quartzite shined, even underneath the layer of dust.

There was dust on everything, just like in her place. She looked at the cabinets, the big island, and finally at the drywall. The McCaigs' contractor was a professional and knew what he was doing. Unlike her place, here she only saw a couple of screws in the drywall that would need to be removed or patched.

*You get what you pay for.*

Eve turned back and looked out the doorway into the dining room, then walked to the end of the kitchen and looked out that door into the family room. And she shivered again, but this time she knew why.

Maybe going without sleep once in a while wasn't so bad, she thought. Maybe it purged the mind the way fasting can purge the body of toxins. Because now she saw it all, every move that Anna McCaig had made. That was the chill, her unconscious mind seeing it all before she knew it. She took out her phone and called Duncan as she headed for the front door.

"Get the crime scene unit down to the McCaig house right away."

"Why?" Duncan asked.

"I found Priscilla's body." She disconnected the call and walked outside, where Eddie still leaned against the patrol car. "Pop the trunk for me, will you?"

He opened the driver's side door again, leaned inside, and pulled the trunk-release latch. The trunk snapped open. Inside there was a first-aid kit, Kevlar vests, road flares, a small battering ram, and a crowbar, among other things. Eve took the crowbar and closed the trunk just as one of the CSU vehicles and Duncan's car came speeding down the hill. She waited for them at the front door, crowbar at her side.

Nan came first, carrying her kit. "Detective Pavone says you found the body."

"That's true," Eve said.

"I don't see how that's possible. We thoroughly searched the house."

"Yes, we did." Eve waited for Duncan to join them, then led them inside. "Have you ever remodeled your kitchen?"

"No, I haven't," Nan said.

"I'm doing mine now. It takes four times as long as they say it will and the demolition and construction creates a lot of dust. So, to prevent the dust from getting all over the house, they put big sheets of plastic up over the doorways of the room they are working on." Eve gestured to the open doorways to the kitchen in the dining room and family room. "But not here."

Eve ran her finger along the coffee table, a bookshelf, and finally the dining room table.

"And yet there's no dust." She held up her clean finger. "I have the plastic up and I still have dust everywhere."

The rest of Nan's team came inside and stood, waiting for instructions.

"I agree. Anna McCaig keeps a clean house," Duncan said. "What's your point?"

"She also keeps it very cold," Eve said. "Like a meat locker."

Duncan saw what Eve was implying. "My house is cold, too, but that doesn't mean I'm storing any corpses. It means my wife has hit menopause and now I've got to sleep in a parka. Everybody has a different metabolism."

Eve picked up the grocery store receipt off the dining room table. "She also bought four boxes of baking soda. What does she need that for? She has no appliances for baking. What else is baking soda good for? Absorbing nasty odors."

Nan sighed impatiently, looked at her team waiting, then turned to Eve. "It's been a long day for us. You said you found a body. Did you or didn't you?"

"I got a little ahead of myself," Eve said and Nan turned to go. "Wait, just one more minute, and I'll show you."

"You have thirty seconds," Nan said. "Or I'm going home."

Eve led them into the kitchen.

"There's a lot of sloppily installed drywall in my kitchen, because I hired a crime scene cleaner to do the job, but in this one, there is only one piece that's poorly done. Right here." She pointed to a screw buried deep in the drywall. "It's screwed in too tight, tearing the paper. That's because Anna removed this piece of drywall and screwed it back in . . ."

Eve jammed the sharp edge of the crowbar into the seam between the two pieces of drywall. She jerked the crowbar, tearing away a big chunk of drywall, revealing an arm wrapped in dusty plastic.

". . . after she stuffed Priscilla's body in here, wrapped in the plastic from the doorways."

Eve stood, crowbar at her side, looking at everyone and waiting for their reaction. Duncan was wide-eyed, but Nan glared at her.

"What?" Nan said. "Are you expecting applause? This isn't an episode of *Columbo*. In the future, don't waste my time indulging yourself in theatrics. Just show me the damn body. Now get out of my way and let me do my job."

Eve set the crowbar on the island and walked out into the dining room, Duncan following behind her. The rest of the CSU team moved past them into the kitchen to get to work.

"She didn't have to be rude," Eve said to Duncan. "I was sharing my thought process."

"Nan doesn't care about that," Duncan said.

"Do you?"

"Yes, but you should have told her where the body was and then you and I could have talked about how you found it, and why we missed it the first time we searched the house."

"Anna planned this all ahead of time. We didn't find blood because she spread the plastic from the doorways onto the floor before she killed Priscilla and cut the baby out of her."

"Ah-ha."

"Then she broke a few of Priscilla's bones with a mallet or something so she'd be malleable, wrapped her and the knife and a couple of opened boxes of baking soda in the plastic, and duct-taped everything closed. Then she stuffed her into the wall, screwed the drywall back in, cranked up the AC, and hoped for the best. It's no wonder she had to take sleeping pills that night."

Duncan sighed, and it seemed to Eve that his whole body sagged, weighed down by every one of his fifty-plus years and the hundreds of cases he'd worked in his career.

"I should have retired months ago," he said.

"We all missed this the first time through," Eve said. "It has nothing to do with you being on the job too long. I just got lucky."

"What I meant was, if I'd left this job earlier, I never would have caught this case, or our first one together, and I wouldn't be haunted by these gruesome memories for the rest of my life."

"I know what will make you feel better."

He gestured to the food stacked against the wall. "That box of Ding Dongs?"

"Let's go arrest Anna."

"She can wait. She's not going anywhere for twelve more hours," Duncan said. "I just need a few minutes."

He grabbed the box of Ding Dongs and took a package out.

"To eat the Ding Dong?" Eve asked.

"No." Duncan unwrapped the pastry and took a bite. "I have to apologize to Daphne Grayle."

He headed for the door. Eve started to go with him, but he held up his hand in a halting gesture. "This is on me. You stay here and observe the evidence collection."

As horrible as that was going to be, Eve couldn't help feeling that she was the one getting off easy.

# CHAPTER NINETEEN

The Northridge Hospital Medical Center was located at the corner of Roscoe and Reseda Boulevards, which Eve considered one of the dreariest, bleakest, and ugliest intersections in the San Fernando Valley, a washed-out concrete and asphalt wasteland of gas stations, auto mechanics, convenience stores, and payday loan rackets, crisscrossed above by power and telephone lines. So she thought the view from the window of Anna McCaig's room in the psych ward didn't exactly lend itself to peace of mind, tranquility, and reducing despair. But it was a view of paradise compared to what Anna would be seeing from her prison cell for the rest of her life.

Anna sat on the edge of her bed wearing hospital-issued clothes that resembled surgical scrubs and the kind of disposable slippers that hotels and spas offered to their guests. She glared at Eve and Duncan, who'd pulled over two guest chairs.

"I'm going to read you your rights," Eve said.

"You already did that."

"I'm doing it again." She repeated Anna's rights and also asked her to acknowledge that their conversation was being recorded on Eve's phone.

"That's all fine, but I don't understand the point," Anna said. "I've already admitted that I found the baby in my dumpster. Do I really need to say it all again? I know I shouldn't have pretended it was mine, and that I dragged you and the paramedics to my house for nothing, but surely locking me up in a loony bin for two days is punishment enough."

"Not nearly," Duncan said. "Neither is life in prison. But, unfortunately, the law doesn't allow us to burn you at the stake or stone you to death for your crimes."

"What are you talking about?" Anna said. "The baby was already dead. I tried to save him. What I did wasn't a crime. It was an act of kindness."

"Anna, look at me," Eve said and Anna met her gaze. "We found Priscilla Alvarez's body in your kitchen wall. She was wrapped in plastic with a hacksaw, your bloody clothes, and four open boxes of baking soda."

Duncan said, "You call that an act of kindness?"

Anna looked down at her hands, and picked at some dry skin on her thumb for a moment, before answering in a calm, matter-of-fact tone.

"Yes," she said. "The boy would have had a much better life with me. I'm sure she would have appreciated that."

Her reply disgusted Duncan, who gave Eve a look that conveyed he couldn't stand another minute with Anna. He got up from his seat and walked to the window, turning his back to both of them.

Anna looked over her shoulder at him. "You know it's true."

Eve was disgusted, too, but Anna's reply was a confession of sorts, indicating that she'd accepted it was all over for her and that she might be willing to tell all, if properly coaxed. Eve decided to be nonjudgmental, to adopt the same tone as Anna.

"When did you decide to take Priscilla's baby?"

"The day Jeff left for Berlin. He promised that when he came back, there wouldn't be any more trips, that he'd stay with me until the baby was born. That terrified me. It meant I had to have a baby before he gets back next week."

"Why not just fake another miscarriage?"

"It would convince Jeff that I can't have children," she said. "He'd dump me and find someone more fertile. That's why he left his first wife. He's probably already got another woman lined up. He wants a child and is tired of waiting."

"Why did you pick Priscilla?"

"I saw her walking past my house every week. She kept getting bigger and bigger. It was like she was mocking me. It was so unfair. All the people who work here are poor, uneducated, and illegal. The only thing they're good at is cleaning toilets and getting pregnant. Nobody would miss her," Anna said. "So I told our contractor to take the week off, that my doctor said I needed quiet and rest before delivering my baby. Once he was gone, I opened up part of the kitchen wall, laid the plastic on the floor, and waited for her to walk down the hill to catch her bus."

"What made you think you could perform a C-section?"

"I watched some videos on YouTube. It didn't seem too hard, and it wasn't, really. The difficult part was what to do with the body. There were no YouTube videos for that." Anna grinned, which sickened Eve. "It took some thinking, but I figured it out."

Eve noticed that Anna never used Priscilla's name. That would have humanized her victim too much. But Eve kept repeating her name anyway, even at the risk of irritating or shutting down Anna's confession.

"How did you get Priscilla into your house?"

"I went outside and stopped her as she was walking by. I asked her if she could maybe squeeze in another client after she had her baby. Of course she said she could, because those people are always desperate for money, so I invited her in to take a quick look at the house and give me a price."

"She wasn't worried about missing her bus?"

"She was, but I promised her I'd drive her home if that happened," Anna said. "I led her into the kitchen, and once she was standing on the plastic, I pulled a bag over her head and strangled her."

The casual way Anna said it, as if it were something people did every day, was frightening. But Eve kept her emotions in check, forcing herself to respond with the same flat, conversational tone as Anna's.

"Did it occur to you that strangling her would also suffocate the baby?"

Anna gave her a bewildered look. "Is that what happened? Well, now that I think about it, I guess that makes some sense, though I tried to work very fast."

"Was the baby already dead when you called 911?"

"I think so. It was such a disappointment. But I didn't have time to dwell on it. I had a plan to follow, and I stuck to it. I got undressed, smeared the maid's blood on my thighs, because it wouldn't look right if I wasn't bleeding, then I put her body in the plastic with everything, taped her up, and stuck her in the wall. Then I called 911. That's when I could let go and feel my pain."

Her eyes actually started to well up with tears, as if she were the one who'd endured the suffering, not Priscilla and her baby. Eve found herself at a loss for words.

Duncan turned away from the window and looked at Anna. "What were you going to do if you got away with it? Just leave her in your wall?"

Anna wiped away her tears. "Of course not. What if we remodeled again or if we sold the house someday? It was too risky. So before Jeff got home, I was going to take the body out to the desert, somewhere off the highway on the way to Victorville, and bury it. Even if the body was found someday, nobody would know who she was. She was here illegally. She wasn't anybody."

"Tell that to her husband and children," Eve said.

"What about me?" Anna said. "That's the sad part. I would have been an amazing mother."

◆ ◆ ◆

They arrested Anna for murder, handcuffed her, put her in the back seat of the Explorer, and drove back to Calabasas. There were a dozen satellite TV news vans parked outside the Lost Hills station when they arrived, with cameramen setting up lights and placing microphones at a podium in front of the main entrance. A press conference was coming. Eve hoped that Captain Shaw hadn't leaked the news about Anna McCaig's arrest. This was not a case she wanted to talk about on television or see sensationalized, though she knew it would be.

But none of the press paid any attention to them driving in, or going through the gate, and Eve took that as a good sign. The media was here for something else, but she had no idea what it might be.

They brought Anna inside for booking and she finally spoke again, asking for a public defender. They asked if she'd like them to contact her husband, who was still in Berlin, for her and she was adamant that she didn't want them meddling in her marriage. Since Eve and Duncan had no reason of their own to talk with him, they abided by her request. So Duncan went off to arrange for Anna's public defender while Eve finished the processing and put her in a cell to await her transfer to the jail downtown for her arraignment.

When Eve walked into the squad room, she saw Garvey standing at his cubicle, all dressed up in a nice suit, checking himself out in a mirror that Biddle held up in front of him. Duncan was at his desk, watching with amusement as Garvey primped.

"Looks like someone is getting ready for his close-up," Duncan said.

"Set your DVRs, it doesn't matter which station, because we're gonna be on all of them." Garvey licked his finger and smoothed his eyebrows.

"What happened?" Eve asked.

Biddle said, "We found the Ferrari that hit the surfer on PCH. It belongs to Justin Marriott."

"Who is that?" Duncan asked.

"You don't know?" Garvey said. "He's a singer. The kid made his first $10 million before he was eighteen with a song about jerking off constantly because he can't screw the girl of his dreams."

"How did I miss that?" Duncan said. "Sounds like my kind of song."

"I'd never heard of him, either," Biddle said. "We arrested him for vehicular manslaughter and felony hit-and-run. Now he's sitting in a cell, going through extreme Twitter withdrawal. We may have to call paramedics."

"Every newscast and talk show in America wants this," Garvey said. "My Twitter is going to explode."

"You have a Twitter?" Duncan said.

"I also have electricity and running water," Garvey said. "You really are a dinosaur. If you aren't on social media, you might as well be dead."

Captain Shaw opened the squad room door a crack and stuck his head in. "Pavone. Ronin. Can I have a word with you in my office?"

Duncan got up and the two of them stepped out into the hall, where Shaw was waiting. He led them down the hall.

"What Biddle and Garvey did was solid, old-fashioned police work," Shaw said. "No flash, no high tech, just diligence and shoe leather."

"A dying art," Duncan said.

Shaw beckoned them into his office and closed the door behind them. "I wish I could say the same about your investigation of the fetal abduction."

His comment confused Eve. "The crime is extraordinarily rare and the case wasn't nearly as straightforward as a hit-and-run."

The captain walked around his desk and took a seat behind it. "It would have been if you'd thoroughly searched Anna McCaig's house the first time."

Duncan stepped up to Shaw's desk. "I could have searched it a thousand times and wouldn't have made the deduction that Eve did today."

"Then perhaps it's a good thing you're retiring."

Eve moved up to Duncan's side. "That's a cheap shot."

"*Cheap* is not a word that applies to this investigation," Shaw said. "We kept a man parked outside McCaig's house for twenty-four hours and executed a totally unnecessary search of another home. That's a huge amount of wasted man-hours, resources, and money. We do operate on a budget, you know. Next time you do a search, I expect you to be more thorough and detail oriented."

"That's a load of horseshit," Duncan said.

"What did you say?"

"What matters is that we caught the killer and she made a full confession, an outcome that wouldn't have happened if it wasn't for Eve seeing things that a veteran homicide detective and an entire crew of forensic investigators with tens of thousands of hours of combined experience completely missed. So how about congratulating her for a job well done instead of bitching that the job wasn't easy?"

Shaw stood up and glowered at Duncan. "I could suspend you right now for insubordination."

"I could also walk outside, go to that podium, and tell the press about this nightmare case, how Eve solved it in two days without sleeping, and that your reaction was 'What took you so fucking long?' How do you think that'll play?"

Duncan didn't wait for Shaw's answer. Instead, he simply walked out, leaving the door open behind him. Eve looked at the captain, who waved her away, too.

"Get out of here," he said. "I want your reports on my desk in an hour."

Eve caught up with Duncan at the door to the squad room.

"I can fight my own battles," she said. "You didn't have to say that."

"You didn't have to tell him he took a cheap shot, which I deserved, by the way."

"No, you didn't. I just got lucky."

Duncan leaned against the wall and looked at her. "It isn't luck, Eve. It's instinct. You're a natural at this. What you haven't learned yet is how to do it without making enemies."

Eve tilted her head toward Shaw's office. "Like what you just did?"

"I'm at the end of my career, you're at the beginning. If you want to make it as long as I have, you have to stop antagonizing everybody you work with and take better care of yourself. You look terrible."

"Gee, thanks."

"No, I mean it. You need to get some sleep."

"I will," she said. "Right after we file our reports."

They went to their desks, divvied up the paperwork, and got to it.

An hour later, ten minutes past Shaw's hastily issued deadline, Eve was still finishing up her work when a uniformed deputy approached her.

"Eve Ronin?" he asked.

She looked up at him. He was squat, in his thirties, with a buzz cut and a weight lifter's body. His name tag read PRICE. "Yes? What can I do for you?"

Price handed her an envelope. "This is for you."

She took it. "What is it?"

"Consider yourself served," he said, gave her the finger, and walked out.

Eve opened the envelope and pulled out the papers inside. It was a wrongful death lawsuit, filed by the widow of the deputy who'd killed himself during the course of her last investigation, the one prior to the home invasion case.

She'd been expecting the lawsuit, but even so, it still felt like a punch in the stomach. Duncan glanced over at her.

"Bad news?"

"I'm being sued for $10 million."

"Is that all?" he said. "I figured it would be at least twice as much. Is the department named in the suit as well?"

"Yes," she said.

"Then you're golden," Duncan said. "They're insured for stuff like this. The insurance company will settle for a million and you won't have to do a thing."

"I hope you're right."

"Are you done with your paperwork?"

"Just about," she said.

"That's good enough," he said, standing up. "You're done. I'm taking you back to your hotel. I don't want to see you until at least noon tomorrow. Better yet, take a sick day."

"You're going to miss the Hilton's breakfast buffet?"

"That should tell you how concerned I am."

They went outside, got into Duncan's Buick, and drove out. They were almost to the Hilton, and Eve was already half-asleep, her head against the window, when she remembered something important. She sat up straight.

"Wait, you can't take me home yet."

"Why not?"

"We need to talk to Mr. Alvarez. Face-to-face. He can't learn about what happened to his wife and unborn child from the evening news . . . or in a phone call."

"I haven't forgotten. I'll handle it before I go home."

"I'll go with you. You shouldn't have to do something like this alone."

"It's better if I do, especially with you like this," Duncan said. "You don't have the strength left, emotionally or otherwise, to deal with it."

Eve knew he was right, but even so, she felt like she was neglecting her duty. But she was also relieved. Because the truth was, she was terrified to face Alejandro Alvarez and tell him the horror story that would destroy his life. How could she do it without breaking down herself? She needed to learn that skill. But it wouldn't be tonight.

"I'm sorry," she said.

"Don't be," Duncan said. "You solved the case. Let me close it."

She started to get out of the car, but then stopped. "How do you tell somebody something like this and not fall apart yourself?"

"I've got a calloused heart," he said.

# CHAPTER TWENTY

Eve slept for fourteen hours, awaking at noon. But instead of feeling refreshed, she felt like she'd been beaten. She took a long, hot shower, got dressed in casual off-duty clothes—a V-neck, short-sleeve top and jeans and her off-duty weapon, a Glock 42, in an underwire bra holster—and walked over to the Commons for lunch.

She went to the Corner Bakery, ordered a club panini and a Diet Coke, and carried her number to the back table facing the door. Someone had left the *Los Angeles Times* behind, so she took a look at the front page.

Garvey's arrest of Justin Marriott was the lead story, apparently judged by the editors to be of equal, or more, importance to Los Angelenos than a mass shooting in Milwaukee or a tsunami in Thailand. The story about Anna McCaig and the fetal abduction was buried in the California section, but Eve suspected that was only because the news came in shortly before the paper's deadline. Neither she nor Duncan was mentioned by name, which she was glad to see. There would probably be a larger follow-up in tomorrow's paper with all the sordid details. She wondered if McCaig's husband had heard about his wife's crime yet in Berlin. If she were him, she'd stay there for a while and put the house on the market, though it would be a hard sale to make.

Thinking about owning a home that was a violent crime scene reminded her about the death that had occurred in her condo and the lawsuit that had been filed against her. She had to start thinking about her defense.

The waiter delivered Eve's sandwich. She wolfed it down, as if someone might take it away from her if she didn't hurry, and then called the County Counsel's office to find out what steps the department was taking on the lawsuit. The County Counsel provided legal advice and representation to the county's various departments and agencies, as well as to the board of supervisors and other county officers.

Eve was transferred several times until she finally managed to reach the lawyer assigned to the case, a man named Peter Monsey. She introduced herself and told him that she'd been served.

Monsey said, "Actually, we were served with the lawsuit some time ago and I'm pleased to say that we've negotiated a settlement."

Eve felt a wave of relief. She'd been dreading this suit for weeks and it was all for nothing. "Wow, that was fast."

"That's the power of reason. The wrongful death suit attempted to hold the county liable under section 1983 of the Civil Rights Act. Such cases usually involve excessive force, coerced confessions, or fabricating evidence, none of which applies in this case."

"So the lawsuit was baseless."

"Not entirely. Their argument was that you, in your official capacity, harassed someone so badly that it led him to his suicide. To hold us liable, however, they would have to prove that your conduct reflected department policy, written or unwritten, which it didn't, or that you were acting under a superior's direction, which you weren't."

"But you settled the case," she said.

"Yes. I convinced them they wouldn't ultimately prevail against us in court, and we negotiated a confidential settlement, but I can tell you it was in the low six figures, far less than the estimated legal costs of defense, and, of course, there was the ever-so-slight risk that we could lose."

"So we're done."

"We are, but you aren't," he said. "The case against you can proceed."

Eve felt a stab of anxiety in her chest, an entirely different ache than her sore, mending sternum. "Are you negotiating a settlement with them on my behalf?"

"We have nothing to do with your case. Our position is that you acted on your own, therefore we won't represent you or indemnify you for damages if you lose."

Anger now tempered her anxiety. *How could they take that stand?*

"That doesn't make any sense. I was working for you when this happened and I wasn't disciplined or penalized for my actions in the investigation."

"That doesn't mean you won't be nor should it imply that your conduct was authorized."

That was a very lawyerly, protect-our-asses answer, she thought. "You're just throwing me to the wolves."

"I wouldn't put it that way. I'd say you're representing yourself in this matter and we wish you the very best."

Eve hung up on him. They were sacrificing her. It was the department's way of punishing her for the scandal that was created by her investigation. But they were letting the lawyers do their dirty work.

Now she had to find herself an attorney and could only think of one place to start. She called Rebecca Burnside, the assistant district attorney she'd worked with since she'd transferred to Lost Hills. Burnside was smart, ambitious, and straightforward, and although they didn't always agree, Eve trusted her. That didn't mean Burnside would always have her back, but at least she wouldn't put a knife in it.

She managed to catch Burnside on a lunch break from court, grabbing a taco and Coke from a food truck, and quickly filled her in on the situation.

"I'm not surprised," Burnside said, talking with her mouth full. "It's the position I would have taken if I was in the County Counsel's seat."

"Gee, thanks."

"His job is to protect the county's exposure, not yours. It was an easy call. That doesn't mean it was right."

"Do you think they have a case against me?"

Burnside took a moment to swallow her food and wash it down with Coke.

"Honestly, yes, I do. You need a top criminal defense attorney. But they aren't cheap."

"How much is not cheap?"

There was a crunch as Burnside took another bite of her taco, then chewed it a bit before answering. "It could be as much as $500 an hour."

Eve gasped. She could forget about buying a new car. She'd have to buy some of those tree-shaped air fresheners to dangle from her rearview mirror instead, though she might not be able to afford those, either.

Burnside said, "Your homeowner's insurance might cover it. Some policies have protections against liability lawsuits like this."

"I've pushed it with my insurance company already on the remodel of my condo," Eve said. "They may cancel me rather than face more expense."

Her auto insurance already did after all the accidents and vandalism she'd filed claims for. Her new policy, with some sketchy company based in Barbados or someplace like that, cost three times as much as her old one.

"Sorry," Burnside said. "I'll email you some names and numbers."

"Thanks. Now there's an arrest warrant I'd like to talk with you about . . ."

Eve filled her in on Sherry Simms, her role in the home invasion spree, and her disappearance.

"I'll do it, out of pity for you, but she's small fish," Burnside said. "No department in the state, much less in the country, is going to make her their public enemy number one. I doubt it's worth the effort."

"Justice is always worth it."

Burnside groaned. "I've never met anyone who talks in pretentious movie taglines the way you do. What's worse is that you actually say it with a straight face."

"Because I mean it."

"We'll see how you feel about that when you're facing a judge and jury for what you did."

"I didn't make the deputy kill himself," Eve said. "His guilty conscience did that."

"And you don't think saying things like 'justice is always worth it' paints you as somebody who believes she's everybody's conscience? That's a load I wouldn't want to carry."

Eve ignored the comment, genuinely thanked Burnside for her help, and disconnected the call. Feeling sorry for herself, she got up and ordered a maple pecan bar and brought it back to her table. The thought of spending $500 an hour defending herself was terrifying.

How could she afford that?

She could only think of one way, so she called Linwood Taggert. His assistant answered with her perfect, *Downton Abbey* British accent.

"Linwood Taggert's office," Downton said. "How may I help you?"

"This is Eve Ronin. I'd like to talk with him."

"Let me see if he is in."

The artifice of that response annoyed Eve. Obviously Downton knew if he'd walked past her out of his office or not. What Downton really meant to say, in her possibly fake British accent, was "Let me see if you're someone he wants to talk to or if I should blow you off."

But the next voice Eve heard was Linwood's. "Did you like the script?"

"I haven't read it yet. I have a question for you. When do I get paid?"

"You already received the $5,000 option money."

It was only a small percentage of what she'd get if the project went forward and would be tapped out in just ten hours of consultation or work with the attorney.

"When do I get my next check?"

"When someone buys Simone Harper's script."

"And after that?"

"When we get the green light for production of the pilot or, if we're lucky, a straight-to-series order," Linwood said. "Then you get paid as each episode is completed, unless you exercise your option to be a full-time producer. Then you're paid weekly."

"Thanks." Eve disconnected and decided that she'd read the script today. Because the sooner Linwood sold it, the sooner she'd be able to afford to defend herself. She decided to take her maple pecan bar home and eat it while she read.

Before she got up, though, her phone dinged. It was a new email notice. Burnside had sent her the list. She sat back down to read it.

The names meant nothing to her. Eve would have to google each name, and look at the criminals they'd defended, and then decide which attorney was the least detestable choice to work with. But first she'd read the script. If it was terrible, and she walked away from the project, there was no way she could afford a top attorney.

A man's voice said, "Is this seat taken?"

She looked up to see Ethan Dryer, owner of Big Valley Security, standing in front of her with a cup of coffee in one hand and a piece of coffee cake in another.

"I was just leaving." Eve started to get up.

"Hold on a minute, please. I think we got off on the wrong foot the other day. I owe you an apology."

Eve sat back down. "Really?"

Dryer dragged a chair away from the table with his foot and sat down across from her.

"I thought about how I'd have felt, back when I was on the job, if a guy like me showed up on my crime scene. I would have treated me the same way you did. I'd like a reboot." He set down his coffee and held his hand to her over the table. "I'm Ethan Dryer, and I'm pleased to meet you."

Eve decided to acknowledge the apology, and the courtesy, even if she felt it was probably insincere. He simply wanted to get her on his good side for the future. She shook his hand.

"Likewise. How is Grayson doing?"

"He's on leave, but I'm not sure if he will come back."

"Is he too traumatized by what happened?"

"On the contrary, I think it has lit a fire under him," Dryer said, starting to nibble on his coffee cake. "He might take the sheriff up on his offer and join you in the big leagues."

Seeing him eat prompted Eve to start in on her maple pecan bar. "Why didn't he try before?"

"He did, with the LAPD, but didn't pass the tests. Some people just aren't good at them. But he won't have to worry about that with the sheriff's department, not with that medal around his neck."

It was true, Eve thought. Lansing would love the PR aspect. Grayson would have a charmed career. "But you hired him anyway."

Dryer shrugged. "Our requirements aren't as rigorous as the LAPD's and the job isn't nearly as tough. Our guys sit in guardhouses at businesses or gated communities, or stand in stores as a deterrent to shoplifting, or respond to home alarms, which are mostly set off accidentally by the homeowners themselves."

"Don't you also do private security for celebrities?"

"For that stuff, we hire ex–law enforcement officers like you."

"I'm not available."

Dryer looked at her over the rim of his coffee cup. "Yet."

Now his desire to reboot their relationship, as he called it, made more sense to Eve. He wanted to recruit her.

"Do you know something I don't?"

Dryer took a sip of his coffee and smiled. "I'm always looking for good people. But the kind of Hollywood job you might get when you're ready to leave LASD, producing a TV series about yourself, is more attractive than the Hollywood job I could offer you."

"Babysitting celebrities and getting them out of trouble?"

"Somebody has to do it."

"Talk to Stan Garvey. It's a job he might enjoy." And, in her mind, he was already doing it.

"He's on my speed dial."

"I'm sure he is." Eve was almost finished with her maple pecan bar. "How come you couldn't keep Justin Marriott out of trouble?"

"He's not one of our clients."

"But if he was, I'll bet his Ferrari wouldn't have had a scratch on it when our detectives showed up at his door."

"You've misjudged me, Eve. I'll protect a client from embarrassment, but not from a felony. Once a cop, always a cop," Dryer said and she got the feeling he actually meant it. He just went up a notch in her judgment. "That's how I know that, once you leave the sheriff's department someday, you won't be satisfied producing a TV series about yourself."

That was probably true, Eve thought, scooping up the crumbs of her maple pecan bar with her sticky fork. Nothing was going to waste on this plate. "What will I do? Become a PI?"

"Like Kinsey Millhone? No," he said. Wow, she thought, a reader, too. He was full of surprises. "But you could lend your name to a security service."

Ah-ha, she thought. So he wanted to leverage her reputation someday to offer bespoke security and investigation services to celebrity clients, the way he'd used his experience at the LAPD to open Big Valley.

"It's something to consider," he said. "And having the right partner would allow you to get up and running immediately."

It felt good to be right. It should also have been a comfort, Eve thought, knowing she had two avenues for income to pay her legal fees or to support herself if she got thrown off the force. It was a wealth of opportunities. But somehow, it only made her feel icky. So many people out there were ready to profit from her fortune or misfortune and had no real interest in her. And that included her own parents.

Was it Hollywood that did this to people or something else?

But Eve set aside her reservations, told him she'd keep the offer in mind, and left the restaurant. She was eager to get back to her room and read the *Ronin* script.

Eve emerged from the elevator at the Hilton and saw a maid's cart a few doors down from her room. That changed her plans. Her room was a mess, smelled like pizza and dirty socks, and desperately needed to be cleaned. She'd have to quickly straighten up her room so it wasn't an obstacle course for the maid and then go read the script in the lobby to get out of her way. Daily maid service, along with fresh towels and sheets, was a luxury she'd definitely miss when she moved back to her condo.

Eve hurried into her room and began by gathering up all the fast-food containers and stuffing them into the ridiculously small trash can. That done, she picked up yesterday's clothes off the floor. When she scooped up her jacket, several sheets of paper covered in handwriting tumbled out of the inside pocket. She snatched up the loose pages. It was the list of license plates for the vehicles that left Oakdale on Tuesday, the day of Priscilla's disappearance. Eve had given the list to Clayton, and he'd returned it to her with the owner information listed alongside the license plate number and time code showing when the vehicle appeared on the gate video. The list was irrelevant now, but she set it on her laptop to put in the McCaig murder book, the complete record of the case, when she went back to the station tomorrow.

Eve gave the room another once-over, seeing if there was any other clutter she had to stuff into the trash, a drawer, or a suitcase, didn't see anything, and reached for the script beside the laptop. Her gaze flicked over Clayton's list, and her eye caught a name beside one of the license plates.

*Green's Greenery.*

That struck her as odd for two reasons. She didn't recall seeing a Green's Greenery truck enter or leave the community on the security gate video from Tuesday and Michael Green had told her himself that he wasn't there that day.

She sat down, opened her laptop, and booted it up. She clicked the link to the Oakdale security camera videos for Tuesday and scrubbed to the time code by the vehicle license plate number.

But it wasn't a Green's Greenery box truck in the image. It was an Amazon delivery van.

That didn't make sense.

She double-checked the license plate on the Amazon van against the one on the list. The plates matched.

The maid knocked at Eve's door. Eve got up, opened the door, and smiled politely at the woman.

"Can you please come back in an hour? Or put it off until tomorrow? There's work I have to do."

The maid nodded, and even seemed a bit relieved, and Eve went back to her computer.

She opened her file directory for the home invasion case and checked the license plate against the list of vehicle owners that were at each of the communities when robberies took place.

Green's Greenery and Amazon delivery were on the list.

That, in and of itself, wasn't suspicious. But she still felt a chill.

She called up the Vista Grande footage from Monday and fast-forwarded through it until she found a Green's Greenery box truck entering the community. A few minutes later, an Amazon van came in. She checked the plate on the Amazon van against the one on Clayton's list. It didn't match. She fast-forwarded some more. Another Amazon van came in. She checked Clayton's list.

*It had Green's plate.*

Now she knew how the home invaders got into and out of the gated communities, and that Michael Green was their ringleader.

What she didn't have yet was anything tying Green to Dalander, Colter, and Nagy, the three dead robbers.

Eve fired up Safari and browsed Green's website. It showed off his fleet of trucks, featured the faces of his happy workers, and talked about his community involvement. His office was in Calabasas and he proudly supported Bay Laurel Elementary School, A. C. Stelle Middle School, and Calabasas High School activities and events. There were pictures of his booths at school fairs and his logo on team uniforms. He'd also sponsored and coached a soccer team in a valley youth league.

She felt a jolt of excitement, picked up her phone, and scrolled through her photos until she found the ones from their search of Paul Colter's room.

And found what she was looking for: the soccer trophy Colter won for just participating in the sport. She zoomed in on the team name and the date.

It was the team that Green sponsored and coached.

Now she could tie Green to Colter. But what about Dalander and Nagy?

Eve opened up the virtual drive of Nagy's computer, went to his library of thousands of personal photos, and began scrolling through the ones taken during the school year listed on the trophy.

While she scrolled through the pictures, her phone buzzed multiple times, all calls from reporters, undoubtedly seeking a quote from her about Anna McCaig and the investigation. They wouldn't be getting one from her, not today, not ever. She ignored her phone and kept searching the pictures for soccer balls, soccer fields, or soccer uniforms or any familiar faces besides Nagy and his family.

After forty minutes, just when she was beginning to think she'd hit a dead end, she found a picture of Nagy at soccer practice. She slowed her scroll. There were more pictures of Nagy and his team at practices and games. She enlarged a few of them.

And there they were. They were younger, ganglier, and geekier, but still instantly recognizable. Dalander and Colter, on the same team as Nagy. Green was there, too, with a big Tom Selleck mustache that he no longer had.

They weren't the only faces she recognized in the photos and it changed her perspective on the whole investigation.

Eve called Duncan.

"Did you just wake up?" Duncan asked. It was late afternoon.

"I've been up for hours."

"I hope you're taking it easy."

Eve stared at the team photo, at those young faces, and thought about the fate they'd met and her part in it. And the part she still might play. "I've barely left my room."

"Too tired?"

"Too busy," she said. "I've discovered how the home invaders got in and out of the gated communities and what ties the three men together."

"Holy shit," Duncan said. "How did you do that?"

She quickly explained what she'd found, right up to the soccer team photographs of Dalander, Colter, and Nagy. She held back the last surprise. She wanted to get him on board with her theory first.

"You think the robbers came in as part of Green's landscaping crew or hidden inside the fake Amazon van," he said. "Or divided among the two vehicles and left the same way."

She wasn't sure from Duncan's tone of voice if he was on board yet, so she elaborated.

"It was a clever strategy. Everybody in the gated communities thinks it's a given that the guard has checked out everybody who comes in. And nobody is going to think twice about seeing an Amazon deliveryman carrying boxes to or from a house or landscapers working on a property. For instance, Green's crew was working beside the sting house the day we were hit."

"Yeah, I noticed. So you believe they all met back when Green coached their soccer team and somehow, for some reason, they reunited years later to rob homes."

She was bothered by his choice of words, by the "somehow" and "for some reason," interpreting them as signs of his skepticism.

"What do *you* think?"

"I think it's amazing what you can accomplish after a good night's sleep."

What did that mean?

"I'm asking you about the crime. Do you think we've solved it?"

"Not we, you. And yes, I believe you have," he said. "Now all that's left to do is arrest Green."

That was a relief. Now she felt comfortable dropping the bomb.

"Actually, there's more. And it creates a big problem."

She took a deep breath and told him. His reaction was succinct and summed up her feelings perfectly.

"Oh, shit," he said.

# CHAPTER
# TWENTY-ONE

The next morning Eve, Duncan, Rebecca Burnside, and Sheriff Lansing all gathered in Captain Shaw's office. It was a tight fit. Eve was the only one standing and her laptop was close by on the coffee table.

Burnside was in a tennis outfit but somehow wore it like one of the suits she wore in court. It was every bit as stylish and wrinkle-free, and perfectly highlighted her curves without being in-your-face sexy. Her makeup was also perfect. Eve wondered if she'd applied it for the game or for the meeting or never went out in public without something on her face.

Shaw was clearly pissed off at Eve and his anger radiated like a heater. He'd had no role in calling this meeting and only found out about it when the sheriff and Burnside showed up. He spoke up the instant everybody was in the room and the door had closed.

"If there's an emergency situation that merits the sheriff and the ADA being called in here, in person, on a Saturday morning, I need to hear about it first and I'll decide whether it requires all hands on deck," Shaw said to Eve. "Does chain of command mean nothing to you? Who the hell do you think you are?"

Eve had a direct line to the sheriff and she intended to exploit it, chain of command be damned, when it served her cases.

"You're right, of course," Lansing said to Shaw. "Her actions display a blatant disrespect for your authority and, ordinarily, I wouldn't let it stand. But she's cashing in a marker, whether she realizes it or not. This isn't the first time Eve has organized an urgent meeting like this. In that case, I disregarded what she had to say, and it nearly cost a child's life. So I'm willing to hear her out and then decide if disciplinary action is in order."

"Thank you, sir," Eve said. "We've solved the spree of home invasion robberies but—"

"Oh, for God's sake," Shaw interrupted. "That's old news. You closed that case four days ago. You dragged everybody in here for that?"

"This time we've really closed it and tied up all the loose ends, some we didn't even know we had before. We've finally identified and nailed down everyone involved."

Shaw waved off Eve's clarification. "So you tracked down Dalander's girlfriend. That's hardly urgent and it doesn't change anything."

"Actually," Duncan said, "she's still at large."

"What else is there?" Shaw asked.

"We stumbled onto a key piece of evidence in the home invasion case while we were investigating the unrelated fetal abduction at Oakdale," Eve said. "And it completely changes our understanding of the crime."

Eve explained about Green's Greenery, the fake Amazon delivery van, and Michael Green's connection to Dalander, Colter, and Nagy.

"I get it now," Lansing said. "You're saying I was wrong when I told the media that the case was closed at the awards ceremony for Grayson Mumford. I appreciate your concern about the potential embarrassment to me and to the department, but don't worry about that. I'll play up that you two kept at it, going above and beyond, because we never quit. In fact, this will reflect very positively on the department. It shows we're tenacious and not worried about public perception. But I agree with the captain—this wasn't an urgent matter and doesn't justify dragging us all down here."

Burnside studied Eve. "There's more."

Lansing looked at Burnside, as if he'd forgotten she was there. "What?"

"That's only the beginning. She's not done," Burnside said. "I wouldn't be here if that was all there was to it. Look at her face. The other Manolo Blahnik hasn't dropped yet."

Lansing turned to Eve and he could see that Burnside was right. "This won't be good. Go on."

"There was an inside man, someone who smoothed the way in and out of the gated communities for Green and picked the homes to be hit." Eve went to her laptop computer on the coffee table, opened it, and displayed a photo of Green's soccer team. She pointed to one of the teenage players. "Grayson Mumford."

Shaw squinted at the screen and shook his head. "Just because Mumford was on the same soccer team as the three dead assailants years ago doesn't make him part of the robbery crew. By that logic, we should arrest the whole team."

Duncan said, "But the rest of them aren't working as floating front gate security guards at every community that was hit."

Eve tapped a few keys on her laptop. "I'd like you to take another look at the video of the grocery store shooting."

The video and sound from the confrontation played out from various camera angles on her laptop screen.

Colter charged into the grocery store and went straight for the liquor aisle, Grayson tracking his movements on a parallel course.

"It was no accident that Colter is here," Eve said. "He'd just walked into a trap and saw two of his friends get killed. He blamed Grayson for it. Colter carjacked a vehicle and fled. But when he realized that there was no chance of escaping, he veered into the shopping center and decided to use his last moments of freedom to confront him."

On the screen, they could see Colter at the end of the aisle, holding a vodka bottle in one hand and his gun in the other, half turned away from Eve toward the back of the store, where Mumford was hiding.

Colter said, "I know you're here. Show yourself. Don't be a coward."

Eve, on the video, stepped into the aisle and said, "Here I am."

Colter turned toward her and that's when Grayson stepped out and shot him.

Eve paused the video.

"It wasn't me that Colter was calling out. It was Grayson. I distracted Colter for a split second, and Grayson saw his chance to save himself. He executed Colter to keep him from talking."

Lansing said, "And that's the guy I chose as the first civilian in history to get our Medal of Valor. What a fucking mess." He stood up and looked at Shaw. "Eve did the right thing calling this meeting and briefing us all at once." Shaw held his hands up in surrender, but Eve was sure he'd still hold a grudge. "Let's set aside, for the moment, how this looks for the department." Lansing shifted his gaze to Burnside. "Do we have a case?"

"Against Green, yes," Burnside said. "But not against Mumford."

"He gunned down Colter," Duncan said.

"To save Eve," Burnside said. "You can't prove Colter was calling out Mumford and not the relentless cop who'd chased him from Vista Grande."

"Okay," Eve said. "So we arrest Green and get him to flip on Grayson in return for a lighter sentence."

Burnside shook her head. "There's still no case. Mumford's attorney will argue that Green is lying in a flagrant and despicable attempt to reduce his sentence and tarnish the reputation of a true hero. The sheriff gave Mumford, a civilian, the Medal of Valor, for God's sake."

"No need to rub it in," Lansing said, pacing in front of Shaw's desk.

"The defense attorneys and the media certainly will," she said, "so you might as well get used to it."

Shaw cleared his throat to get everyone's attention. "There's another alternative."

Everyone looked at him. "We arrest Green and tell him his only hope for leniency is if he gets Mumford to implicate himself."

Lansing stood in front of Shaw's desk and looked at him. "You want Green to meet with Mumford and wear a wire?"

Shaw leaned back in his chair. "We have nothing to lose."

Eve thought about it a moment, then said, "We don't know who else at Green's company is involved in the robberies. What if Grayson gets word that Green has been arrested from someone in his office or among his landscaping crew?"

"We raid Green's Greenery tomorrow," Shaw said, "when they are closed and his crew isn't around, and we arrest him at home. We make the deal and have Green set up the meet right away."

"And if he doesn't take the deal?" Eve asked.

Burnside answered before Shaw could. "He'll take it. Guaranteed."

Lansing turned and addressed the room. "It was all an elaborate charade."

Eve said, "With all due respect, sir, I think Grayson was improvising as he went along."

"I'm talking about the Medal of Valor ceremony," Lansing said. "That's how we explain it. We say we suspected Mumford was involved in the robberies from the start. But if we hadn't acknowledged his heroism, he would have suspected we were onto him. It was all a charade on our part. We wanted to lull him into a false sense of security, and the Medal of Valor did that spectacularly."

Burnside chuckled. "Do you really think the media will believe that?"

Lansing glared at her. "Do you have a better idea, Counselor?"

"Tell the truth. It's a lot more convincing."

Eve had to give Burnside credit for backbone, but the ADA could afford to be blunt with the sheriff. She didn't work for him.

"The DA would love it if I did that," Lansing said. "It would give him one more thing to embarrass me with when he runs against me for mayor."

Burnside stood up and brushed imaginary wrinkles from her tennis shorts. "Politics aren't my concern, Sheriff. Let me get to work on the warrants." She turned to Eve. "What do you hope to find at Green's place of business?"

"Stolen goods, the phony Amazon van, weapons, ammunition, and the cars belonging to the three dead assailants."

"Why would their cars be there?"

Duncan explained what they'd learned from tracking the cell phones of all three assailants and how each man had turned off his phone before leaving home on the days of the invasions. He told her their theory that it was done so nobody, if one of them was caught, would be able to track where they'd left their cars.

"Very clever," Burnside said. "You'll have the warrants by the end of the day." She looked at Shaw. "When do you think you'll make your move?"

Shaw, in turn, looked at Duncan. "Where's his office?"

"Here in Calabasas."

"Where does Green live?"

"Out in Oak Park."

"So we'll have to bring in the Ventura County Sheriff's Department with us on the arrest," Shaw said, then addressed Burnside. "We'll handle Green's arrest and the searches of his properties in the morning and set up the sting for the afternoon."

Eve was still worried about word of Green's arrest spreading, and possibly reaching Grayson Mumford, if they apprehended him at home and searched it.

"I think we can avoid arresting him at home and get him to come to us," Eve said. "I met him at Oakdale and he gave me his card. I could ask him to drop by my house to give me an estimate."

Lansing nodded. "I like that idea. Go back to the Realtor who found the sting house and see if he can find you another one that's remote and easy for us to control. We can search Green's house afterwards, and not make a multijurisdictional show out of it."

Burnside said, "After we have Green in custody, and I've made him cry, then I'll pursue the warrant for the wire."

Lansing nodded and got to his feet. "Good luck tomorrow. Keep me informed."

Eve and Duncan left the office. They were halfway down the hall to the squad room when Lansing caught up with them.

"Hold up for a second. I should have said this before. I want to thank you both for your work on this case and for your discretion."

Duncan tipped his head to Eve. "Thank her. I had nothing to do with it." And before Lansing could argue the point, Duncan walked into the squad room, leaving the two of them alone.

Eve turned to Lansing. "The other day you said you'd always have our backs. Did you mean it?"

"Of course I did."

"So why isn't the department defending me in the wrongful death lawsuit?"

Lansing looked around, then lowered his voice to answer. "The department is behind you on this. I argued vehemently that we shouldn't settle, that the son of a bitch was corrupt and a disgrace to the badge, and that representing you was the right thing to do. But in the end, it's the County Counsel's decision. I have no authority. They've settled a lot of cases that I wanted to fight in court."

Eve didn't believe him, but she knew it was true that it was the County Counsel's decision, not his. "I feel like I'm being sacrificed."

"You're not. You'll have the full weight of the department behind you."

"What does that mean, exactly?"

"We'll say you did nothing wrong."

She looked him in the eyes. "So what I did was in policy?"

He shifted his gaze. "No, I wouldn't say that. I'd say that you were diligently investigating a case and that your only motivation was uncovering the truth and getting justice for the victims."

Now she had her answer. She was being sacrificed. "But you don't condone my methods."

He looked around again. "This really isn't the time or place to discuss all the details. This will be settled before the case goes to court."

"I won't settle," she said.

"Then I'm sure the jury will rule in your favor. The public loves you."

He patted her on the shoulder and walked out. Eve didn't feel reassured.

Eve spent the evening in her hotel room reading the *Ronin* script, which was an unsettling and surreal experience. There was nothing that could have prepared her for reading a fictionalized telling of her recent life, one that set her up as some kind of iconic detective hero.

The first time she read the script, all she noticed were the liberties that Simone Harper had taken with her life and with real events. But Eve knew some of that was inevitable when trying to compress months, and a lot of dull investigation, into an entertaining forty-four-minute show.

The second time she read it, she tried to accept that it wasn't a documentary and judge if the story, in general, was true to how events actually played out. But she still kept bumping on the character of "Eve Ronin." This Eve Ronin wasn't her but some idealized and yet also deeply flawed and somewhat unlikable version of herself imagined by someone else.

Was this how people saw her? God, she hoped not, because this was not the woman she wanted to be. But at least she wasn't portrayed as a martial arts superstar with blonde hair, big boobs, and a sports car. The question she had to ask herself was not whether this was a good series character but if this characterization of her was one that she could live with.

It wasn't the character's inexperience or procedural mistakes that bothered her, even if they weren't factually correct. What bothered her was the heroine's political gamesmanship and, in particular, her ridiculous heroism, blindly running into danger without a second thought. This Eve Ronin felt no fear. Her heroics seemed overwrought, as if written for a bombastic orchestral score. All of that would have to be toned way down. But, overall, after four readings, Eve wasn't as troubled by the script as she thought she'd be. She could work with the writer on a rewrite that might not be an accurate reflection of who she was, or aspired to be, but at least would be an image she could live with, if not necessarily live up to.

Eve called Linwood's mobile number, which she found on her phone from the multiple times he'd tried calling her after the shoot-out story broke. He answered after one ring.

"Stop hounding me with all of these calls," he yelled. "You're not my only client."

"I've only called twice in the last two days."

"I'm being sarcastic. Where's your sense of humor? That's two more times than you've ever called me before. I'm in shock. Have you read the script?"

"I have and I think it's okay for now."

"What do you mean, 'for now'?"

"As a sales tool, for you to sell the script and get a network to order the series," Eve said. "But before a frame of this is shot, there will need to be some significant changes."

"Like what?"

"The police procedure is all wrong, more TV than reality."

Linwood snorted. "Have you seen *Law & Order*? The trials are held a week after the bad guy is arrested."

"I understand the need for compression for dramatic reasons, but some of what Simone has got here is just ridiculous." Eve listed some of the errors and wild deviations from reality.

"That's all minor stuff. Easily fixed. Is that all?"

"I never said or even thought a lot of the things coming out of my character's mouth, so that needs to go," Eve said. "And the character is too manipulative and premeditated, immediately seeing how to leverage any situation for her own personal political advantage."

"That's you," Linwood said.

"No, it isn't, and even if it is, that's not how I want to be portrayed on TV."

Linwood laughed. "Do you also want her to be ten pounds lighter?"

"Are you saying I'm fat?"

"No, I'm just saying a perfect character is boring. She has to have flaws, even if you don't."

"The flaws are fine. I like them better than the insane bravery and sanctimonious heroics. But I don't want to be seen as someone who puts her selfish interests first and her job second."

"Got it. Lose the Wonder Woman outfit and Lasso of Power."

"I believe it's a Lasso of Truth," Eve said.

"You would know. But overall, did you like it?"

Eve thought about that. It wasn't a simple question. "Simone treated me fairly and handled the murder case with sensitivity."

"Does this mean you trust Simone now to tell your story?"

"It means I can work with her. It will take a lot more to earn my trust."

"Have I earned it?"

Now Eve laughed. "You're a Hollywood agent!"

"So?"

"That is the *Oxford English Dictionary*'s definition of untrustworthy."

"Okay, baby steps then. I can live with that," Linwood said. "Okay, I've got to go and make you a million bucks."

She hoped he wasn't joking, though there was a fifty-fifty chance if he succeeded that every penny would probably go to the lawyers and the family of the corrupt deputy who'd killed himself.

At least she wouldn't end up living under an overpass in a cardboard box on urine-soaked dirt.

She called Michael Green on her cell phone from her desk at the Lost Hills station at 9:00 a.m. as Duncan and Shaw stood on either side of her chair. They'd researched Green prior to the call. They'd learned he was a divorced father of two teenage girls, who now lived with their mother in Riverside. He owed years of back alimony and child support and his business was on the ropes. He had no prior criminal record.

Green answered with a cheery hello.

"Mr. Green? This is Eve Ronin, we met a few days ago in Oakdale."

"The detective who traded her Rolls-Royce for a Subaru."

"That's the one. You gave me your card and I've been thinking about it ever since."

"I'm glad I paid the extra money for the glossy paper. The printer said it would leave an impression."

Eve faked a laugh, which she hoped sounded genuine. "I'd like to talk to you about relandscaping my house, which isn't saying much. It's mostly dirt and weeds."

"What we in the trade call 'a blank canvas.'"

"It could certainly use your artistry. Do you think we can meet? I know this is last minute, but I have a very unpredictable schedule in my line of work and I'm actually free today."

"I would be glad to. I can imagine how hard it is for anyone in law enforcement to make appointments and keep them," he said. "You never know when somebody might get killed."

"Sadly, that's true." Eve gave him the address of an empty house in a cul-de-sac in Calabasas, in an older neighborhood known as Saratoga Ranch, less than half a mile from the Lost Hills station. "If you come at noon, I'll even throw in lunch. I make the best sourdough grilled cheese sandwiches in the galaxy."

"How could I turn that down? See you at noon."

Eve disconnected and looked at Duncan and Shaw. "We're on."

Shaw nodded. "I'll set the teams in motion."

"I want Duncan, Ross, and Clayton with me," Eve said. "I need to know I have backup I can trust."

"You can trust me," Shaw said, but didn't wait for her reply. As soon as he was gone, Duncan turned to her.

"Is that true about the grilled cheese sandwiches?"

"It is. That's why I was able to sound so convincing."

"How come you've never made me one?"

"I'm saving it for your retirement," she said.

# CHAPTER
# TWENTY-TWO

The Saratoga Ranch neighborhood was tucked between the Ventura Freeway and the Calabasas landfill, which had been dug out of the hills north of the homes and was steadily being filled with the county's trash, supposedly on top of a layer of toxic waste from the Rocketdyne weapons labs that had once operated in the nearby Santa Susana Pass. Eve couldn't imagine why anyone would want to live here, breathing exhaust fumes and rotting garbage all day, and possibly having their bodies baked, on a genetic level, by radiation. Just thinking about it made her wish she was wearing a hazmat suit.

But it made perfect sense to her why the ranch-style house had been for sale for months and already had three price reductions. There was a lot more going against it than the exterior's 1970s vibe incongruously matched with the faux "renovated barn" roofline. The front yard was all dirt that was so hard and dry that weeds wouldn't even grow.

Eve's Subaru was parked in the driveway and she waited inside the empty house. Duncan, Ross, and Clayton were hiding in the back rooms. She was dressed casually, but she had a gun in her bra holster, just in case, and a set of cuffs in her pocket.

Green arrived promptly at noon in a ten-year-old BMW 3 Series rather than one of his logo-emblazoned trucks. He emerged with a clipboard in hand and surveyed the front yard for a moment before walking to the door. Eve opened the door to greet him before he got there.

He gestured to the yard. "I thought you were exaggerating about the dirt and weeds."

"I was," Eve said with a smile. "Do you see any weeds?"

He laughed, and Eve stepped aside and beckoned him into the house with a sweep of her arm. Michael walked past her and immediately noticed the empty living room.

"Did you just move in?"

Eve grabbed him by the right arm, yanked it behind his back, and shoved him face-first against the wall, though she gave him an instant to turn his cheek to the surface before impact. He dropped the clipboard and let out a surprised cry.

"You're under arrest for fraud, armed robbery, and murder."

That same instant, Duncan and the two deputies spilled out of the other rooms in case she needed backup.

"What are you talking about?" Green said. "I haven't done anything."

Eve used her foot to spread his legs and her free hand to pat him down, pulling out his wallet, cell phone, a pen, and a set of keys, all of which she passed along to Duncan, who dropped them into evidence bags.

"Give me your other arm," she said.

He did. "You're making a mistake."

She cuffed him, read him his rights, then spun him around to face the four of them.

"We know you were the ringleader behind the home invasion robberies that Dalander, Colter, and Nagy committed," Eve said. "And we know about the fake Amazon van you used to get them in and out and we know about the help Grayson Mumford gave you."

The color drained from his formerly ruddy face. Now he looked like he might be sick. Duncan stepped forward, getting into Green's face.

"We have search warrants for your business and your home," he said. "If you don't want us breaking down the doors and making a mess, you'll give us the keys."

Green's shoulders slumped, a defeated man. "You've already got them. The two Medeco keys at one end of the ring are for the warehouse. The single Medeco key at the other end is for my house."

"Thank you," Eve said. "Now I want you to think about what we're going to find at your office and your home and how it's going to strengthen our already airtight case against you."

"I want my lawyer," Green said.

"That's fine. We'll take you to the station for booking and let you give him a call. Tell him to come right down. In the meantime, we'll conduct our search and then we can all get together to discuss your bleak future."

Eve nodded to Ross and Clayton, who took Green to the garage, where their patrol car was hidden.

Duncan held up Green's key ring. "Which do you want—home or office?"

"Office."

Duncan took the two Medeco keys off the ring and handed them to her.

Green's Greenery was located in Craftsman's Corner, an industrial pocket of unincorporated land north of the freeway and at the base of the weedy hills that gave the city of Hidden Hills its name. Calabasas was decades into the process of annexing the neighborhood, which the city ultimately planned to raze and turn into a new downtown, with a performing arts center, a big plaza, and other amenities, by the 2030s.

However, one thing wouldn't change. The Los Angeles Pet Memorial, the final resting place of Tarzan's Cheeta, Hopalong Cassidy's horse Topper, and Humphrey Bogart's dog Droopy, took up ten acres on the northwest side of the neighborhood and was protected from development by state law. Eve was glad for that. She'd often visited the quirky cemetery with her mom, sister, and brother when she was a child and loved it.

She also liked the history, which was a microcosm of the shady land deals and corruption that epitomized the valley's growth in the early twentieth century. Craftsman's Corner was formerly the country estate of financier Gilbert H. Beesemyer, who was arrested in 1929 for stealing $8 million from Guaranty Building and Loan, a crime that shocked Hollywood and remained the biggest embezzlement in US history for the next three decades. Beesemyer gave investing advice to all the stars and studio heads of the day and was a key player in the development of the San Fernando Valley, which he never saw again. The terms of his 1940 parole from San Quentin, after serving less than a quarter of his prison sentence, required that he never step foot in California.

Green's Greenery was a corrugated-metal, flat-roofed building that looked like a shipping container. It sat on cracked asphalt on the east side of Douglas Fir Road, which ran along the eastern boundary of the pet cemetery, and was up against a weedy hillside that abutted the southwest boundary of Hidden Hills.

The building had only one door and one window, both in front, and roll-up garage doors along the back, which Eve could see as she drove up, followed by a CSU van. Green's cyclone-fenced back lot contained two logo-emblazoned box trucks, a pickup truck, pallets of planting soil, and stacks of planter pots and trays.

Eve got out and unlocked the front door, then she and two evidence collection specialists, Fred and Dale, went inside. The front office was empty, the Formica countertop and two metal desks behind it cleaned off. He'd let his office staff go a long time ago. The linoleum floors were scraped, scuffed, stained, and torn from years of use. Straight ahead of them was a door leading to what she presumed was the warehouse/garage and a short hallway that led to an office, a small kitchen, and a bathroom.

Only one of the offices appeared occupied. It was filled with papers, boxes of files, and catalogs, dirty fingerprints on just about everything. The desktop computer was filthy, the keyboard caked in dirt, and the leatherette desk chair was patched with duct tape.

"I don't think he gets many guests," Fred said. "What are we looking for?"

"In here? Stolen goods like credit cards, wallets, jewelry, designer bags, that kind of thing," Eve said. "Also guns, ammo, and uniforms for Southern California Edison, Spectrum Cable, Pacific Bell, Amazon, and other utilities and delivery services."

"That shouldn't take long."

Eve backtracked with Dale and opened the door to the warehouse/garage. The space was large enough to contain a Bobcat mini-bulldozer, a propane-powered forklift, several pallets of fertilizer, numerous lawn mowers, a few eight-gallon propane tanks, several gasoline and oil cans for equipment, rows of gardening tools, Weedwackers and air blowers, racks of PVC pipes, bins and shelves full of various sprinkler and outdoor plumbing parts and, behind all of that, an Amazon van and three vehicles covered with tarps.

She walked over to the vehicles and yanked the tarps off them, revealing a Hyundai Sonata, an old Mercedes C-class with Uber and Lyft stickers in the windshield, and a Toyota Corolla.

It was the three cars belonging to Dalander, Colter, and Nagy, minus their license plates.

"What's on our shopping list?" Dale asked.

Eve slipped on a pair of rubber gloves. "First I'd like to find their cell phones. But otherwise, the same things your partner is looking for."

"He's not my partner," Dale said. "I can barely stand to look at him."

"Why is that?"

"He's sleeping with my girlfriend," he said. "Well, she *was* my girlfriend, now she's his."

"Ouch," Eve said.

She opened each car and checked the glove compartments. No phones. Green was stuck with the cars but wisely disposed of the phones, which were easy to destroy and throw away.

Eve left Dale with the cars, went over to the van, and opened the back doors. The interior was full of empty Amazon boxes and several uniforms and hats for Amazon, Southern California Gas Co., Pacific Bell, and Edison.

Pay dirt.

She went back and checked the office. Green was too smart to leave any stolen goods in plain sight or even in closets or drawers, but Fred did find a gun, a box of ammo, a carton of unopened burner phones, and three license plates in a shoebox. The plates belonged to the cars of the dead assailants.

"This is helpful," Eve said. "It's none of my business, but did you really have an affair with your colleague's girlfriend?"

Fred shrugged. "She's freaky for forensics guys. I'm the third one she's dated in the unit. I wouldn't be surprised if she's already looking for her fourth."

"But you're staying with her until then?"

"Never had so much action in my life. Five, six days a week. The downside is she gets off on me being dressed for work—Tyvek suit, gloves and masks, the whole outfit—and processing her body for evidence as foreplay. At least she's naked. Then she—"

"TMI," Eve interrupted, holding up her hands, signaling him to stop.

"So why'd you ask?"

Eve stepped outside and called Duncan, who was out at Green's house in Oak Park. "Guess what I found."

"Three cars, the Amazon van, and Amelia Earhart's plane."

"Two out of the three. There were no cell phones in the cars but the van was full of utility company uniforms and empty boxes. We also found a gun, ammo, and burner phones," she said. "Have you had any luck?"

"Nope. If he had any stolen goods, he's already unloaded them. Unlike his crew, he didn't keep any bling for himself. But you've found enough to convict him several times over."

"And he knows it."

"By the way, I met his attorney."

"He came to the house?"

"He's Green's next-door neighbor," he said. "Millard Himmel. He's primarily a divorce attorney, but he has some experience in criminal defense. He's on his way to the station."

Eve ended the call, left the CSU team to process the cars and the Amazon van, and headed back to the station.

Eve and Burnside sat across a table from Himmel and Green in the interrogation room. Burnside was dressed for court, even though it was Sunday, in a suit that accentuated her figure rather than exploiting it. Himmel was a round-faced, pale, chubby man in a polo shirt, pleated shorts, and slip-on loafers and he seemed a bit disoriented. This wasn't how he'd planned to spend his day.

Burnside took charge. "This is an open-and-shut case, Mr. Green. A slam dunk. A no-brainer. A lawyer just out of school, who has never tried a real case before, could effortlessly win this one. We don't even need to question you."

Himmel harrumphed. "So why are you here on a Sunday instead of working on your bikini tan?"

Burnside nailed him with a sharp look. "Is that a sexist remark, Mr. Himmel?"

"I'm genuinely admiring your tan, speaking as someone who sunburns easily, and making an observation. I'm not a criminal defense attorney by trade, but I know nobody likes working on Sundays. So if what you say is true, you must want something from my client."

Burnside glanced at Eve to answer the implied question.

"Grayson Mumford," Eve said.

"What makes you think my client knows this individual?"

Burnside took that one. "Mr. Mumford, like the three dead men, was on the soccer team Green coached, and he was a floating security guard at every gated community Green's home invasion crew hit in Calabasas. He eased their way in and picked the homes that they robbed."

Eve looked at Green, who was slumped over the table, examining the scratches as if they were ancient Sanskrit he was attempting to decode. "But this time he sent your crew into a trap and got Dalander and Nagy killed. Colter was so mad, he fled to the grocery store where Mumford was working security to confront him. Mumford gunned him down to save himself."

"And you, Mr. Green," Burnside said, and slapped her palm on the table, startling Green. "But that part didn't work out so well, did it? Grayson Mumford is going to walk while you do twenty-five years to life in prison."

"I didn't kill anyone," Green said.

"Be quiet, Michael," Himmel said. "I'll do the talking."

But Burnside ignored Himmel and directly addressed Green.

"You're the ringleader. You brought them into Vista Grande, aiding and abetting in the crime . . . which led directly to their violent deaths.

That's accomplice to armed robbery and felony murder. We have all the evidence we need against you but nothing on Grayson Mumford."

Green snickered at that. "You're the fucking clowns who gave him the Medal of Valor."

"Yes, we are," Burnside said. "But you're the fucking clown who can either do the full ride in prison, while Mumford remains free and pursues a career in law enforcement, or you can reduce your sentence by helping us."

That got Himmel's full attention. "What would helping you entail?"

Now Burnside addressed him. "Mr. Green gives us a full and detailed confession now, including the names of anyone involved in committing the robberies or selling the goods, and then he arranges a meeting with Mumford, which we'll record."

"You want him to wear a wire and get Mumford to incriminate himself."

"That's right."

Green had no choice and, from the look Eve saw on his face, he knew it. So did his lawyer.

Himmel pretended to consider the offer for a moment. "If you drop the murder charges against my client, and agree to recommend that the court impose the most lenient sentence possible on the armed robbery charges, he will consider your offer."

"It's a deal but it expires in ten minutes," Burnside said. "We can't risk Mumford learning that Green has been arrested, so we have to act fast."

"Deal," Green said.

Himmel's head whipped around to Green. "We need to talk—"

"About what?" Green interrupted. "Mumford is the only leverage we have." He glanced at Eve. "Does he really want to become a cop now?"

"So I'm told."

Green shook his head. "If only his brain was as big as his balls."

Burnside left to get the warrant for the wire and Eve got Green to give her the details on his home invasion racket.

Green confirmed that the robbers came in as part of the landscaping crew and left in the Amazon van, or vice versa, depending on the situation. He wasn't worried about any of his landscapers causing any trouble or going to the police. They were all Hispanic day workers, mostly illegal immigrants, that he picked up on street corners or in Home Depot parking lots throughout the valley. Most of them didn't speak English and didn't want anything to do with the police out of fear of being deported.

The idea of doing home invasions was born from desperation, resentment, and chance. Green's landscaping business was being crushed by "mow-and-blow illegals," as he called them, who radically undercut him on price.

"The stinking rich are fucking cheap," Green said. "Which is how they stay rich and why they stink."

His problem was that he operated a legitimate business that paid taxes, was licensed and bonded, and carried insurance, all costs his "mow-and-blow" competitors didn't have. That meant he was already priced out of the market before he could even make a bid for a job.

"I had to let office staff go," Green said. "I was behind on all my bills and facing bankruptcy."

That was about four months ago. It was also when he saw Grayson Mumford working the gate at Mountain Oaks. They had a few beers that night and discovered they were both at dead ends in their lives and that they shared deep bitterness toward the wealthy people they were working for. Over a few more nights, and a few more beers, they hatched their home invasion scheme. The only issue was finding a crew that would blend into the neighborhood.

"White people," Eve said.

"That's right," Green said. "Nobody notices some white guys in the neighborhood who don't belong because all whites belong."

"How did you find Dalander, Colter, and Nagy?"

"Mumford stayed in touch with them from the soccer team days, mostly because their lives had gone nowhere, just like his. Dalander was still working at Burger King, Colter was still living with his parents, and Nagy was a no-talent writer barely getting by as a reader, gleefully preventing other writers from getting the work he wanted, not that it got him anywhere. The three of them were broke, bored, and eager to come on board, as much for the excitement as the money. They walked out of the houses they robbed with hard-ons, not that anybody but Dalander had a woman who might appreciate it."

That was a mental image Eve didn't need.

Green explained that Eve was right, that Mumford's job was picking the houses to hit, checking out the homeowners, and running interference on security issues, while Green did the close-up surveillance of the target homes, then planned and executed the jobs. Most of the bags, wallets, shoes, and watches they stole were sold online and the jewelry was fenced through a shop in Sherman Way run by another former soccer coach. The split was 60 percent for Green, 10 percent each for the other four participants.

He got the lion's share because he was carrying the operating expenses, like creating the Amazon van and offering his landscaping services to homeowners at well below cost just so he could stay in the gated community. By the time he covered all the costs, he walked away with a little over 10 percent himself. Or at least that's what he told the other four and they believed him.

Green was aware that his three men skimmed some for themselves, but he wasn't going to jeopardize the operation over it.

Mumford picked the sting house and said the old man and his jailbait girlfriend would be easy pickings.

"Of course, it all went to hell," Green said. "I was about to shit my pants when I saw Colter run out of the house and carjack an Escalade. I'm just glad he had the good sense not to come to me."

Now Eve knew that Green had lied when he'd told her before that he wasn't in Vista Grande that day, but she let that go for now. "Colter was running for his life. But when he saw he couldn't escape, he changed his plans. He decided to use his last few minutes of freedom to confront Mumford instead."

"I can't blame him for that or Mumford for shooting him first."

"Did you call Sherry Simms and warn her?"

Himmel cleared his throat. Eve and Green both looked at him. "That wasn't an objection. You can answer her question."

"Yeah, I called her the second after it happened," Green said. "I knew you'd be showing up at her place and she needed to ditch her computer. Instead, she ditched herself, too."

"There's just one thing I don't get," Eve said. "After things went so spectacularly, violently wrong, why were you casing Oakdale a day later in your fake Amazon van?"

"I was looking for another house to hit. We had a good thing going and I couldn't afford to give it up."

"But you didn't have a crew."

Green dismissed her comment with a shrug. "There are a lot of guys I coached whose lives have gone nowhere. I even found the perfect house to hit."

"Which one?"

"You'll like this. The McCaigs'." He smiled ruefully. "This just isn't my week."

# CHAPTER
# TWENTY-THREE

Eve went with Green to his office, where the LASD technical team installed hidden cameras in the front office but didn't bother with the warehouse. Green insisted he and Mumford wouldn't have any reason to go in back. Green was given a cell phone that would constantly broadcast to the LASD mobile command center, which was parked among the mobile homes and campers at a recreational vehicle rental facility down the street and around the corner from Green's office.

Shaw was in the command center, where the video and audio would be recorded and he could coordinate the operation. Two deputies were hiding in a van parked at the muffler repair shop next door. Eve and Duncan would be parked in her Subaru at the storage facility across the street, watching and listening to everything going down in Green's office on her phone. Once Mumford arrived, an LASD patrol car would arrive to block the end of Douglas Fir Road, just to be safe.

It was 4:00 p.m. The technical team had just gone, leaving Eve alone with Green in his cluttered, filthy office.

"Give him a call," Eve said.

Green picked up the phone and dialed. Before Green could utter a greeting, Mumford said, "Are you insane? What are you calling me for?"

Eve figured Green's name came up on Mumford's caller ID.

"Why do you think?" Green said. "To congratulate you on your Medal of Valor, of course. You must be so proud of yourself."

"What do you really want?"

"We have unfinished business," Green said.

"Our business is finished. In fact, it's dead and buried."

"That's exactly what we need to discuss. Face-to-face."

"Forget it. We're done. You're welcome. Have a—"

Green interrupted him. "Come to my office in an hour, you smug motherfucker, or I'll burn your family's house down with them in it."

He slammed the receiver down. Eve glared at him.

"Did you have to threaten his family?" Eve was worried about how that bit would play in court when Mumford was tried for murder.

"You wanted him to come, didn't you? Now he will. Actually, I was planning on having this conversation with him anyway, just without an audience or facing prison time."

"What are you going to say to him?"

"You'll see."

Eve and Duncan sat in her car, the minutes dragging on like hours. But it was only forty minutes after the call when Shaw's voice came through their earbuds from the mobile command center.

"Mumford just passed us on Craftsman," Shaw said, "heading your way in a gray Chevy Malibu."

The words were barely out of Shaw's mouth when Mumford's car cruised slowly up the street.

Deputy Ross, in the van in the muffler shop parking lot, radioed in: "He's scoping out the area, looking for surveillance."

Eve and Duncan slid down in their seats as the Chevy passed.

She said, "I don't like this. He already suspects something."

"He's just being careful," Duncan said.

Mumford drove past Green's office to the dead end, turned around, and came back down again, paused for a moment in front of the building, then drove into the parking lot.

"Here we go," Duncan said.

Mumford got out, went to the front door, and walked inside without knocking. Now Eve and Duncan shifted their attention to her phone, where they watched a live feed from the four cameras inside the office.

On her earbuds, Eve heard Shaw notify everyone that Grayson Mumford was inside and order the patrol car to move into position across Douglas Fir Road.

On the screen, Mumford looked around the front office, peeked into the empty offices, and opened the door to the warehouse.

"It's a good thing we didn't put anybody inside," Duncan said. "The kid is cautious."

Green called out to Mumford, "I'm in my office."

Mumford stepped inside and saw Green behind his desk, pretending to finish up some paperwork.

"Glad you could make it. I know how busy you are with TV appearances and autograph signings these days."

"Fuck you, Mike. What do you want?"

Green leaned back in his chair, in no rush at all, and gave an appraising look at Mumford, who stood in front of his desk. "You aren't wearing your medal. I'm disappointed. I was hoping you'd let me kiss it."

"You should, you ungrateful piece of shit. I saved your ass."

"From your own epic fucking mistake. You sent us into a trap."

"How was I supposed to know that?"

"It's what I paid you for." Green leaned forward now, his elbows on his desk, and glared at Mumford. "You were supposed to fully check out each homeowner before we hit their place. Instead, you got everybody killed. You even shot Colter in the face yourself."

"I did us both a favor. He would have talked. So unless you asked me here to thank me, I don't see what the point is of . . ."

His voice trailed off and he got a strange, lost look on his face.

Eve said, "What is wrong with him?"

"I don't know," Duncan said.

Green stood up. "The point is that you're a big hero now and I want a percentage of everything that's coming your way. Endorsements, movies, whatever." Mumford's expression didn't change. Green snapped his fingers in Mumford's face. "Look at me when I'm talking to you, asshole."

Mumford blinked hard and met his eye. "It's like when the bad guys get together on a TV show."

"What is?"

"You spending the last five minutes telling me what we already know. It's for the benefit of the audience."

Mumford pulled a gun from under his shirt, shot Green twice in the face, and bolted from the office before the body fell.

Eve jumped out of her car, drawing her gun as she ran across the street, Duncan behind her, and Deputies Ross and Clayton rushing out of their van next door. In her ear, she heard Shaw frantically yelling "Move in! Move in!" as if they needed to be told.

Eve took the lead, Ross, Clayton, and Duncan backing her up, as she went to the door. In her ear, she heard Shaw say, "We've lost visual. He's in the garage."

She opened the door and went inside, moving straight to the door to the garage. Going through the door would be dangerous. Ross and Clayton took one side of the door, Eve and Duncan took the other. She could smell gasoline. That wasn't good.

"On the count of three," Eve said, reached for the doorknob and, on three, flung it open and spun low into the garage.

Time seemed to slow down. The smell of gasoline was intense. In the next second, she saw that the fertilizer pallet was drenched, several open gasoline cans and propane tanks were in front of it, and a trail of liquid led to the far end of the warehouse. She also smelled the rotten-egg odor of leaking propane gas. Just as she registered the meaning of all that, she saw the flash of a road flare arcing through the air and landing in the trail of gasoline, lighting it like a fuse . . .

. . . to ignite the fertilizer, packed with ammonium nitrate, the easy-to-find explosive of choice for terrorists everywhere.

*"Run,"* Eve yelled as she spun around, pushing Duncan toward the front door. The four of them ran out of the building, Eve's feet hitting the asphalt of the parking lot just as the building exploded.

The concussive force sent Eve flying, and probably saved her life. She smacked down on the asphalt as jagged, flaming sheets of corrugated metal peeled off the building and whirled through the air like spinning helicopter blades. Tongues of flame licked out over them as bits of glass and wood and plaster rained down all around.

Eve lifted her scratched face from the ground, hearing only the ringing in her ears, and through the smoke saw Mumford darting across the street, heading west. She scrambled to her feet and chased after him, nearly toppling with dizziness on her first step.

She willed herself not to fall and kept running, half wobbling as the ground seemed to shift like rolling surf under her feet. Of course, she knew it wasn't the ground—it was her inner ear, her balance shot by the blast.

*Is Duncan okay? What about the others?*

She couldn't look back or think about that now.

*Focus.*

*Don't stop running. Don't let Mumford get away.*

Her face stung all over, blood or sweat trickled down her cheeks, and each breath she took as she ran brought a sharp pain in her chest.

*Have I broken my sternum again?*

Mumford was fifty yards ahead of her, running across the storage unit parking lot. He scaled a low cyclone fence in the back and dashed through the vacant dirt lot beyond, disappearing down a slope.

Eve reached the fence, tried to scale it fast, and her blouse got caught on a sharp barb. There was no time to free it. She threw herself to the dirt, using her body weight to free herself, the wire ripping the side of her blouse and cutting her flesh. But at least she was free of the damn fence.

She ran across the lot, stumbling over gopher holes and mounds of dirt, slowing as she got to the rise. Below her, the pet cemetery spread out in front of her, a wide-open expanse of lawn, spotted with mature trees and mostly flat tombstones decorated with paper bouquets and spinning, colorful whirligigs at some plots. A creek lined with steep four-foot-tall slabs of vertical concrete bisected the park, east to west. The culvert was crossed at various points with arched wooden foot-bridges and narrow roads, the trickle of brackish water flowing through a large pipe underneath them. To her left, in the center of the park, was a vehicle roundabout, a flower bed in the center with a statue of Saint Francis of Assisi in the middle, arms out in greeting to cemetery guests, a carved bird resting on his shoulder.

There was no sign of Mumford, but she knew he was down there somewhere, likely waiting for her to come out in the open so he could shoot her down and then make his run for it. There was no one else in the cemetery, either. The park closed at five and the gates were locked. That also meant no backup vehicles would be able to get in right away.

She realized at that moment that she'd lost her gun, that it must have fallen out of her grip in the explosion. Luckily, she still had the backup weapon in her bra holster. She'd been carrying it since Green's arrest.

Eve moved down the hillside, staying low and using trees for cover, until she got to the edge of the culvert, which reminded her of a World War 1 trench. That gave her an idea. She'd use the creek for cover, as a way to traverse the park without making herself an open target. She got down on her knees and carefully dropped into the culvert, slipping the instant she landed, falling on her side onto the slick concrete bed.

She sat up, pulled her small Glock from under her soaked, torn shirt, and moved along the trench, peering up now and then, looking for any sign of movement.

Behind her, the ground was rocked by another explosion from Green's Greenery. She lost her footing and something whizzed past her head, shattering the carved bird off Saint Francis' shoulder.

*A bullet.*

She hadn't heard a thing, the blast and her ringing ears combining to muffle the sound of the gunshot. But she knew the trajectory.

Eve whirled to her right, gun held out, her back to the south culvert wall, eyes scanning the northern slope, dotted with trees. Nothing moved. If Mumford was up there, he would have been able to see right into the trench, except where his view was blocked by trees. But when he saw an opportunity for a shot, he'd taken it.

*Where was he now?*

He'd probably changed position, she thought, perhaps moving closer.

She ducked, and scrambled forward, but she was running out of trench. Up ahead was a road that crossed over the culvert. A pipe carried the water under the road, like a tunnel, to the continuation of the culvert on the other side. That presented a problem. If she climbed out and went over the road to drop into the other side of the culvert, she'd be exposed for a long moment and become an even more vulnerable target than she was now. That left her only one other option.

*Can I crawl through the pipe?*

Just as she was considering that, and beginning to bend down farther to examine the pipe opening, Mumford popped up in front of her like a jack-in-the-box from the culvert on the other side of the road, using the crossing as his cover.

Eve threw herself to her left, slamming into the concrete wall as he fired. She felt the hot bite of the bullet grazing her right shoulder and then she dove forward as he fired again, the shot passing over her head.

The instant she hit the creek bed, she flattened herself and fired three times through the pipe that ran under the street, shooting into darkness.

But it wasn't darkness. It was Mumford's midsection, blocking the pipe opening on the other side of the culvert. She knew that she'd just blasted three bullets into him.

He collapsed, disappearing from view.

Eve rose to her feet, aiming her gun over the roadway, and saw Mumford on his back in the culvert. He was gurgling, his gun out of reach of his grasping fingers. She looked over her shoulder and saw Duncan, Ross, and Clayton coming down the hillside against the backdrop of a dark sky roiling with smoke and flame.

*They're alive.*

She holstered her gun, lifted herself out of the culvert, crawled across the roadway, climbed back down into the trench, and made her way over to him.

Mumford was hit in the thigh, stomach, and chest. She guessed that he must have caught the last bullet as he fell. Blood seeped out of his leg, bubbled out of his mouth, and trickled out of his nostrils. He was bleeding out externally and drowning in his own blood internally at the same time. He was conscious, but couldn't speak, his eyes wide with terror.

Eve got on her knees beside him in the muck and blood, took his trembling hand in hers, and looked into his eyes. He weakly gripped her hand, afraid of what was coming next. She held his hand tight, making sure he knew that he wasn't alone, that she'd stay with him until the end.

It came an instant later. His hand went limp, his pupils became wide and black, and his body seemed to deflate, like a punctured air mattress.

She'd killed him.

# CHAPTER
# TWENTY-FOUR

In the wake of Michael Green's murder, Grayson Mumford's killing, and the explosion that shattered windows throughout Craftsman's Corner and burned down two buildings, a hillside, and two estates in Hidden Hills, Captain Roje Shaw accepted responsibility for the debacle and wisely took an early retirement.

No civilians were injured or killed in the blast. But Duncan broke his left arm and opened the wound on his face again. A piece of metal punctured Ross' left side, narrowly missing his heart, and had to be surgically removed from one of his ribs. And Eddie Clayton broke his sunglasses.

Eve was immediately placed on leave, very much against her will. The Officer-Involved Shooting investigation unit determined the shooting of Grayson Mumford was justified, but the department psychologist, who Eve was ordered to see, declared that she needed to take some time off to cope with the psychological toll of the killing.

But a vacation was the last thing Eve wanted. She'd had enough of that already over the last few months while recovering from the injuries she'd sustained on her first two major cases.

She'd only suffered some lacerations, some nasty bruises, and a ruptured eardrum, so she felt that she wasn't really wounded this time.

Not physically anyway and, as long as she kept busy, she wouldn't be emotionally, either.

That's why at the start of her second week of involuntary leave, she took an early-morning flight to Raleigh, North Carolina, rented a car, and drove straight to Durham for a very late lunch at Edna's Chicken and Waffles.

The place was downtown, on the ground floor of an old art deco–style building that was once a Kress department store, the name still etched into the stone. The dining room was packed with Duke University students in logo clothes, retirees, and a couple of uniformed Durham police officers.

Edna's was famous for buttermilk fried chicken, waffles, and biscuits, all slathered in flavored butter and maple syrup and drizzled with candied pecans. It was death on a plate, but that was basically all there was on the menu—only the choice of butter and waffle flavors, types of drizzles, and the number of pieces of chicken changed.

Her waitress was an attractive young woman whose bottle-blonde hair and pale-white skin stood out among the largely African American staff and clientele. She could have been a college student working her way through school, waitressing between classes to take some of the financial burden for tuition, room, and board from her parents. Or a single mother struggling to support her child by working three jobs. Eve had a vivid imagination.

"What can I get you, ma'am?" the waitress asked. The "ma'am" sounded awkward somehow coming out of her mouth.

"I've never had fried chicken and waffles before," Eve said. "Should I have it with the cinnamon butter, the maple syrup, and candied pecans on top or on the side?"

"Slather it all on. Go for the full experience," she said. "Trust me, it's delicious."

"You talked me into it. How many times a month can you eat here without having a heart attack?"

The waitress motioned to an old couple. "I'm told that they've been coming here just about every day for years and they seem to be doing fine."

"How about you? Was the six pounds of grease, salt, carbs, and sugar a shock to your system the first time?"

The waitress laughed. "On the contrary, it's Southern Crack. You'll be back again for dinner and again for breakfast in the morning. You'll have to wean yourself off of it."

"How long does it take?"

"At least a week," she said. "If you have the willpower."

"So how's the second week going for you?"

"Not so good. I foolishly got a job here." She started to turn away, then hesitated, turning back. "I forgot to ask. What can I get you to drink?"

Eve smiled at her. "That's not what you really want to ask me. You're wondering, How did she know I've only been here a week?" The waitress looked past Eve to the two police officers sitting behind her at the other table. Both of them were looking at her. "And why are those two cops, who come in here all the time, staring at me when they haven't paid any attention to me before?"

She looked at Eve, really looked at her this time. "You're from Los Angeles?"

"Calabasas." Eve took out her badge-wallet and flashed it for her. "Detective Eve Ronin, Los Angeles County Sheriff's Department."

Sherry Simms sat down at the table, resigned to her fate. "How did you find me? I tossed my phone and my computer. I've stayed off the grid and completely out of touch with everyone I've ever known. I've paid cash for everything and only stayed in towns I've never been to before."

"Your Mustang ratted you out."

"I've changed the license plates a dozen times."

"But it's the same car," Eve said.

245

"There are thousands of Mustangs out there just like it."

"When you bought the car, you registered for the FordPass app, though you've never used it. It's really handy. It can tell you where your car is parked if you forget, or it can tell the police where you are if they're looking for you."

Eve held up her phone, opened the FordPass app, and showed her the map display with the pinpoint where Sherry's car was parked. The idea of using the app occurred to Eve the morning after the pet cemetery shooting.

Sherry sighed. "There's no such thing as privacy anymore."

"Certainly not where you're going to be for the next few years."

"Am I allowed a last meal?"

Eve passed her the laminated menu. "Would you like to join me for chicken and waffles?"

"I thought you'd never ask." Sherry used the menu to flag down a passing waitress. "Hey, Molly, can we please get two number ones and two ice teas? Thanks." She looked at Eve again, ignoring the confused expression on Molly's face. "I can't believe you came all this way just for me. Selling stolen goods isn't that big of a crime."

"You're the only one involved who is still alive," Eve said. That news shook Sherry, making her left eyelid twitch. "Grayson Mumford and Michael Green are dead now, too."

"Who killed who?"

"Grayson killed Green. I killed Grayson."

Eve hadn't thought a lot about Mumford over the last few days, but she couldn't stop thinking about his sister, who'd been so eager to have her picture taken with her, the woman who'd soon kill her brother. That thought haunted Eve when she had time to think, which she tried hard not to have.

"I've never met a killer before," Sherry said.

"How do you know?"

"Why bother coming for me?"

It wasn't a bother. It was a requirement.

"Somebody has to be punished."

The waitress studied her face. "I think it will be both of us."

Eve was afraid that Sherry might be right. Her phone vibrated. She glanced at the screen. It was a text from Linwood Taggert.

Ronin is a go. We sold the TV series.

# Author's Note and Acknowledgments

This book was inspired by a fetal abduction case I learned about at a homicide investigators' training conference for law enforcement professionals. I am grateful to Jason Weber, the public safety training coordinator at Northeast Wisconsin Technical College in Green Bay, for the opportunity to attend the conference.

Danielle R. Galien, an associate professor of criminal justice at Des Moines Area Community College and a fifteen-year veteran crime scene investigator with the Des Moines Police Department, attended the same conference I did, was familiar with the case, and gave me an enormous amount of help.

I am also indebted to Pamela Sokolik-Putnam, a supervising deputy coroner investigator for the San Bernardino County Sheriff-Coroner Department, for sharing her experience and advice.

I owe special thanks to retired cops Paul Bishop, Robin Burcell, and David Putnam for letting me hit them up with procedural questions at all hours of the day and night.

Eve Ronin's continuing adventures exist because of the enthusiasm, insight, and support of my editors Gracie Doyle, Megha Parekh, and Charlotte Herscher, the marketing brilliance of Dennelle Catlett and Megan Beatie, and the negotiating finesse of Amy Tannenbaum.

Finally, the city of Calabasas, California, is a real place, and many of the locations that appear in this book, like the Lost Hills sheriff's station, the Hilton Garden Inn, and the Commons shopping center, actually exist but the events and characters I've described are entirely fictional. I've also taken some creative liberties with geography, police procedure, and other inconvenient aspects of reality that got in the way of telling my story.

# About the Author

*Photo © 2013 Roland Scarpa*

Lee Goldberg is a two-time Edgar Award and two-time Shamus Award nominee and the #1 *New York Times* bestselling author of more than forty novels. He has also written and/or produced many TV shows, including *Diagnosis Murder, SeaQuest*, and *Monk*, and he is the cocreator of the *Mystery 101* series of Hallmark movies. As an international television consultant, he has advised networks and studios in Canada, France, Germany, Spain, China, Sweden, and the Netherlands on the creation, writing, and production of episodic television series. You can find more information about Lee and his work at www.leegoldberg.com.